NORTHERN
WINTERS
ARE
MURDER

RendezVous
Crime

NORTHERN WINTERS ARE MURDER

Lou Allin

RENDEZVOUS PRESS

Toronto, Ontario, Canada

Cover art: Alan Barnard

Le Conseil des Arts
du Canada
depuis 1957

The Canada Council
for the Arts
since 1957

We gratefully acknowledge the support of the Canada Council for the Arts for our publishing program.

Napoleon Publishing/RendezVous Press
Toronto, Ontario, Canada

Printed in Canada

07 06 05 04 03   5 4 3 2

Canadian Cataloguing in Publication Data

Allin, Lou, date-
    Northern winters are murder

A Belle Palmer Mystery
ISBN 0-929141-74-1

I. Title.

PS8551.L5564N67 2000   C813'.6   C00-931969-7
PR9199.3.A3963N67 2000

Dedicated to
George Norman Allin (1910-1999),
in memory of 1001 nights at the movies.

Acknowledgments

Many thanks to those who helped me along the way. Marilyn, a veteran crime writer, gave me confidence. Caroline, Sheila and Tim read faithfully and kept me on the mark. Sylvia offered a berth at RendezVous Press and made the editing process as entertaining and instructive as any Shakespeare play. Jan, for both our sakes, refused to read a single word before publication.

Any similarities to actual people, events, businesses or places are intended as fiction. Though the plot weaves through the Nickel Capital and its wilderness, I have made some of the geography my own creature.

PROLOGUE: A SUMMER NIGHT

Neutral tones dissolved white into black. Clouds of tarnished pewter hid the moon. Not even a whisper of wind feathered the lake, its glassy surface catching the reflected light. Twinklings of cottages rimmed the crater lake like stubborn fallen stars. There was a brief splash as a merganser duck led her paddling brood to shelter, the smallest perched on her wide back, struggling for purchase.

On a shelf of shimmering granite beside the water, a girl knelt, spilling the liquid crystal over her hands. Dressed in a simple white chemise, a slip perhaps, she crooned to herself, oblivious to the hum of ravenous mosquitos unfettered by the still night. Her hands crumpled the lacy needles of a tiny cedar sprouting from a rock cleft, and she brushed the rich perfume into her long hair. A dark, irregular pattern spread across the lap of her dress, or was that a trick of light?

From the house far above floated the strains of a violin concerto, Paganini, the rippling, fluid tones of Itzhak Perlman. The girl nodded her head to the music. Sudden silence, then a raucous country tune faded in and out, interrupted by static. The radio snapped off, replaced by a hurried conversation.

"I don't know. She's not in her room."

"Find her. The way she has been acting…shouldn't have been left alone."

Footsteps sounded on the stairs, tentative at first, then

heavy and deliberate across a wooden platform to the granite shelf. "Come inside. It's late." A hand reached out to her, and the girl swayed as she stood. At last the moon found a chink in the drifting clouds and dyed the dress burgundy with the intrusion of a single frame of technicolour.

"Oh, my God. What have you...?"

She took the arm, leaning against it, and struggled to walk, blinking at the face as if emerging from a dream, or entering, confused and delighted, stunned and saved at one gesture. Her lips moved as she counted. She climbed the stairs, resting every three steps and sank to her knees at the top, where other hands reached out. The warbling sob of a loon echoed across the lake.

ONE

The Ojibwas called it Crust-on-the-Snow Moon, the full moon of the coldest month in a climate which suffered no fools. Technology had tried to even the odds, but people in Northern Ontario knew the illusory line between safety and danger. Snug behind triple-glazed windows, Belle Palmer scanned the lake to watch the bloodless sky ghost surrender to the sun. At -28° Celsius, this February morning was dead quiet. No loons ululating, no rain pelting from the eaves, no crickets chirping on the hearth or anywhere else.

The harsh growl of a snow machine near the deck caught her in a customary T-shirt, spoiled by the woodstove which warmed the house like a bakery. She yanked on sweat pants, opened the door, and was shoved aside as her German shepherd charged at a tall figure in a snowmobile suit. Then the man removed his helmet and the dog, transformed from attack to welcome mode, waggled up for a pet. "Hey, Freya, didn't you recognize me?" he asked.

"Jim Burian, you cowboy," said Belle. "Only the young and strong and crazy would be out in this. I haven't seen you since Thanksgiving dinner at your mom's."

"I guessed that you were up. The smoke looked like a fresh morning fire. Shouldn't have gone out at this temperature, but I counted on stopping here on the way to the lodge." He cocked a thumb at a boy throwing snowballs for Freya in the driveway. "The kid's turning blue, too, though he won't admit it." He dropped his heavy boots at the door and called, "Come in here, Ted, before your nose falls off."

"Coffee's on. And I've got cocoa, too." Though Belle disliked unannounced visitors, Jim she could talk with eight days out of seven. Ethical, hard-working, completely without pretensions, the Burians were golden currency in the region. Years ago she had discovered his family's lodge at Mamaguchi Lake with its friendly charm. He'd been having trouble with grade ten English when they first met, so with her literature background she'd tutored him as a favour; then they had become good friends. Twenty-three now, having spent a few years as a Katimivik volunteer in the Hudson Bay area, he was a crack wilderness instructor who paddled the local canoe routes like the familiar streets of a neighbourhood. His course at Shield University was demanding most of his time, so they hadn't talked much since the summer.

"Jeez, what a sauna! Strip tease," he said, peeling off the suit, two sweaters and a pair of wool pants, leaving him in the same outfit as Belle, her mirror image, give or take twenty years. His face, chafed by the cold, had filled out from a gangly adolescence and recalled a young Tony Perkins. He brushed a hand through his thick, curly brown hair and got comfortable on the sofa. Just one flaw marred his even features, the traces of a harelip operation, camouflaged by sprouts of a new mustache. At age three he had been sent to Toronto for reconstructive surgery, and a more recent operation had repaired facial nerve damage. His crooked smile didn't match his innocent presentation.

Ted, a younger version of Jim, happily retreated with Belle to her computer room, carrying a plate with toast and peanut butter, a mug of cocoa and a hint book to the game "Grim Fandango". When she returned, Jim was sipping his coffee with

4

obvious relief and rubbing his stockinged feet back to life. "Selling any properties lately? Or is the market quiet?" he asked.

Belle pursed her lips in mock despair. "With Madame Quebec's constant threat to leave the marriage bed, nervous interest rates and depressed nickel prices, not much is moving." The International Nickel Company, aka Mother Inco, had been until recently the town's major employer.

As Jim leafed through Canadian Geographic, jade-green eyes reflecting the sun pouring in through the walls of six-foot windows, Belle engineered a giant omelet filled with chopped artichoke hearts and mozzarella. With a quiver of guilt and some minor salivation, she ripped open a package of hollandaise sauce mix. "Been saving this for someone special. You're not a high-cholesterol time bomb yet, are you, laddie?" He shook his head. "Good, because after this concoction, your arteries will need an ice auger!"

Minutes later, they forked into the fluffy pillows of egg, oozing with mellow cheese and golden sauce, exchanging appreciative smiles instead of words. Finally, Jim slowed up enough to mention that his family had opened the lodge only a few weeks ago. "Too cold in January to bother. Seven weeks of -35° each night and -25° by day. This winter no one's going to get his money's worth from that megabuck snowmobile trail pass. Why don't you come on up and see us?"

"I'd like to check out your new hunt camp, too, just value my toes and fingers too much. Where is the place?"

"About ten miles north of our lodge, Larder Lake area." He rummaged through his suit and unfolded a topographic map. "Right here. Has a great stream, even runs all winter so I don't have to melt the snow. I've been recording virgin pines in the area, hoping to get evidence to prevent that new park from being built."

"Yes, I was sick to hear about such a stupid proposal. Tell

me what you learned. Put me on the inside track."

He gave her an unusually dark and serious look which surprised her. "It's an ecological disaster in the making. You know that country, Belle. Those dirt roads the tourists will use cross some pretty sensitive areas. It's on the edge of the only big tree country within fifty miles. We're having a rally at Shield, March 15. I hope you can come."

"I'll spread the word to my neighbours. None of us wants any more activity on Lake Wapiti. We like living twenty miles from the nearest convenience store. It concentrates the mind." Belle spooned up the last drop of hollandaise. "Well, on to happier topics. How's Melanie?" She wiggled her finger under her nose. "And very fetching, by the way, but is it Gable or Hitler?"

A blush crossed his face as he gave a cover-up cough and shifted his feet. "Couldn't be better. Melanie's in the nursing program, so we see each other for lunch or coffee. Study at night together, too. I took her on some of the old canoe routes in the early fall. Remember the Elk Lake loop?"

"When it rained for five straight days, and I nearly got hypothermia? I'll say. We should have stayed in camp, except that we were tired of salty rice and noodle dinners and the same Agatha Christie novel. I'd read a page, rip it off, and toss it in the fire to lighten my load," she said, laughing.

Jim pushed back his empty plate, wiped clean with toast. "Boy, can she carry a pack! Forty pounds is no problem." He rotated his coffee cup in reflection. "Taught that city girl everything she knows about the woods. Call me Caliban, the monster of the forest. 'I'll show thee the best springs; I'll pluck thee berries; I'll fish for thee and get thee wood enough.'"

Belle realized how much Jim had matured in the last few years. His parents had confided that as a boy he had been so insecure, especially with strangers, that he had refused to meet anyone's gaze. "I see you remember the Shakespeare we read for your grade twelve finals. I thought that you hated it."

He nodded at the reference.

"Besides," she went on, "Caliban was my favourite. He had substance, and he smelled out hypocrisy. Miranda was so boring with all that 'Brave new world' stuff." The back of her hand swept over her forehead in a stage gesture.

Jim's smile widened as the sun brightened the room. "I'm happy with Melanie. We're so easy together, so easy that it's a miracle."

Belle knew him well enough not to pry further about his plans; he guarded his privacy like a Cayman Islands bank account number.

He downed the last gulp of coffee. "Got to go now, but how about a tour? I haven't seen your house since it was framed."

"The computer room," she said, leading him down the hall, following the salsa beat as Manny Calavera, travel agent for the dead, voyaged to the Underworld to save his client. Needing no help, Ted was operating the controls like a pro, flipping through Manny's inventory, manipulating his scythe.

"If you're short on ideas for my Christmas present," Ted said to his brother, "this would be great."

Belle cleared her throat. "I, uh, got the system more for the information connections. Our business webpage, too. I belong to several forums, tropical fish, mystery, classic films. But don't ask about alt.sex. It might as well be old.sox at my age."

"I'd kill for an Internet account at school. Our research facilities are pretty feeble," Jim replied.

Belle escorted him to the TV room where she trained her Chaparral system on Ted Turner's sanity-saving TNT classic film network. "How long have you had your satellite dish?" he asked. "It's quite the piece of art on the dock."

"Ha! Art would be cheaper. The cement base was poured in September, but I finally saved enough this month to add the electronics. Too bad aerial reception is so poor out here. Cable's a century away. Maybe man wasn't meant to live in the boonies."

On a sturdy stand by the window, her fish family splashed in their fifty-gallon aquarium, bumping the glass in hungry frustration. She turned off the pump, sprinkled on some dried shrimp and dropped in a few food tablets. "It's always Tanganyika or the Amazon rainforest for these lucky brats," Belle said. Mac, the African knifefish, paraded his spots, eight on one side and thirteen on the other. Li'l Pleco, the plecostemus, leisurely rolled onto his back to suck food from the surface like a boat turned turtle, confident that a stray pellet would drift into his sucker maw in payment for rasping the algae from the tank. In contrast, Hannibal the needlefish lurked at the top in imaginary weeds. Prisoner of his genes, he ate only live prey and had been spoiled by the summer's excellent minnows, now reduced to an occasional goldfish. "He was a #2 pencil, now he's a pregnant Orson Welles," Belle said.

After the tour, Jim reassembled his clothes with a sigh. "Hate to go back into that cold, but I think I'm stoked enough to ward off frostbite for the half hour to the lodge. Thanks for the meal. Drop by if you can. I'll be out at the hunt camp during break week to work on my paper." He started to fasten his helmet, then paused. "Say, I wanted to ask. Have you seen any small planes around the lake, seen lights in the night?"

Belle cocked her head, trying to recall. "Maybe once. I thought it was a fluke because I know they're not allowed to land after dark without instrumentation. What's up?"

"Nothing good." He rubbed Freya's ears, and the dog gave an imitation of a purr. "I spend a lot of time in the bush, especially at odd hours coming back from the hunt camp. I've heard small prop jobs at night and seen signs of ski landings on Obabika, Stillwell, places no one should be."

"See any people?"

"Are you kidding? They're in and out in minutes. And why go there anyway? Those lakes are way off the main trails, too shallow for fish. It's a transfer, Belle, and I'm talking about drugs. What else?"

She nodded. "Used to be that was just an American problem. Then a big city problem. Everything's twenty years late up here. We've been lucky."

Jim's hands trembled as he pulled on his mitts, and his voice grew cold. "They're going after kids now. Ted's in grade nine, for God's sake, and several of his classmates have used that junk. If anyone ever tried to turn him on, I'd take care of them." He punched his fist into his leather gauntlet. "I love that little guy."

Ted had to be pulled from his game, but he thanked Belle before he left, which earned him an approving wink from his big brother.

As the machine faded into the distance, Belle found herself worrying about this new side of Jim, a personal rage against drugs. If she read him correctly, serious anger was not an emotion he'd had to deal with much in the past. Well, he was a grown man now, not a high school student. Shrugging off her concern, she beamed into the weather channel. It always cheered her to see that compared to the Arctic, her world was relatively tropical. It was -45° in Rankin Inlet up in Hudson Bay, -40° in Resolute, and a whopping -48° in Iglulik. For a sweet minute she felt toasty...until she noticed a monster blizzard sweeping down from Superior. Another day of grace before the plowing would resume.

The phone rang, and a grizzly voice asked, "How about a

run to Mamaguchi Sunday? It's me, Rocket Man." Her neighbour, Ed DesRosiers, had just sold his plumbing business and retired. She envied Ed his racy new Phazer snowmobile with its killer headlamp housing sitting up like a beacon. It was as unlikely a machine for a fat old coot with a dickey hip as it was for a sort-of-middle-aged woman hourly expecting arthritis.

"Why not? There's a storm on the way, but it should clear by then."

"Come out to the ice hut around ten. Only ling biting, but it helps to pass the time. Hélène's going to early-bird bingo, but she's making a batch of *tourtières*."

Belle's neighbours were few, especially after the cottages closed up for the winter. Those hardy souls who wintered over were well-bonded, tolerating each other's idiosyncrasies in exchange for the loan of a handy tool, an egg or cup of milk, some gas, a newspaper or videotape, and most importantly, a watchful eye for strangers. In this primitive cooperative, one person was good with electricity, another with pumps, another with snow machines; one had a plow, one had a backhoe and one handed around fresh vegetables or fish.

Hanging up, she heard a deep rumble from the main road, probably the wood she had ordered. Usually ten or twelve cords handled the vicious winters, but the record cold had melted her pile to a few odd ends of junk cedar harvested from her acre lot, stuff that went up like cotton and lasted about as long. Several calls had finally located a supply of "dry" maple. Green wood, seasoned less than eight to nine months, gave no heat and was difficult to light. Of course, she had propane back-up, but she wasn't about to shell out five hundred dollars a month to Cambrian Fuels if she could avoid it.

Down the driveway, scraped to satin by Ed and his plow, bumped an ancient dump truck. A young lad, cigarette in mouth, jumped out before he realized that Freya was slavering after him. He leaped for the cab. "Whoa! Call your dog, lady." Belle reserved this ploy for new tradesmen. Ninety pounds of hairy muscle rampaging like a rabid wolf discouraged unwelcome callers. Ever the tease, Freya could be depended upon to veer off at the last minute, but the uninitiated rarely stood still long enough to discover this for themselves.

"Sorry. I'll get her." She led the barking dog inside, tapping her gently on the head and scolding her for effect.

A tutored glance showed that the wood was seasoned maple, a good sixteen inches, not short-cut like the townies with pretty stoves wanted. "Over here, please." Belle pointed at a cleared space near some pallets. "Watch the telephone and hydro lines." When the pneumatic lift pumped up, the driver opened the tailgate, the wood crashed down and the door clanged shut.

The boy walked over, presenting a paper. "Five cords of dry maple. Sixty a cord comes to three hundred and tax of forty-five."

Belle caught his eye and arched her brow. "Cash?" Two-thirds of Canadians admitted to avoiding the onerous provincial and federal sales taxes. The underground economy was alive and well even if the primary one was still ailing.

"Sure. Three hundred even," he said without flinching and accepted the three crisp brown bills she withdrew from her parka. He surveyed the mammoth deck to the endless lake beyond. "What a great spot. Wish I could live here. Do a bit of fishing." He paused and seemed to be counting the windows. "Big family?"

Belle was ready. "Oh, several of us. And a hungry dog," she added. Taking the hint, he inhaled a last meditative drag, and soon the guttural chug of the motor faded into the distance. Isolated places were free Wal-Marts for thieves. It helped to have a vehicle visible at all times, even a junker, so she let Ed leave his plow truck by the propane tank to free up his small parking area.

Later that evening, just before she packed Spenser away (poor man was on a heavy case in tropical San Diego; did people get paid for working there?), Belle thought she heard a plane. She stepped out onto the mini-deck off her second floor master suite and tried to home in on the sound. The temperature was back to -30°, and the trees were snapping like rifle shots. Though the moon illuminated the white surfaces and the house lights radiated across the lower deck, a steady snow was beginning to obscure visibility. She turned her head slowly, shutting her eyes to concentrate. Too low and too noisy for a regular airport flight. It came closer, so much so that she ducked involuntarily. A small cream Cessna ski-plane landed and taxied to her dock, where the dish sat collecting snow. Was the guy crazy? Belle threw on a heavy coat, boots and hat and followed her snowmobile path to the lake.

"Good thing I saw your dish," a man said, getting out of the plane and letting the motor idle. "Where's Dan? Place sure don't look like a lodge."

Belle propped her hands on her hips and yelled over the engine noise. "What are you talking about?"

The man squinted at the house while the snow danced circles around his waist. "Say, isn't this..." He wheeled as he bit off the words and climbed back into the cockpit, throttling up and off in a swirl. She watched him fly down the lake until he disappeared in the shrouded darkness. Too small for instrumentation gear, yet he hadn't seemed low on fuel or in trouble. She made a note to call Steve Davis, a detective on the Sudbury Force. Besides, Steve owed her a dinner.

TWO

For once, the predictions had been accurate. The vicious storm which had buffeted the area left behind perfect conditions for snowmobiling, only -15° C with lots of fresh powder. Across the lake nestled pockets of fog, trapped in the line of low hills, a parfait of white and green to burn off in the bright daylight. The dog looked up expectantly. "Next time, Freya," Belle promised. "I'm going too far today."

Winter fought fairly on its own primitive terms: strap on cross country skis or snowshoes, or drive a snow machine. Sudbury's graying population of retirees from the mining industry was well-represented, since the "sport" required little more than a strong right thumb and a resistance to cold; youth and muscle were secondary advantages unless breaking trail or attempting aerial stunts. Belle's compact red Yamaha Bravo 250 lacked the benedictions of reverse gear, instrumentation, automatic start or cushy suspension, but she had installed handwarmers, a cheap but blissful fix. The dependable Volkswagen of the snow machine world got her where she wanted to go, and better yet, allowed her to view the scenery instead of just an eye-watering blur.

Freya moped in the computer room, her ample poundage curled up impossibly in her "cheer," a stuffed plaid monstrosity shredded by long-gone cats and banished from polite company. Remaining there through the tempting aromas of bacon frying and toast browning signalled a grade-A sulk. Despite the pats and nuzzles, the dog pointedly ignored her, turning her head in a classic snub. Belle buried her face in the thick neck hair, inhaling the comforting smell of a clean, healthy animal. "Back in the Cro-Magnon caves, girl, you'd have kept me warm and safe, fleas aside," she said as Freya finally sighed in resignation.

Can't let a dog run your life, Belle told herself, collecting her gear: long red "thunderwear," T-shirt, sweater, sweat pants, a versatile woollen cowl, felt-pack Kodiak boots and the bulky snowmobile suit. Dressing in deep winter seemed like running a Mobius strip, so she left everything in layers and piles, burrowing in and out with acquired skill. Under her helmet and face shield she wore a balaclava; heavy mitts which reached up her arm completed the outfit. The luggage container held extra oil, topographic maps, spark plugs, tools, lighter and a sinister pick designed for escape from a fall through the ice, useful in summer for preparing ice chips for drinks. Her survival gear, which included a tube tent, thermal blanket, rope, flare and chocolate, stayed permanently in the rear carrier.

Except for a few islands and its southern shore where Belle lived, most of Lake Wapiti was undeveloped Crown land or First Nations Reserve. Scientific opinion had called it the site of a meteor crater, a smaller version of the meteor bomb which had christened the Sudbury basin "Nickel Capital of the World." Roughly eight miles in diameter, a crude circle, the lake was over three hundred feet deep in the centre. In winter, the sleeping giant opened onto thousands of miles of snowmobiling trails, stretching north to James Bay, east to Quebec and west to Manitoba and Michigan. It was an amazing secondary transportation network, complete with signage, restaurants and motels, slipping through small towns happy to snag the tourists in winter. Teenagers in outlying districts drove the machines to school, often following hydro tower trails to avoid the roads.

Since the day was clear, the sand cliffs or "Dunes" at the North River loomed sharply. This tributary had played a vital role in the lumber trade at the turn of the century. Millions of board feet of pine, oak and maple had floated down it, bypassing rapids via wooden plank runways called "flumes." The logs were gathered near the river mouth to be transported by a narrow gauge railway straight to town. Much of the wood had rebuilt Chicago after the fire. Within a ten-mile radius of the original smelter in adjacent Copper Cliff, the acid fumes of the open pit nickel smelting, which continued until 1928, had destroyed the remaining growth. Once the vegetation vanished, the fragile topsoil ran down the hills, leaving the notorious moonscape where astronauts came to train.

In a long-overdue response to the ecological disaster, not to mention the embarrassing publicity, forces from industry, government and the community had joined to arrest and repair the damage. The erection of the 1250 foot Superstack in 1972, aggressive liming and reseeding ("Rye on the Rocks") and summer programs which hired students to plant thousands of trees had started coaxing the shell-shocked landscape back to life. It was a slow process, but by the nineties, black was becoming green again.

Stopping at a pressure ridge where the ice plates collided to form sinister hedges, Belle searched for a safe passage around the weak spots. No one was in danger of going through on such a massive lake, though. Most drownings occurred farther south when novices pressed the season's start or finish, or on smaller lakes where springs ran all winter, even at 35 below. The year's snowmobile death toll stood at forty in Ontario, most from crashes into fences, rockcuts, other machines and even trains. She passed one ice hut village and drove on to the next, where trucks and cars were gathered round, chimneys puffed out warmth and hardy children flew Canadian flag kites in the stiff breeze. Although a few lone huts parked over personal hot spots, most people preferred togetherness over privacy. Ice fishing was a social event complete with card games, meals and matching beverages. At the shack beside the customized Phazer reading "Rocket Man" on the hood, she cut her engine and knocked at the plywood door. Inside, his feet propped up near a small tin stove, sat Ed DesRosiers, warming half a *tourtière* on an aluminum pie plate. A freshly opened pack of Blue Light made her shake her head, but only one bottle had been opened.

"Ready to go?" Belle asked as she settled into a battered lawn chair next to one of the holes, jigging the bait and peering down a turquoise crystalline tunnel of ice to the waterworld below. Raising a polite eyebrow at Ed, she broke off a piece of the meat pie, sinking her teeth with satisfaction through the flaky lard pastry to the spicy filling seasoned with a touch of nutmeg, Hélène's signature.

"Let me pack up and get my duds on. Got to run this brew back to the house so's it don't freeze. Fire's nearly out," he said.

Behind the carton of beer, a yellow-brown form with black mottling lay still on the floor, chin whiskers and tubular nostrils giving it a prehistoric look. Belle felt a small shudder. "Ugh. Talk about the Creature from the Black Lagoon. What in God's name is that thing?"

Ed finished his bottle with a happy burp. "Cod's name, you mean. Freshwater, otherwise known as ling. My *grandpère* used to call it burbot, mud fish. Lots of people throw them back on account they aren't so pretty, but they're tasty—white and flaky flesh. Smoked is even better." He stroked his catch with affection and tucked it into his carrier. "No scales to speak of, but the skin is some tough."

"Say it's trout if you serve it to me. I don't want to know."

Shortly after, they gunned up the steep hill to the top of the Dunes, sand base exposed from the traffic. Accessible by an old logging road in the summer, the Dunes had served for decades as an unofficial park where locals planted their trailers Newfie-style to enjoy the beaches and the fishing. The proposed development would bring thousands of tourists from crowded Southern Ontario, as well as the United States, at a high cost to the environment. "Sad to see this wilderness disappear if that plan goes through," Belle said as she flipped up her facemask. "We've had this bush to ourselves for so long. The casual camping is dangerous, though, especially because of the fires. That should have been stopped years ago. No manpower for patrols, I guess."

"You can say that again," Ed said. "I see them bonfires clear across the lake June to August. Let the wind come up and she could burn every hectare between here and North Bay, never mind how many water bombers they keep at the airport."

"Last year, when that big one hit at Chapleau, you could smell the smoke across the province. And on a clear day a charred birch leaf dropped onto my lawn like a silent message," Belle said, remembering the filigreed threads, a telegram of gray lace.

"Lotta money for somebody, though. Killarney's full up all summer. Crazy fools in Toronto willing to drive three, four hours on weekends just to get out of the Big Smoke. The lodge owners will do a fancy business in boat rentals, not to mention food, booze and bait. The Beaverdam, Dan Brooks' place on the lower east shore. That's the nearest."

"I wouldn't care if the Beave closed up forever," Belle said with a snarl. "Its traffic goes right by my house, one pee stop away. Two a.m. on weekends, I'll bet ten or fifteen guys stop at my dish like a landmark, yelling to each other and roaring their motors so loud I need a second set of earplugs. Anyway, I heard Brooks was going under. His old dump hasn't had a facelift since his father built it."

"Funny," Ed said, "because Paolo told me that his nephew was hired last summer to build new cabins. At least ten. Would have to mean a big septic system, too. That'll cost."

They gazed up the frozen North River, more inviting than a hilly trail, but too undependable for travel with its treacherous currents beneath the smooth snow. "Stumps show where the old bridge used to be," Ed pointed. "Great place for pickerel. Those Belcourts who drowned were fishing there when the storm came up. One boat went to the shore; the other fool went straight across."

"What happened? That was before my time."

Ed shook his head as if he wondered how anyone could have been so stupid. "New motor was too big. That's how they tipped. Then night hit and no one could go after them. Had to stay with the overturned boat, and you know how cold this bugger lake is. Only the two kids left by dawn. And the poor old aunt never come up." A common rumour had it that the chill and depth of the water often kept corpses from surfacing.

The Drift Busters Club Bombardier groomer ("Your trail pass money at work") chugged by. A tall tank with a heated cab, it inched along on huge treads. Sometimes Belle watched it creeping across the lake at night, a powerful beam reaching out like a cyclops eye. Now the trail to the lodge was level and wide, offering ample room for seeing around tricky corners. There was a speed limit, but how could a few volunteer marshalls enforce it on endless wilderness trails? And snowmobile horsepower had risen dramatically thanks to the competition for market share. Belle's Bravo 250 was a baby; 650cc was common, and trade magazines reported that the new Thundercat 1000 was capable of over 180 km/h on a lake. The weekend before, two riders had collided on Lake Nipissing, sending up a fifty-foot flame on impact which had melted their expensive full-face helmets.

Once underway, the pair passed through the typical Boreal forest at a steady pace. Stretching across Canada, Russia and Scandinavia, this hardy microclimate consisted of deciduous aspen, balsam poplar and white birch as well as the conifers, white and black spruce, tamarack, balsam fir and lodgepole, and jack pine. Since Sudbury also skirted the southern forest, the spectacular hues of maple, oak and yellow birch hardwoods painted the fall like an artist's palette.

Half an hour later, into the Mamaguchi territory, pines three feet thick towered over cathedrals of spruce and cedars bent by heavy snow. A chickadee flock rustled the birch bark for grubs and the pads of a lynx pair crossed the trail and exited in lengthening strides after the tell-tale triple prints of a rabbit. An arrow with a large happy face marked the turn for the Burians' lodge.

Finally they reached a tiny clump of log buildings dwarfed by massive pines on the shore of a long, narrow lake. Ted, with a fat black Lab ambling around him, was unloading jerry cans of gas from a Bombardier hauler. The small lodge sold fuel to those too lazy to carry their own, but at a high premium. A dollar-sixty a litre, nearly eight dollars a Canadian gallon. The gas and provisions had to be lugged eighty kilometres from town, including the last twenty by sledge on a snowmobile trail. "How many last weekend at the poker run, Ted?" Ed asked, cutting his engine.

"We fed over a hundred," the boy said proudly. "Mom was

stirrin' up spaghetti out of everything she could find."

Belle gave the dog, Tracker, a quick pet as she and Ed shed their helmets and heavy jackets before entering the small main building. Inside were a large kitchen, a dining room with a homemade industrial drum woodstove and four pine tables, and the entrance to a sleeping nook for the family. High over the stove hung a simple but effective clothes dryer: a metal bed frame for wet mittens, scarves and boot felts. A black bear head with whimsical antlers bore a brass plate reading "Old Ned, 1982."

Mrs. Burian greeted them, face flushed from the steam and flour dusting her apron.

"Hello, Meg. I finally made it. What's cooking?" asked Belle.

"Spaghetti, garlic bread and apple crisp, with plenty of country cream to fatten you up, Ed, from my brother's dairy in New Liskeard," the woman replied as Ed snapped his suspenders. Her gray hair was yanked into a sensible bun, but in her dervish toils, wet tendrils framed her face. Belle had rarely seen her sitting; if she weren't preparing food or cleaning, she was hanging washing out to freeze-dry. A minute later Meg plopped two chipped, steaming mugs before them.

"Jim stopped by and told me to get myself up here," Belle said. "He seems to be doing well at the university. You must be proud of him."

She had hit the right chord. Meg's face lit up like a generous April sun, hands framing her ample hips. "Likes his course in Forestry Management real fine. All As last semester. Right now he's at one of our hunt camps to write up some project. Had the big storm, so I guess he's taking his time getting back. Sunday supper, he'll make it. Moose stew's his favourite."

"What do you people think about that new park?" Belle

asked her as two more snowmobilers came in with a rush of cold.

Meg opened up the stove and tossed a birch log into the flickering flames. "None of us is too happy, I guess, more people, more trash, more problems. In the summer, of course, it might bring canoe trade, but that's our vacation time. And then there's the pictographs." She pointed to some black and white photographs on the wall which outlined vaguely human shapes, stars, circles and crosses on a rock face. "Ben took me up there canoeing on our honeymoon. Better than Niagara Falls. Those red ochre images have been on that old Champlain canoe route since God knows when but won't last long now, people get to rubbing at them. Jim tell you about that rally at the university?"

"Sounds like a good idea for us cottagers to go, too. It's rush hour every Saturday night the Beaverdam is open. The noise never stops," said Belle as she and Ed dug into the spaghetti. Alphabet letters dotted the tangy sauce, but it tasted sublime. And the dessert surpassed all promises, thick swirls of cream over tart apples.

As they paid the token five dollars each, Belle asked after Ben. Meg opened the door and peered out, shielding her eyes from the reflected sun off the snow. "Here comes Pop. Took the sled over to the ridge to pick up some down-and-dead." In certain wilderness areas, the Ministry issued permits to harvest fallen trees and widow-makers.

"So where have you been? First time all year," Ben said, hitting the kill switch on the small sled designed for light bush work. He picked up an axe and lifted a five-gallon gas can over his shoulder. "Loading up on Mom's special, I'll bet." A lean sixty, his face tanned and creased from outdoor work at the small lodge on weekends, Ben had retired early from Falconbridge,

Inco's little brother, a mining corporation. He passed a few minutes with Belle and Ed complaining about the weather.

"Don't go yet," Meg called as she ran up bearing a small jar wrapped in a calico cloth. "Wild gooseberry jam. Jim picked me a bounty last summer, and I forgot to give you one at Thanksgiving." Belle thanked her and wedged the jar firmly into the carrier.

"I could have stood a nap after that meal," Ed said.

"No wonder Hélène calls you an old bear."

The slap of -10° C revitalized them as they topped up the machines from a carrier jug. Ed and Belle had marked a trail north through a ridge system, down through Laura Lake and back to Wapiti. After a half hour, they stopped at an unusual pine loop. "Might make a good picture," she said. Then they noticed a track snaking into the bush. Not many drivers left the main routes, and with good reason. Without a snowshoe path, machines had rough going breaking trail, especially on fresh, heavy snow. Travelling unbroken lakes was even riskier, since a layer of melt often lurked under the pristine snow blanket. Yet it looked sooooo good, so tempting, that a rider just had to make a track across, put his mark on the landscape, cut the birthday cake. A machine could, however, be trapped in this treacherous slush until a freeze allowed its owner to round up burly friends to chop it out of the ice. Rescue by helicopter was an expensive proposition. "Looks firm enough. Trapper's cabin? Good fishing hole?" Ed wondered as he backed up, then revved his engine like a young kid. "Might lead somewhere interesting. Want to have a go?"

"Why not? It's only two o'clock," Belle said. "At the first sign of a problem we'll stop. Neither of us has the muscles to budge these machines if they bog down."

"Speak for yourself, little lady," Ed snorted, though he

rubbed his hip thoughtfully. Already a few yards past the cut, Belle began the laborious process of turning the Bravo, first shifting the skis by tugging on the metal loops, then lifting the heavier rear of the sled. "I'll have reverse next time even if I have to mortgage the dog. No more bullwork for me," she said, wincing at an ominous twinge in her back.

Following the path was a jerky trip, with Belle's skis slipping in and out of wider ruts, drifted over in places. Shimmying and sliding, they followed a roller coaster trail through heavy spruce, the laden boughs dropping snow down their necks as they passed. One sharp turn cut around a massive glacial outcropping of rock twenty feet high, shrouded in snow. Finally they spotted the frozen lake, ringed with dark firs, cloudless cerulean blue above, the picture of serenity… except for a ragged, refrozen hole with a hand beckoning, pointing at that same blue sky.

THREE

S omeone's gone down!" Belle cried, braking at the shoreline. A round pool of new ice, a lake within a lake, had formed in the older snow cover. A sled had travelled perhaps forty feet before breaking through and left only the pale blue hand locked into the new surface.

"Looks like he never even swam for it. Jesus, poor bastard," Ed said, testing the edge with his boots and shielding his eyes against the glare. "See anything?"

"A flash of red just below. That fresh ice is a couple of inches thick already, but I'm not walking out on it. Too deep to spot anything else. We'll have to go back for help. The police will bring a diver. And they'll need an axe."

They drove back quickly, pushing into the lodge as a surprised family of four lowered forks from their spaghetti. Belle called toward the kitchen. "There's someone broken through about a half hour north." She chose not to mention the hand.

"I'd better get Ben ready," said Meg, a small line worrying her forehead as she gave a huge iron pot a stir. "You don't think..." she murmured as she rushed out in search of her husband, leaving her coat hanging on the rack.

Since the area was well outside the city's jurisdiction, Belle used the radio-phone to call the Ontario Provincial Police, then stood by helplessly while Ben packed his gear and rounded up some sleds, speaking softly to his wife as he gave her a hug. "I know what's on your mind, and you can stop it right now."

"But where is he? He's always back way early for Sunday dinner. And the storm's long over. Been clear since morning."

"It's the boozers and daredevils have the accidents. Jim knows how to handle himself in the bush. Maybe he had some problems with his research, Meg. Or worked extra hard for those exams," Ben said as he lifted the cover from his largest machine, packed the rescue gear and, with an efficiency born of second nature, attached a fibreglass cargo toboggan.

Belle rubbed at her numb ears in the rising wind. "The O.P.P. said to wait until they arrived with the air ambulance. The plan is to leave the helicopter here where there's plenty of space. That swamp lake is too dense with bush. I told them that we hadn't touched anything at the site, not that there was anything to see." Only one thing, she thought with a shudder.

While they warmed up on coffee, the drone of the rotors filled the still air; sound from above travelled far in winter with the dampening effect of the snow and the bare trees. A short man, whose confident bearing added a mental foot, climbed down and walked over, two constables on his heels. "I'm Al Morantz. I understand that a body was found. What can you tell me about the site?"

Belle made the introductions. "Ed and I found the lake following a trail not too far from here. Probably doesn't even have a name, a little swamp like that. Track goes to the edge, and the rest is a refrozen hole."

Morantz looked around. "We're short on personnel, or I would have had our machines meet us here. I understand from what you said on the phone, Miss Palmer, that we can use the lodge's."

"Thought of that," Ben said and gave the officers two sets

25

of keys as he pointed toward the shed. One of them retrieved his diving gear from the helicopter.

Meg appeared in a patched-up snowmobile suit, carrying a thermos of coffee. "No arguments, Pop. I'm going with you."

A barely perceptible frown from Belle with her lips framing a "no" got through to Ben. "Don't think you should, Ma. You might be in these folks' way."

Arms folded, Meg got onto the two-up seat in stubborn silence, while Al and his men started the lodge's other machines. Driving in cortège, unsmiling and heedless of the packs of laughing drivers on the trail, they reached the lake and cut their motors. Before anyone had time to react, Meg ran to the shore, her agonized voice breaking the sudden stillness. "My God. Oh, my God in heaven. That hand." While the diver stripped to his wet suit, she inched forward on the dark surface of the new ice, her eyes exploring the shadowy grave until she slumped over in a sob, hugging her knees. "The little patch of red down there. That's the scarf his grandmother knitted him for Christmas. I know it is," she said, trembling as if she had aged a hundred years.

To the collective chill of the onlookers, the diver wielded an axe to break the surface. Tossing it back on to the shore, he disappeared with a stoic shake of his shoulders into the murky water, bubbles rising in his wake. His face around the mask was exposed, and the pain was evident on the second surfacing. "Can't see too well. Could be ten feet to the bottom. One arm of the coat is hung up on a branch. Guess that pushed the mitt off."

No one spoke. Finally, with the help of several officers, he hauled the body to the shore, bulky and sodden in the heavy suit and boots. Ben waved the men aside and unstrapped the helmet. It was Jim, or his pale double, a light slate cast to the features, sandy hair freezing brittle in the wind and jade eyes dulled by a final curtain. Ben knelt as if in prayer, his shoulders shaking, as he gently brushed the boy's forehead. "What in the name of Christ were you doing out here?" he whispered.

Belle turned away, leaning against the solidity of a huge pine for support as Ben rocked the boy back and forth, and the rest of the group fell silent. "He's cold. He's so cold, Meg."

His wife spoke slowly and deliberately, her voice struggling for control, wiping her tears away with the rough nylon of her suit. "No. No. No." A litany of pain in a single syllable. "Jim never would have come to a place like this alone."

Morantz waited a few moments before taking the Burians aside so that the rescue team could prepare the body for transport. The couple held each other, Ben shielding his wife's face. With some firm and steady pressure on the stiffening limbs, the team arranged the body on the toboggan with dignity. Another man winched the small Ovation to shore, weeds and muck hanging from its handlebars. Attached neatly to the rear carrier with a shock cord was his duffel bag. Like a slate wiped clean, the lake began freezing again, guarding its secrets as tightly as the earth itself. Belle glanced around, any possible evidence trampled to mush by the footprints and machine tracks of the rescue effort.

"What happens now?" she asked Morantz.

Morantz tried to write a note on a small pad, then exchanged the pen for a no-fail pencil. "Just like an auto accident. First we'll get him back to the hospital for an autopsy. Check for alcohol and drugs. Go through that gear on the sled. Get his medical records and rule out heart attack or seizures." He paused. "But, Miss, I want to be clear about one point. You did say that his was the only track? No sign of another person?"

She gestured uselessly as if in violent denial of the facts.

27

"One track straight to the lake. No sign of turning around, no other sled. But what in heaven was he doing here in the storm? Could he have been documenting an old trapper's trail when it hit? Or taken a wrong turn trying to get home?" Belle asked, though experience told her otherwise.

"The storm was a bad one." Morantz shrugged and closed his notebook. His conclusion was obvious; without other evidence, this tragedy was just another fatal human error, another statistic for the bean counters. The last frame in a shattered film script saw Meg tucking her scarf around Jim's neck as if saying a loving goodnight, Ben standing stiffly aside, Jim's helmet dangling from his hand. And then the convoy, a northern funeral procession, headed back to the lodge as a jay screamed through the diamond-chipped air.

Belle gestured to Ed, and they set off in silence. As they parted later in front of his house, he asked, "Come in for a drink? Maybe it might do you good to talk to Hélène. Her car's back."

"Talk? Talk about what, Ed? You were there, weren't you? Jim's dead. There's no resurrection." She saw his face sag, and instantly she regretted her brusqueness. "Sorry to be rude. I just lost a good friend and at my age, I can't spare any. What just doesn't make sense is what he was doing there."

"Well, we took the trail to check it out. Why not him?"

"Maybe, but when? I suppose the time of death might give us a clue. God knows how rigor mortis works in those icy conditions. Anyway, take care of yourself. Hélène, too." She slapped his arm with her glove and drove off.

Only as she opened her own front door and tripped over her briefcase did she remember that she had an appointment in town.

Evening work was a negative reality of her job, but that

night the distraction was welcome. She had scheduled a preliminary visit to a newly divorced woman in Chelmsford who wanted to move home to her parents in Val D'Or.

Belle left the house in a charcoal wool pantsuit and white turtleneck under her parka. Pulled over her ears was an incongruous blue and red Norwegian soft felt hat, which used to prompt cries of "Smurf!" from rude children. Clutching her briefcase, a newspaper and a thermos of Bavarian Dutch Chocolate coffee, she tested the van doors. Frozen again! Third time this week. Belle swore softly and began the usual procedure with her de-icer spray. If that didn't work, Plan Two involved her hair drier and a series of lively expletives.

She finally broke in, only to find the power antenna had seized. Nothing but static on the radio. Belle grabbed a tape of her favourite musicals and tucked it into her bra with an "eeeek". Twenty minutes of body heat would thaw it enough to play. Whoever said that women's liberation began in the seventies hadn't listened to the grand old babes of the sixties, Lucille Ball in *Wildcat*, Tammy Grimes in *The Unsinkable Molly Brown* and Roz Russell in *Wonderful Town*. Those tough ladies made their own rules, and men loved them for it.

Edgewater Road was a winding, hilly six-mile run, which passed the Santanens' at the final turn to the main highway. Derek Santanen had served eight months in the Sudbury Jail for drug dealing. His parents' tiny place clung like a limpet to a narrow strip of land. It was built long before the road arrived, when camps were accessible only by boat or snowmobile. At well over three hundred pounds, Derek often turned to crime for its easy profits. Belle suspected that he favoured the house for its remoteness and for the many hidey holes for his stash. On one occasion, a police search had the cottagers lining the road and passing around pop and chips, while police divers explored his waterline fifty feet off shore to discover prime Acapulco gold in watertight containers. Derek Santanen might make a good starting point for any inquiries about the area drug trade.

Just before eight she arrived in Chelmsford, a quaint, predominantly French town. The glorious church and its spire anchored the village with the infinite grace of bygone centuries, every pink granite stone carted lovingly from the surrounding hills and carved by local masons. It might have stood in the Quebec townships. An ominous growl from the midriff reminded Belle that she hadn't eaten since lunch. She stopped at a small grill and stationed herself at the counter behind a blonde girl barely eighteen and dressed in the same size. The girl's eyes widened as Belle lip-read the menu, sucked in her breath and mumbled, *"Une moyenne poutine."* A brief pause, then her voice jumped an octave. *"Non, une grande poutine, s'il vous plaît!"*

"La même chose pour moi," Belle added quickly. Growing up in Toronto had not been the place to learn colloquial French, and her fledgling vowels amused shopkeepers so much that she was glad when they smelled her accent and switched gears into English without missing a beat. She watched the waitress anoint the mounds of crispy fries with tender chunks of cheese curds swimming in gravy, the lifeblood of the North, especially in winter.

Belle ferried the steaming plate of sin to a table and opened the *Northern Life* to scout the offerings of her real estate competition. She knew every lake and cottage for sale within one hundred miles, and considering that the Regional Municipality counted over ninety named lakes within its boundaries, that was a feat in itself. Holy moley, another Ramsey Lake cottage lot was on offer, probably one of the last. Central to downtown, the largest city-contained lake in the world, only Ramsey's most remote sections remained undeveloped. Water and sewer were on their way, which would jack up the lot price by thirty thousand. Might be worth it, though. "Lakefront," Uncle Harold had growled philosophically, "they ain't making any more."

Lights were off at 2334 Brentwood, but Belle was early. Well-prepared for such cold delays, she sipped the aromatic coffee, started the engine every ten minutes and played tapes. *Nashville* was a favourite, its parodies of country songs so true-to-form that they passed for legitimate. "He's Got a Tape deck in his Tractor" always made her grin. Belle had been drafting a song in memory of the better parts of her mother. After all, she told herself, there are only about one hundred words in country music, so why not mine? She tapped out the chorus:

> Come on up to Mama's table,
> If you're hungry or you're cold,
> If you've got too many mouths to feed
> Or if you're growing old.
>
> She'll shelter and she'll feed you,
> She'll have a hug to greet you.
> You'll always feel real welcome
> At my Mama's kitchen door.

The pencil got a chew. Oops, "have a hug to greet you" should come before the "shelter" part. At this point, the tune didn't concern her. Maybe a music student from Shield could compose the score.

Startled by the sudden lights of a car, Belle spilt the coffee on her coat. As usual, she had forgotten a napkin, so she dabbed at the liquid with a tampon from the glove compartment.

Out of a battered Escort struggled a woman trailing three small children, one of them bawling like a frustrated weanling. "You must be Ms. Palmer," the woman shouted as Belle rolled down a window. "Sorry for the delay. I had to go to the lawyer's in town, and then all the kids wanted hamburgers. Come in and make yourself comfortable. I'll settle them in the rec room while we talk." She hefted the screamer over her shoulder like a sack of potatoes, cooing and patting it for good measure.

"Do you mind if I look around upstairs first, Mrs. Mainville?" Belle asked. "It might save us some time, and you look like you've had a tough day." Nothing like womanly understanding.

"Call me Joan," the woman answered with a smile as she hustled the kids down the basement stairs.

Conventional suburban living with a country advantage: three bedrooms, newish kitchen, dining room in name only, living room with a view overlooking a pasture. Big yard for children. Too bad someone had sparkle-plastered the living room ceiling and installed red shag carpet half-way up the wall. It suggested a planetarium designed by Hugh Hefner. After making notes, Belle joined her client downstairs where Barney was mumbling mindless platitudes as the kids giggled. Both women winced at the numbing chorus. "I hate it, too, but what can you do?" Joan said.

"Better than violence...or is it?" Belle replied. "All kiddie shows should carry a warning sign."

Joan took her into the laundry room to point out with shy pride an amply-stocked cold cellar. "I'm a fool for canning," she said. "Don't know how I'm going to take all of this to Mom's, though." Here sat the winter wealth of resourceful Northerners, jars of pickled beans, carrots and beets, and the inevitable green tomato chow, an innovative answer to a short growing season. "Guess my neighbours might like them." The spotless jars and shelves pleased Belle, since a clean place always showed better, and she found herself accepting a jar of chow. Amenable to suggestions about the value of neutral colours, Joan waved a cheerful goodbye. Somehow Belle couldn't mention the crimson carpeted wall; maybe if the place didn't sell quickly...

Back home, she noticed the blinking light on her answering machine. A female voice spoke softly but deliberately. "My name is Melanie Koslow, Miss Palmer. I was engaged to Jim. I need to talk to you about the accident...in person if you have time. My schedule's pretty full with my nursing course, but I'm usually at Tim Horton's on Regent Street before class every morning at eight. Just look for a red wizard hat and pile of books. If those times aren't good for you, call me at 233-4566 at the Shield Nursing Residence."

Abruptly, her mind returned to Jim, the hand in the frozen lake and the the accident that—just maybe—wasn't.

Later, as the moon circled the house, Belle curled up with a book, trailing Dave Robichaux through the bordellos of sultry New Orleans. The book snapped shut at eleven, and Belle fingered the light switch. A churchgoer only as a child, she maintained a cautious belief in a personally-designed afterlife. Prayers were a convenient method to take stock of the day and remember old friends. No one had ever answered her calls, and, while this silence perturbed her at first, in the long run it was saner. A premonition about not getting on a certain plane to Buenos Aires was fine; constant suggestions and recriminations from the other world would be not only distracting but might send the listener to a madhouse. So she maintained a one-way conversation with Uncle Harold, her grandparents and her mother, imagining a host of patient advocates nodding and blessing her each night. "Help me take good care of the old man, Mother," she asked, gazing up at a framed silhouette of someone her own age "and keep us safe from all harm." Somehow she just couldn't call on Jim. Not yet.

FOUR

Though she opposed new development on Wapiti out of principles both selfish and unselfish, Belle had no objection to trading in established properties, in this case, a large piece by the marina. The original owner had bought cheap, tacked up a small camp and outbuildings, then squatted on it for decades, paying only minimal taxes. Then about twenty years ago, as lakefront grew scarce, land values had started to climb. The price had risen to 95K for each of three lots in the last hot market. Why Julia Kraav wanted to purchase all three properties was a puzzle. Perhaps she had a big family.

In order not to waste time and effort, Belle had vetted her client as carefully as the law allowed. The older woman had been almost embarrassingly frank in disclosing her financial assets. Not only a fine brick home on York Street but over 700K in rock-solid investments. How had the Kraavs saved so much, the husband a Sudbury Transit driver and the wife a salesclerk? Then Julia had described their life plan: no kids, a tiny house shared with her parents, every cent banked, the last ten years in GIC's when the rates hit double-figures. A year of retirement and Tomas had died of liver cancer, she had added with bitterness. "Congenital heart disease killed all of my family before fifty-five. And here I am, alive and kicking after two operations, and my darling man is gone. Life is not rational."

As Belle rolled down the driveway, she wondered if Julia were intending to sell her house as well; if so, the broker's commission would be impressive. The open garage beside the house held trailers with a Seadoo and a 40 horse bass boat, strange toys for an elderly woman without children. A fancy Jeep Cherokee with leather interior was parked in the drive, its fender suspiciously creased. Evidence of costly landscaping peeked from the snow: new tie beds and pink crushed stone as expensive as marble. Life-size bronze statues of a doe feeding and a buck boasting ten-point antlers graced the front lawn. A hedge of small cedars from the walkway to the house gave way to a row of six-foot junipers. Belle had priced one of those charmers before shouldering her shovel and heading to the bush for a handy pine.

As she stepped up to the porch, Belle peered into every Northerner's dream: a Florida room containing a hot tub, heavy-leaved tropical plants, and floor-to-ceiling glass, probably low-E, which regulated the heat transfer for efficiency. What a spa. Take a trip and never leave the farm. Suddenly she wished that she and Julia were better friends. Answering Belle's knock at the stained glass door, her client stood in a velvet morning gown. "Come in, dear. I've been expecting you." Even thinner than when Belle had last seen her, Julia glittered with feverish excitement, massaging her tiny hands, a blinding diamond on the ring finger. "I have such plans!" A younger look-a-like, conservatively dressed in jeans and silk blouse, sat on the couch, twisting the tassel of a pillow; she was introduced as Emily, a "baby" sister, and her eyes were afraid.

"I have been in touch with Mr. Converse," Belle said as Julia took her coat and showed her to a wing chair. "He is willing to offer all three adjoining properties as a package for

$70,000 each. That's quite a drop, but winter is a bad time for cottage lots. Nobody wants to buy what they can't use immediately. A bargain for you, though."

Pacing back and forth, the woman beamed as she waved a double checkbook. "I can give you the money now. I'm just so thrilled to have found the perfect place for my project. And now everything will be completed by summer."

Belle glanced at Emily and felt some misgivings at the concerned expression on her face. If Emily had doubts about the value of the purchase, perhaps reassurance would help. "It is excellent property. You'll have over 750 feet in lakefront with three acres across the road. A sandy beach and plenty of room for septic. There's a dug well, but for my money you'd be better off pumping out of the lake. Less iron."

"I remember the day you took me there, when we drove over the hill and saw the trees and the lake beyond spread out like the promised land. I closed my eyes and saw my vision come to life. So many good people to help. Isn't God wonderful, Emily?" Her sister sat mutely tearing a tissue into bits, a thin smile in answer.

"I'm a bit confused, Mrs. Kraav. What do you mean by 'so many people'? These are just cottage lots," Belle said, suddenly aware that she was clicking her retractable ball-point pen like a set of worry beads.

Julia shuffled a pile of letters across the coffee table, passing Belle envelopes with hand-written addresses, the crabbed alphabet of the barely literate. "Look at the responses to my ad."

Julia's too-merry laugh, just a tone below hysterical, raised the tension. "Oh, you don't understand. It's Tomas, my husband, as I told you. He came all this way as a boy from Estonia without a penny in his pocket. Didn't know a word of English either. What a story. I'm writing a book about our life, and I'm up to 1955 with the first three chapters. It'll be a best-seller, you watch. Even a movie eventually. Anyway, this whole development is for him, something really special to keep his name alive long after I'm gone." She picked up another sheet. "Here's the notice I placed across the country in the major newspapers," she said.

It read: "All Estonians are welcome to relocate to Northern Ontario to live at the Tomas Kraav Memorial Apartments. Moving expenses paid, free rent, a lakefront for recreation and nursing care for the elderly. Apply Box 23432 Sudbury, Ontario." Belle passed from Julia's radiant face to Emily's pale terror, struggling for words which she feared would destroy this illusion.

"But the land isn't zoned for multiple dwellings."

"Oh, you." She tapped Belle's knee with her fingers, drew out the words coyly, as if being teased. "My builder told me, 'No problem, no problem at all.' The whole east side will be developed along with that new park. Maybe a mall for shopping and a theatre. Won't that be a miracle for those poor souls? Many of them have never had a decent meal or a warm bed." As Julia clapped her hands, Belle saw through a shift in her gown a deep burgundy scar traversing her thin breastbone, which rose and fell with her quick breathing as if nourishing itself upon impossible dreams. The sight reminded Belle of a baby robin, blind, featherless, heart beating in a fierce rhythm to keep warm.

Belle scribbled a few meaningless notes to buy time, not knowing how to continue. "Do you think I could have a glass of water?"

"Oh, certainly. Hostess with the leastest, aren't I, Emily? Just excited. Would you prefer coffee?" When Belle shook her head, Julia floated her gown out of the room, leaving a faint trace of Estée Lauder.

The sister spoke quickly. "You're an honest woman, I can see. This scheme will break her, take every penny. She can buy the land and put up the buildings, but what then? There'll be nothing left for the support she promised them, or for her own expenses. It'll be a nightmare."

Belle sighed. "Of course. And she'd need an act of Parliament to change the zoning. That's single residence only. How do you want to handle this? She looks pretty fragile."

"Yes, she's been mixing Tomas's drugs with whatever garbage she could scrounge from her doctor. We're preparing to get a court order by Friday to lock up her finances until she can manage on her own again. Maybe you saw some of the toys she's been using to attract her friends and relatives. She wants to buy the world for anyone who loves her. Thank God she didn't hurt anyone with the Cherokee. But it's Tomas's death, you see. That's the centre of it all. I'm trying to get her into grief therapy."

Having invented some plausible stall technique which involved another meeting with the owner, Belle crossed town and logged in at the office. Uncle Harold had converted the downstairs of a splendid Victorian house in an older section of town lined with elegant cottonwoods. The upstairs rented to a retired couple who wintered in Florida but needed a Canadian address to maintain their medical coverage. Belle's realty company was no giant, but she had a long term, loyal clientele. In the earlier property boom, many wannabes had jumped on the bandwagon to make a fortune by selling real estate "part-time". These opportunists had long departed, and a $2,000 licensing fee kept the field lean and mean. Belle ran the business with an answering machine, a cellular phone and Miriam MacDonald.

Her first lieutenant had signed off a lifetime of bookkeeping to join Palmer Realty five years earlier. "There is nothing creative about accounting," she insisted, "unless you're working for an American savings and loan or the Parti Québécois during a referendum." She balanced her work for Belle with a passion for quilting. Her pieces had won awards, but she accepted commissions more for personal satisfaction: "That Log Cabin one for Alderman Winder cost me a month's labour, design and sewing. The $500.00 wasn't worth it." To Belle's embarrassment, Miriam had presented her with a stunning king-size quilt in the classic Whig Rose pattern for her birthday.

"How goes the battle?" Belle called as she pushed open the door.

Gray hair in a frizzy afro, her stockinged feet working a therapeutic wooden roller under her desk, Miriam grimaced, mouth tsking as her pencil checked a list. Gulping at intervals from her mug, she pummelled the computer keyboard and seemed annoyed at what she read on the screen. *"Sacrifice. Hostie."* French Canadian minced oaths always made Belle laugh. How many other languages centred their curses around the church and its trappings?

"Stop swearing about communion wafers. You're a Scot, or so you claim. Problems?" She sidled to the coffee machine and poured a generous cup, grateful for the practicality of black appliances. Wouldn't it be great to be able to afford an office cleaner?

Miriam puffed an errant silver curl from her forehead. "I've got such a chain of conditional sales that I'm a screaming mimi. Even if we're not the first realty on half of them, we'll make out like our former Prime Minister. But there's a fly in the proverbial ointment. Mr. Proulx on Norman Lake wants— get this—" she snarled, stabbing at a blurry black and white picture pinned onto the corkboard, "319K for his cottage. With only 65 feet frontage? It's a fishing shack with an outhouse at a 45 degree lean. Everyone else in line is being quite reasonable."

Belle smiled. "So it goes. He'll come around if he really wants to sell."

"If he really wanted to sell, he wouldn't ask the moon. And the whole house of cards may collapse by then." She muttered to herself, *"Câlice."*

"Chalice. There you go again. But doesn't this beat toting up a balance sheet in that cockroach race? Remember when you worked all night in an unheated shed to cook books for that sheet metal firm just before Revenue Canada hit town?"

Miriam stiffened. "Please don't use terms like that. You know I have never done anything actually illegal. But you're right. I don't relish dancing to anyone's tune. Thirty years of penal servitude was enough. And I'm not going to stew over this. Once I finish with Mr. P., he's toast, as my daughter says, at least this week." Her daughter Rosanne was twenty-three, a graduate from Shield University, now attending teacher's college in North Bay. "I warned her," Miriam said. "She'll have her hands full. Has she forgotten what a rotten teenager she was? I needed an exorcist." Then Miriam skidded to a stop between words and gave Belle a puzzled look. "You don't seem yourself today, and I've been babbling. Thinking about Jim?"

"Oh, I had a call from his girlfriend. Every time I close my eyes, I imagine his body trapped in that swamp lake, turning in the tea-coloured water while the ice freezes over him like a glass ceiling. It haunts me like that Atwood poem: 'The photograph was taken the day after I drowned. I am in the lake, in the center of the picture, just under the surface.'"

"That hand you described would bother me, too. Like an

accusation or a plea." She tapped her forehead in rebuke. "Forget that last part. Guilt is not what you need. Think about this. Suppose you hadn't come along, suppose more fresh snow had hidden the accident. The boy might never have been found. That's a parent's worst nightmare."

"It was pretty remote. What with the occasional wolf and fox in the area, the body wouldn't have lasted long if it had washed ashore in the spring. Still, it's small consolation for the family."

"So what does this girl want?"

"Lord, I have no idea. Perhaps a friend of Jim's to talk to." Her eyes closed for a moment. "The last time I saw him alive, he was writing a poem to her on his own heart. I do and I don't want to meet her. What might have been, and all that Victorian sentimentalism. And I hate funerals and viewings. Probably be an open coffin."

"The theatre of death. Morbid, if you ask me." Miriam rummaged under her desk. "Maybe this will help take your mind from the situation...and don't you dare offer to pay me after giving me every book in Sue Grafton's alphabet."

Belle opened the small parcel with a child's wonderment. "*Wild Orchids!* Do I dream? Where on earth did you ever find this? Surely not in town."

"No such luck. Got it in Toronto at Sam's. They sell classic videos there now. Rows and rows, just like a bookstore."

"You know I have none of the silents, Miriam. Thanks for thinking of me." Belle handled the video with reverence as she studied the cover notes. 1929. Sudbury had passed the bushcamp stage and was manfully trying to grow into a city, entering the Great Depression on its magic carpet of silvery nickel. The Sudbury Wolves played in the NOHA, and 110 acres of parkland on Lake Ramsey had been donated by W.J.

Bell. A World War One cenotaph had been unveiled, and Rudyard Kipling himself invited to pen an inscription. The Grand Theatre, formerly the Grand Opera House, had installed equipment for its first talkie. Maybe this delicate piece of celluloid had been the last silent shown to those lucky miners escaping the night shift, freshly scrubbed with carbolic soap and happy for relief from the dark tunnels beneath the city. She bent over and gave her friend a squeeze.

"Oh, hush up. Just let Rosanne use your computer for her term paper next time she's home. I'd get her one except that Scrooge doesn't pay me enough." Miriam stuck out her tongue and winked.

"No problem. You know she's welcome." Belle paged through her notebook. "Hey, what about that Nelson place you went to last week. Are the Toronto people ready to bite?"

"Funny story, but we lucked out. Nelson had told me that the septic system had, in his clever little words, 'been approved.' When I visited for pictures, all I saw was a pipe sticking out of a partially buried holding tank behind the house. No field bed at all. Wet as a mad hen, I was. Of course those Toronto folks hadn't even noticed. They think everything's hooked up to sewers like in cities, but I saved us some embarrassment. Can you imagine the first flushes? Straight out the back and shut down by the health department." She made a rude but descriptive noise.

Belle agreed. "And woe to us if the sale had gone through. Those weasel words might have held up in court. 'Approved' could have meant 'approved for construction.'"

Satisfied that her paperwork was beaten into submission, Belle made her daily phone call to Rainbow Country Nursing Home. At 83, her father had become confused and tottery in his apartment in Florida. Since he had given up his Canadian citizenship, sliding him over the border at the crucial juncture when he could still walk and talk had been a miracle for which she still gave thanks. "Nursing station? It's Belle Palmer. How's the old man today?"

Apparently he was as cantankerous as ever, with his loud demands, and expecting his usual Tuesday shrimp lunch. She visited him once or twice a week, but their conversation seemed limited to the expected meal, the weather and television. It hurt her to see him diminished, to watch the pieces of identity and independence vanish one by one, his expectations dropping with his capacities. Still, if his world had shrunk to food and media, he was in the same boat as 90 percent of North America. And the spunk that had banished him from the dining room made her applaud; when he lost the spark to roar out demands, his life would fade to a guttering candle.

He might not have been the intellectual giant her mother had wanted in a husband, but he had been a loving, kind and indulgent father, had rolled out a motorbike with a red ribbon on the handlebars when Belle entered university, and had slipped her money to travel to England. And as a booker, he had passed on his love of films. How many other ten-year-olds had white mice named Errol and Bette, or a pet squirrel named Clara Bow? As soon as she could walk, he had taken her twice weekly to the private screening room at his office to watch new releases, "every film ever made," he told everyone later at Rainbow. Once the warm weather came, Belle hoped to take him out, wheelchair and all, to one of the blockbuster movies, or maybe even the impressive new IMAX theatre.

On the drive home, listening to CBC radio relate the eternal scuffles of the world, Belle dithered over dinner options. An ice storm had hit the area that afternoon, so she was pleased to see the sander in front of her until a sudden dirty spurt hit her car. "Whoa, all right! I'm backing off," she said, remembering the price of her last paint job.

When she pulled into her yard and shut off the engine, she heard throughout the woods, a delicate symphony, the clear glaze on the tree branches tinkling onto the ground like broken chandelier crystals as the rising evening winds shifted course. Belle paused for a moment and tuned her ears to the delicate orchestration, a rare combination of sound, sight and texture. She reached toward a drooping willow twig, its soft gray pussies wrapped in a coat of ice melting under her hand as fast as it had formed. Back to reality, she sighed, knowing that she'd never get out of the driveway until she laced it liberally with stove ashes and sand.

Happy to be free, Freya chased a tennis ball around the parking area, dropping it into the snowbank at intervals and pawing it out in self-amusement. Meanwhile, her shoulders to the wind, Belle flung handfuls of grit from her bucket onto the icy drive.

A Thai dinner went into the microwave. Not bad for four dollars, but lemongrass mated evilly with chilies, reminiscent of bath powder. The oaky tang of Australian semillon helped cut the edge. Until just a few years ago, steak, pasta or Chinese had dominated the local culinary scene, but recently gourmet coffee, goat cheese and radicchio had made an appearance, and the largest supermarket, a giant which provided maps and carts the size of Alberta, had even installed an olive bar with eight varieties plus artichoke hearts and sun-dried tomatoes.

Freya got four cups of "Mature Dog" Purina, high in fibre. "I must be cruel, only to be kind," Belle whispered as the last cup dinged into the bowl. "You know you lard it on over the winter, and I don't want to be responsible for hip dysplasia."

The dog seemed to be counting, patiently expecting the usual five. Only when Belle turned did she grudgingly bury her nose in the bowl.

Belle took her decaf to the computer room. On the classic film forum, Dietrich's daughter's biography was raising hackles, her graphic descriptions of the old woman's final deterioration condemned as "ghoulish." Someone else wondered what had ever happened to Zasu Pitts and was surprised to find that the silent star had enjoyed a television career in *My Little Margie*, her zany lopsided grin ever marketable. One of these days I really should stop lurking, Belle said to herself, and get involved in this so-called information highway.

Mutual funds had the next round of home pages. As a recent ruthless capitalist in charge of her father's mutual funds, Belle combed the financial quotations, urging the TSE to retake its position above the DOW. "Try our International Money Market Fund," a local funds manager in a wheelchair, the very soul of trustworthiness, had advised, shoving a colourful brochure across the desk.

"At 3 percent this year? Sounds like a loser. Why should I invest in this?"

He had beamed and puffed on an imaginary cigar like a tycoon. "As a hedge, what else? Diversify. The Danish krone has appreciated by 29 percent this year." Was he really licking his lips? "You see, if the dollar drops big-time, you'll make plenty! An ill wind that doesn't blow some good and all that." That had been the last straw, to invest in the financial collapse of the country. The bank probably had a fund that would rocket only if Quebec separated, or British Columbia joined the U.S.

Slipping a tape into the VCR, Belle kicked back in the blue velvet recliner with a glass of Rebel Yell, bought at discount at the liquor store. That intriguing corn tang of a sunny Tennessee hayfield might someday burrow into the hearts of the rye lovers, but it was an acquired taste. *Susan Lenox, Her Fall and Rise* came on with a clean-shaven Gable as an engineer and Garbo on the run from a leering Alan Hale. How could anyone communicate so well using just the clavicles?

As she switched off the lights in the television room, a gentle hooting of barred owls greeted her from the backyard. She had heard their calls her first spring night in the house and had named the property after them, as a varnished sign at the driveway proclaimed: The Parliament of Owls. They returned in March to lay their eggs, risking sudden spring storms that could freeze them on their nests. Nature's amorality cut deep for animals as well as people.

FIVE

M eg's jar of gooseberry jam on the kitchen table the next morning reminded Belle of Melanie's invitation. She was curious about the girl Jim had taken into his heart and to his treasured places among the woods and streams.

Skipping breakfast and putting the jar out of sight, Belle was down the road by 7:15. The morning was cloudy and dark, the huge snowbanks an eerie source of reflected light. As Belle rounded a corner, her hands tightened on the wheel and she reached for the brake. A black, demonic shape seemed to be flying across the road four feet from the ground, its neon blue eyes trapped in her headlights. She heard no thump as the van moved slowly, now joined by a scrabbling form alongside, all jerky legs and lolling tongue. It was Buddy, a very fat young black Lab at his favourite game. Had he actually been flying or simply moving uphill from the vehicle in an optical illusion? She stopped, rolled down the window, and called him over. "Hi, Budman. Now get home, and I mean it." There wasn't a brain in the dog's head, nor a mean bone in his body. His owners should take better care of him, she thought. Bored dogs made their own entertainment; sometimes it was costly, sometimes dangerous. One more bite at a wheel might be his last.

Tim Horton's was Canada's premier doughnut shop in a country with five times more per capita than Big Brother down south. No surprise that beleaguered Canuckleheads chose a quick sugar and caffeine fix to escape briefly from the arctic temperatures. Tim's number 1000 had opened, and the prosperous chain was branching into sandwiches, soup, pies, cakes and cookies along with the reliable 25 different doughnut varieties available any hour of the day. Even the bathrooms would rate a nod from Martha Stewart. Belle sipped at her mug and checked the mutual fund reports in the *Toronto Star*, relieved not to have taken a flyer into the South American markets.

She lifted the paper periodically to check for Melanie, until she spotted a strange, medieval apparition in the crowd. A red wizard hat, made of soft fleece, cupped the head and ended with a tassel two feet down the back. Harry Potter's choice was worn by a strawberry blonde woman, shoulders bowed over a pile of books. Belle motioned her over, noticing that her eyes were swollen and tired as if she had been up most of the night. The girl's hand trembled as she took Belle's, but her grip was firm.

"Melanie? You look like you could use a coffee." In response to a nod, Belle brought back two mugs and matching giant carrot muffins and resisted the impulse to tuck a serviette under the quivering chin. Was the girl going to cry right there during rush hour?

Melanie brightened as she bit into the muffin. Tim Horton's always had a comforting effect." Thanks. I'm glad we could meet, and, you're right, I haven't thought much about food lately." A generous dollop of cream went into the cup. "You look just like Jim said." Her tone was innocent enough.

"Taken as a compliment," Belle replied, watching the girl's colour return. A few minutes of getting-to-know-you chat convinced Belle that Melanie could handle the unvarnished truth, so with an occasional glance of assessment, she proceeded with the story of her tragic discovery in the lake.

The girl was having none of it. "I don't care what all of you saw, or think you saw. That was no accident," Melanie said with a touch of bitterness and as dark a frown as youth and beauty would allow. "Anyone can tell you how well Jim knew those woods, every lake, tree and branch, down to the last mushroom. Besides, he had no time for bushwhacking. Exams were coming up, and he was part of the Stop the Park group, working on a project to document the diameter of those Granddaddy pines, he called them. Even had names for the biggest ones." She stopped to brush back a tear, sniffing into a napkin and pausing to gather her arguments.

"He mentioned that project when he stopped by for breakfast the last time I saw him. And you're right. The lake wasn't on one of his usual routes.

"That's why I called you. His parents told me that you didn't believe the accident theory either," the girl continued as Belle looked away helplessly. "Jim was the most cautious person in the world when it came to winter travel in the bush. Once he was standing on shore when a young boy broke through trying to cross an open patch. The machine flipped, and the boy was killed. First thing he told me when we went snowmobiling was never, never to break trail on a small lake, no matter how tempting."

"I agree with everything you're saying, but we don't have all the facts yet. Have the Burians mentioned the autopsy?" Belle wondered.

"Apparently Dr. Monroe has already finished. Told Ben that he checked for alcohol, but we all know that Jim never drank more than one beer, and never when driving. It just doesn't add up."

Belle looked into the swirly pools of cream in her coffee as if divining the future. "I'm not a professional investigator, Melanie, just a lowly real estate hack. Sure, we can trade our doubts, but why don't you go to the police? Steve Davis is a good man. Tell him I sent you."

The girl took a deep breath and contracted her brows. "What's the point? They're not taking it seriously. Listen, can we ask around? I'll take the campus, his friends, his teachers. Maybe together we can find out something. Jim did mention those planes near his hunt camp. The Burians said you had travelled the area north of the lake, and I know they wouldn't mind if you went to his new camp to see if he left some papers or notes. I'm sure they'd loan me a sled, but I'm tied up during daylight hours with my clinicals at the hospital."

"Last time I saw him, he was pretty upset about the drug traffic. If he found anyone using the bush for transfers, who knows what he might have done? As for records, Jim was pretty methodical. The camp might be worth a look." Belle pulled out a small notebook and scrawled a few words, frowning at her efforts. "My writing is so bad that it has a shelf life of about ten hours. After that, it's illegible. Anyway, I'll be glad to do some fieldwork. Just don't expect magic revelations. And don't discount the accident idea completely. One bush pilot I knew for twenty years flew right into a mountain near the Sault ski hills one bright June afternoon. There were five witnesses, and even they didn't believe what they saw. Nothing wrong with the plane either."

They sipped their coffees for several minutes, the interview winding down as they both checked their watches politely. Then Belle spoke up suddenly. "Something I didn't ask you, Melanie. The answer is probably obvious, but it is personal."

"Jim was my personal life, Belle." She looked dangerously

close to tears again, but Belle pressed on.

"The ageless question. What about enemies?"

"Enemies? He never had a bad word for anyone. He was a kind and gentle man. I never heard him raise his voice. Oh, except when he got excited about the drug problem in schools."

"Kind and gentle means nothing to some people. They regard it as weakness. Did anyone carry a grudge against him, a disagreement even in principle?"

The girl thrummed at the table with her fingers, a pink flush appearing on each check. "Well, there was Ian, my old boyfriend. Kind of embarrassing, though."

"Just keep it under a hundred words. You don't have to write for the tabloids. What was the story?"

Mel had been engaged to Ian MacKenzie in her sophomore year. He was in pre-law and heading for Osgoode Hall in Toronto. His irrational jealousy in combination with his heavy weekend drinking had spelled an end to the relationship.

Belle seemed surprised. Perhaps Melanie's judgement was not as sound as she had thought. "Did he ever hit you?" she asked.

"Ha! I'd never have stood for that. But the verbal threats were frightening enough."

"What kind of threats?"

"It happened after I began seeing Jim. In the halls, in the cafeteria, Ian never missed an opportunity to make an evil comment. Once he made a pretty ugly scene and called Jim awful names. Even gave him a shove. You know that kind of male posturing. I was proud when Jim put him down with a few choice words."

"And lately?"

"No sign of him. I hear he's been hitting the books to raise his grade point average."

"So he's still in town. One last question, Mel, a significant one. We need 'means' here. Does Ian have a snowmobile?"

Melanie grabbed Belle's arm in her excitement. "My God, yes. A new one every year. His uncle owns the biggest dealership in North Bay."

"Too good to be true, and it probably isn't, if you can follow that. I'll see, though. Give me his address."

Melanie seemed more optimistic when Belle left her. She obviously had a rare combination of common sense and imagination, just like Jim. What a couple they would have... Belle shook herself out of Shakespearean tragedy mode as she crunched on a last maple dip and ordered a box of Timbits for the road.

Early that afternoon, the Bravo took her to the Burians' lodge. No welcoming smoke poured from the main chimney this time. Ben gave her a long hug at the door, the wool from his hand-knit sweater brushing her cheek. "Warmer outside than in today. Sorry we can't offer you anything," he said.

"Are you packing up?"

He touched the cold stove with a sad sigh. "Yes, that's why no fire. Going back to town soon as Ma sorts the food. Don't have the heart to stay. Might even sell, anybody's foolish enough to try to run this dog-eared place. You can list it for us."

Belle met the old man's crinkled eyes and let him talk. "The viewing is this afternoon." He snorted into a handkerchief and apologized. "Halverson's. Will you be there?"

Belle felt as chilled as the dead stove. "Of course. And you probably know that Melanie called me. We had a long talk. I promised her I'd look around the camp."

"Don't know what you'll find of help, but I guess we owe it to Jim to try. Ted and I gave it a once-over, but it was too much for us to handle right off. Broke me down, that picture of Melanie and all his keepsakes. She was almost like a..." His reedy voice broke. "Just met the girl last winter, but it seemed like we'd been a family forever. She was so good for him. Gave him confidence. 'Course he was always handsome to us, but Mel was the best medicine." His voice trailed off.

Belle looked outside and left him with his thoughts. Then she resumed. "Listen, Ben, there's something else. What did Jim say about suspicious plane landings?"

Searching his mind, he flicked a lighter on and off, as if he wanted more than anything to start that stove again. "Well, sure, when you're up in the bush, quiet as it is, you notice everything, specially if it's out of order, odd, if you understand me. Small planes at night. Landing, too, from the sounds and tracks he saw on Obabika. Told me he was gonna have a word with you about it, you knowin' that policeman."

"Where else?"

"On Stillwell and Marmot, too. Come and go in ten minutes. Risky stuff in the dark. Fellow here last winter flipped the plane when his wing touched down. Had to lift the whole damn mess off by 'copter. Wasn't good for nothing but scrap."

"When you were at the new hunt camp, was anything out of place?"

Ben looked out the window to a squirrel digging a pine cone from its store under a stump. "Built it all himself. Axe, hammer and chainsaw. No, nothing was out of place, not that I'd notice. Not much there, anyways, a bit of food, furniture, some of his school stuff. I wish to God he hadn't tried to make it back that night in the storm. Stupid waste." He went to a shelf and picked up a folded topo map.

"See, here's the one. Not so far from that damn lake where he... Look, Belle." He set his jaw and passed his hand over his

54

brow. "How in hell did he get off the main trail when he could have found his way home blindfolded?"

"I see what you mean." Belle ran her finger over the route. "It's as if he headed home, then made a left turn miles before he should have. And then drove on and on, even though he was obviously going the wrong way, finally making another wrong turn. Mistakes that a panicky beginner would make, not a pro like Jim." She checked her watch. "One thing more. How do I get in?"

"Sometimes he didn't even lock the camp, but I'll tell you where the key is anyway. Under the big splitting log."

"Thanks, Ben." As she searched his gray face, today so suddenly an old man, she forced herself to ask about the event she would have preferred to have avoided. "What time at Halverson's?"

"Five o'clock. We made it later so's Jim's friends..." he wiped at his eyes, "could come after classes. Melanie put the word out around the university. Suggested that we start a scholarship fund in the Forestry Program. I would never have thought of that. And she's been a help to Meg." Outside, his wife stood wrapped in a heavy parka, still scanning the silent lake, sparkling silver between the granite hills. It was a postcard, but the wrong one for the moment. Did she still expect to hear a familiar roar come echoing down the paths, to see Jim race in, bringing her a handsome lake trout or a brace of partridge?

By the time Belle reached home, her engine had been coughing and jerking for ten minutes, and she had been chanting, "Please, please, please. I don't want to have to walk. New plug's on the way." The motor gave a final lurch and expired half-way to the backyard. When she unwrapped the new plug, however, with hands stiffened in the windchill, she managed to drop it on the cylinder head and crack the ceramic base. Just one more addition to a wonderful day. Still, the old faithful had made it home. That's what counted.

Later that afternoon, she stuffed herself into a black linen suit, a sop to civilization she had picked up at Eaton's downtown just before the venerable Canadian institution went belly up. There was only one problem. In the supercold, the van should have been plugged in so that the block heater would keep the oil warm. You don't want to go to the viewing and you did this deliberately, she chided herself, as the van door creaked in arthritic pain. She plopped heavily onto the seat, which greeted her with the hardness of the Cambrian Shield. Gingerly she fingered the ignition of the hybrid engine. It ground, ground and then flooded, eliciting curses to every Northern god. No good to wait it out. Fuel-injection did not operate like that.

Bruno's Towing promised to come with the advisement that the jaunt to the boonies would cost an easy hundred. When a man arrived a hour later, she climbed grumpily into the truck and asked him to drop her at Halverson's, before towing the van to Cambrian Ford. Cheaper than a cab, and she was already paying royally, she rationalized with an internal growl.

Halverson's Funeral Home had been an institution since World War One. One of the first brick buildings, it had given permanence and charm to the downtown clapboard in the boom days of the mining city. Over the years it had inhaled competing businesses to gain a near monopoly except for the suburban burial societies. Everyone who was anyone ended his career at Halverson's. It was an expected tradition.

Walking slowly to the door, Belle had to urge herself forward. Her family had hated these ceremonies, preferring simple cremation. Open caskets were the norm in Northern Ontario, maybe a European custom which arrived with the many Greek, Italian or Ukrainian immigrants. Inside the quiet, formal foyer, a middle-aged lady in tasteful shades of gray at a reception desk lifted her pince-nez delicately to consult her program: "The Burian Party, yes, just down to the end of the hall, if you please."

From the hallway, she saw other "parties" gathered to whisper in the adjoining rooms. Music drifted by, very soft and understated, a touch of Pachelbel in the night, or was it Mozart? Belle shuddered, willing herself against all odds to relax. A delicate lily of the valley scent wafted along the corridor mixed with the more cloying perfumes of older matrons. Suddenly, she remembered a story her prim and proper mother had told her. Inching along in a receiving line at her school superintendent's funeral, she had anxiously searched for appropriately consoling words. When she had reached the widow, Terry Palmer had leaned forward, gently taken the woman's hand, and murmured, "Thanks for a lovely day."

Finally, Belle entered a divided room with a sitting area of padded chairs and sofas in Laura Ashley chintz. Homey and reassuring. Turning reluctantly, she saw the casket, taupe with brass fittings, accessorized with palms, candelabra and lavender glads. Several floral arrangements flanked the bier, a white and red rose selection particularly resplendent. What a monumental waste of money when Jim would have preferred the subtle beauty of wildflowers or the spicy resin of pine branches. She walked over to pay her respects, forced her gaze up. And by God, Jim did look good. Healthy, even. And that glowing skin tone. If there were an art to find the mind's construction in the face, Myron Halverson was a genius. The innocence and goodness that framed Jim's life could be read here by the blindest sceptic. She knelt on the velvet prie-dieu, murmured a small non-denominational prayer and stood awkwardly, wondering if anyone was noticing the tremor in her hands. Why did funerals make people feel like actors wandering without scripts? What words could form in a moment beyond the limits of speech?

The Burians were seated in the corner, Meg twisting a handkerchief, Ben thin and stiff in his black suit, and Ted leaning next to his mother, blinking away tears and loosening his collar. Belle was surprised to see old Tracker, grieving in the honest, canine way, ears back, head on her paws, her liquid eyes trusting that Jim would return. "Thanks for coming, Belle," Meg said. "You were such a good friend of Jim's." Belle embraced the older woman tenderly, strangely protective about mothers since her own had died.

"He had so many friends," Belle said, summoning up platitudes and hating herself for the failure of eloquence.

But the Burians were lost in a family tableau missing a central figure. "Yes," Ben said, his eyes shining. "They're all here from the university. And Tracker, too, his special pal. Halverson said it would be OK." There would be no burial, just a crypt until the May thaw, common practice in the North. Graveyards were lonely places from December to April, only the tips of the highest monuments spearing the white desolation.

Belle slipped aside to sign the guestbook as a frail woman with henna hair and a purse affecting her balance tottered with a cane towards the Burians. In one corner, some professorial types, three-piece suits and beards, nodded sombrely. She caught a few words, "foolish...never should have" and bit back the temptation to offer her opinion. What did these ivory tower characters know about the bush and its rules? They might as well live in Toronto, driving their Range Rovers to work. Mel sat at the other end of the room, next to a man in what looked like an actual mourning suit, a fashion more read about than seen. Handsome and compelling, perhaps European, he put his arm around the girl briefly. Melanie shook her head as an answer, looked up, and gestured to Belle.

"Belle, you know Franz Schilling?" she asked

He extended his hand and bowed his head in a courtly manner. For a moment Belle thought he was going to kiss hers, as he raised it slightly and seemed to align his heels. "Hello, Belle. Melanie told me what a comfort you have been. It is very tragic to meet under these circumstances." What else could be said?

They made the usual lump-in-throat exchanges, and then Melanie added, "Franz is in charge of the Stop the Park rally."

Franz smiled and then spoke quietly, his gaze fixed on Belle. Though his hair was silver-blond and groomed to perfection, his darker eyebrows had a hypnotic effect. "And our efforts should have an effect. If only Jim could be there to march with us. What a tragedy his accident was."

The women's eyes met. "Perhaps not, Professor. Some things are not what they seem," Belle said.

He arched an eyebrow and looked over at the casket. "Melanie has told me her doubts, and yes, I found it hard to believe, knowing how careful Jim was as a researcher. But still, I remember the night. Very bad. If he had wanted so much to get home and missed a turn in the blizzard..." His voice trailed to a whisper.

"Yes," Belle answered. "His parents told me how important the Sunday family supper was for him. He always arrived in time, no matter what he'd been doing." Memories of those evenings shared with Jim were too much for Melanie, who started to cry softly.

"I'll bring you some water," Franz said with a slight bow and left for a moment. The girl turned to Belle, struggling for control.

"Have you found anything yet?"

"We can't really talk here. And I'm getting claustrophobic. I can hardly breathe." Belle passed her hand over her clammy brow. "Why don't we meet at the Konditorei in about an hour."

After making a unobtrusive exit from Halverson's, Belle was amazed that she felt like eating as soon as the fresh air hit her. Death could be a great appetite builder, a life-affirming ritual rivalled only by sex, a less convenient option.

An hour later, Melanie eased into the other side of the booth, removing her parka and gloves, her face flushed from the cold. "Were you able to get to the camp yet?"

"Not yet. My machine needs a new plug. Don't get your hopes up. Ben says there's nothing much there."

"But Jim did all his work at the cabin. Said he needed the quiet for concentration and inspiration. Perhaps there's a map showing clusters of the old pines. Maybe that's where he met or saw someone. You could look for clues,"

"Clues. Come on, Mel. Don't be naïve. The only sensible possibility seems to be that he stumbled onto something he shouldn't have. He suspected drug drops, and you know how he felt about drugs. But to meet someone on the spur of the moment? And how would the killer make it look like an accident? Or get him to that lake? It wasn't a landing spot like the ones he mentioned."

"Talk to Franz about the planes. He told me he had seen the same thing, thought he had, anyway."

"Why? Where does he live?" Belle asked.

"On an island near the marina on Wapiti. You must have passed it. Quite a log cabin complex, from what I've heard."

Belle searched her memory. "There are a number of camps on islands, but I think I know the one you mean." Then remembering Franz's courtly solicitude at Halverson's, she asked, "Are you two good friends?"

"Franz and I met when I took his physical anthropology course first semester. Of course all the girls were in love with him, but he was always correct and professional, and besides, you know how strict universities are with these sexual harassment cases. Anyway, a couple of people saw him out to dinner with one of the art teachers."

Belle teased the girl. "He's quite appealing. Reminds me of Christopher Plummer in *The Sound of Music.*"

Melanie laughed hesitantly, as the shift in topics relaxed her. "Come on, Belle. He's not that old." She seemed in the mood to talk, friendly, interested, an ideal nurturer with her pleasant manner and frank eye contact. "Jim mentioned that you were from Toronto, Belle. How did you happen to come north?" she asked.

Sudburians were always flattered that in defiance of the moonscape publicity, anyone would join their community. As their bumper stickers proclaimed, "Proud to be a Northerner," they welcomed newcomers with a frontier sincerity. "I've been here for over twenty years, Melanie. My family lived in Toronto, but I spent every summer with my uncle at his camp on Lake Penage. After majoring in English, I went to Teachers' College."

Melanie looked surprised. "English? But you're not a teacher now. What happened?"

"Ha. I respected literature too much to try to pound it into bonehead teenagers. This revelation came when I was practice teaching tenth graders. That's a wicked age, let me tell you.

Just as I read the line in 'Kubla Khan' about 'Alph, the sacred river,' the class broke up. Who would name a river 'Alf'? The kids laughed so hard that the principal left his office and poked his head through the door. That day I hopped a bus for the North, where I'd wanted to live since I was a kid. Uncle Harold put me through a crash course at Nickel City College, offered me a partnership in his realty business and helped me establish a client base. Then he made sure I got my appraiser's license. It's a steadier income. Best of both worlds."

"Sounds like a great guy."

"Yes, I miss him. Made it to eighty on three packs of unfiltered Camels a day. Now I run the place myself with one other woman."

"Jim told me about your house. You must be doing well on your own."

Belle laughed. "If you saw my bank balance, you wouldn't think so. And speaking of balances, I've got a mammoth account payable coming at the garage. Can you give me a lift?"

Melanie drove Belle to collect her van, which was thankfully ready to go, for a mere $200.00 to cover oil and filter and plug change and the extortionary tow from Bruno. "Coulda done it yourself, lady, and saved yerself big bucks," the mechanic said.

"Oh, just chip the oil out of the pan at twenty below. With a blowtorch?"

Belle tooled out of the garage in a pique; her new gold card Visa bill would have to be sent parcel post. Tuning in the news, she was just in time for the obituaries. A thirty-one-year-old had died when his Corvette had hit a rock cut on Highway 144 to Timmins, a deadly combination. She tugged her seat belt to double-check. A person spent the first four decades going to weddings and the next four going to funerals.

And everyone wanted to die young as late as possible.

Brushing her teeth before retiring, she checked the mirror: the elder elf look, red peppery gray hair, but good skin and clear eyes. What was the use of make-up and fifty-dollar designer haircuts if you had to smash and smear them with toques, face masks and scarves? Living in a city was one thing; living in the bush was another; living in Sudbury fell somewhere in the middle, and maintaining a civilized veneer through a six-month winter of waterline-bursting temperatures or daily avalanches was a fool's labour.

Belle climbed gingerly into her water bed and lined up five cigarettes and the latest Robert B. Parker. She tucked a cigarette into her Adolphe Menjou holder, a delicate filigreed gem from the MGM Studios Memorabilia Shop at Disney World in Orlando. Her father had bought it for her when they had made the rounds of the theme parks after her mother's death. Had he been the oldest person to take the "Back to the Future" virtual reality ride? She could still remember taking his hand, cool and gnarly, as the Delorean rocketed them in dizzying speed toward the mouth of a tyrannosaurus. "Close your eyes," she had said.

SIX

S teve Davis had been a family friend since Uncle Harold had used the young officer for apartment security work back when a few extra dollars were welcome. Though he and Belle sat on different sides of the law vs. justice scales, they met over a meal from time to time when his wife used an argument as an excuse to flounce off to her parents in Thunder Bay. The marriage had been one long, stormy snowshoe uphill, he complained. Why did he keep making the effort?

No police presence had been evident at Halverson's during the viewing. She wondered what countermeasures the department had undertaken to control the drug trade and whether the lake landings had been investigated, so Belle called Steve to set up lunch. The Cedar Hut had opened a Mexican room, a nine-day wonder for the mining town, and Belle wanted to awaken her taste buds after years of drought. From a Christmas in Mexico City, she remembered the drum tortilla makers that sizzled on every corner, jolly *mamacitas* slap-slapping dough onto griddles with the rhythm of a mariachi band.

Knowing Steve would likely be late, she made her selection, eyebrows herniating at the prices. Belle ladled hot sauce on her combination platter of chicken enchilada and beef burrito and lined up a chilled Dos Equis in readiness to quench the anticipated fires.

Just as her pupils were beginning to return to normal after the first bites, Steve trudged in, shaking the snow from his parka, and Belle flagged the waitress for a margarita. He manoeuvered his six-six frame into the booth, flashed his handsome black eyes at her, a legacy from his Ojibwa grandmother who had captured the heart of young Rod Davis, a surveyor for the E.B. Eddy Lumber Company. "Olé!" he said after a quick sip of the margarita. "What is this salty stuff, anyway? It's not bad. Sorry to be late, Belle. A couple of drunks at the Paramount tried to settle an argument about the merits of the Habs against the Leafs. At ten in the morning? What an end to my shift. Say, does Mexican food keep you awake?"

"Not with a supply of Zantac," Belle said. "But count yourself lucky. At least it wasn't a gunfight."

"That's one advantage the police have up north, along with following footprints in the snow. Even the convenience store robberies usually involve knives or bats. Fine with me. They don't go off accidentally." He browsed through the menu and followed her suggestion of tamales with a guacamole salad.

Belle watched him dig into his meal, wary of the green gunk at first, but clearly relishing the flavours. "Well, I can't exactly identify it, not that I'd want to," he said, "but it tastes good. And at least it's food. Remember that Japanese place I tried in Ottawa?"

"Where you ate the potpourri?"

"Yes, problem was, it tasted better than the meal."

They both laughed. Steve seemed in a good mood, so Belle pressed her case. "I need to talk to you about Jim. Has anything else turned up?"

His smile faded as he tightened his lips and let out a long breath. "There's no point in pursuing this, Belle. I knew him, too. Jim's the last one I ever figured would make a mistake like that, but he did. Stop torturing yourself. It's over now." He toyed with the candle lantern, then dipped a tortilla chip into the salsa, crunching noisily as if to drown out her inquiries.

"Humour me for one more chip, Steve, and I'll get the cheque. There is one trail we didn't follow. I wasn't even thinking about it in the rush of the accident. On some of his trips through the bush, Jim mentioned suspicious landings on small lakes. Lakes where nobody had reason to be. No ice fishing, no camps, no roads." She looked at his expressionless face, waiting for some nuance of change.

Steve shrugged and dug into his tamales as soon as they arrived. "Dum da dum dum. Let me guess. You're clueing me in about drugs? Why, the traffic has tripled up here in the last few years. Did I say tripled? More than that. What can you expect when the economy has diversified so fast? Like the cartoon strip goes, "for better or for worse", now that we're the regional centre in the North for health care, education, shopping and government, why not for mind-altering substances as well?"

"In other words, location, location, location."

"You're a fast learner. We're not sure exactly where it's coming from, but east and south, the U.S., port of Montreal. Last week in Newfoundland a bust landed five million dollars of cocaine. The week after that two women were stopped at Mirabel Airport with over half a million. Nice retirement package. Next time Prince Edward Island, home of Anne of Green Gables, for Christ's sake. Now Toronto's getting shipments of khat."

"Whaaaat?"

"Khat, an evergreen leaf grown in Kenya and Ethiopia. It has to be chewed fresh one to three hours before the high is reached."

"Come on! What an ordeal! Who would bother?"

"It's a social event in many cultures, brought over by our

increasing refugee population, but its side effects lead to physical violence."

"Much too energy-intensive for the North." She signalled for coffee. "So if the traffic is increasing, as you say, why choose the bush?"

"Belle, you can't make illicit transactions at our small airport very well, you know, not big deals. Records are kept. Mechanics, security guards, waitresses, anyone might take note. The fewer people, the better." He shrugged. "Then again, these fairy tale landings might mean dick-all. Just fooling around."

"Maybe so, but Derek is on my list for a chat. He owes me a favour."

"Derek Santanen! He'd better know zip if he knows what's good for him. When we finally got our lad last time, he'd have been knitting in Millhaven pen. But no, you felt sorry for his old folks and pulled him early probation with that job at Snopac. Let Mr. Blimp make his own mistakes. The next one will put him on a ten-year diet."

It seemed prudent to change the subject, so Belle asked about Janet. A few months earlier, Steve had been talking about a trial separation. It wasn't the despair that was killing him, but the hope. He and his wife were opposite personalities, his brooding seriousness versus her sunny, carefree disposition. One raw nerve had been their childlessness. Maybe Margaret Atwood and her *Handmaid's Tale* had been prophetic; sperm motility had dropped 30 percent in the last few decades, according to The *Globe and Mail*. This time, however, an unusual brightness lit his eyes as he talked of the latest chapter of their marital saga. "It's a turning point, Belle. Keep your fingers crossed, but we may be able to adopt at last. Our name's on the list, and we're supposed to get a call Friday."

"So soon? For a newborn?"

"You must be joking. We gave up on that a long time ago. Our best bet is a three or four-year-old, possibly mixed race. Janet seems calmer now that we've made the decision, and it couldn't have come soon enough for me. This old man is forty this year. And no, don't put one of those 'Lordy, Lordy, look who's forty' ads in the paper."

When the bill came, Belle handed her Visa to the waitress. Steve could use a treat with the toys and clothes and god-knows-what kiddie stuff in his future. "My part of the bargain. Least I can do for faithful, underpaid government servants."

He shook her hand with an over-under-over seventies move she had taught him. "No contest. What about that Clint Black concert next month? Would you like tickets? I'll get extras for my security duty at the Arena."

"Why not? Poor Clint coming up here to the back of beyond! Sudbury simply must show the colours." Belle laughed. After coffee, they returned to the blasts outside, temporarily warmed by chilies never intended to grow north of Chihuahua.

On the pretext of needing parts for her Bravo, Belle visited the local Yamaha shop, Snopac. Derek Santanen was wiping grease from his meatloaf-size hands as he smiled at her across the parts counter. A mammoth bag of Cheetos Paws lay nearby, spilling its goodies in a little golden avalanche. He seemed good at his job, but Belle had known that his snowmobile mechanics were sounder than his eating habits when she had promised his parents that she would speak up for him in court.

Sweating even at twenty below, Derek seemed to put on rather than get into the rusty VW bug that he bumped along their road. No wonder he told her that he had gone through seven sets of tires. Still, he had pushed her up the worst hill during an ice storm, splitting his pants in the process.

"Derek, I need a set of sliders and a couple of plugs for my Bravo," she said. "And maybe a bit of information."

His mouth opened and closed like a hyperventilating ox as a drift of ancient Old Spice aftershave mixed with sweat wafted across the counter. "I don't know nothing, Miss Belle. Been minding my own business." He rummaged for a handful of Paws and crunched them noisily.

"Don't Miss Belle me, Derek. Stop tugging your forelock. Anyway, you couldn't tell the truth unless you thought you were lying."

He gave a tentative laugh and passed her the bag, which she summoned heroic willpower to refuse. Paws had just the cheesy flavour and toothsome resistance which had contributed generously to her ten pound Christmas bulge. "I been clean as these here sliders I'm getting for you," he insisted as he plucked a box from the shelves. His huge Barenaked Ladies shirt rode up his back, revealing overlapping folds of fat, pockmarked chicken skin and coarse black hair. Poor guy.

"You may be clean now, and I say may..." she said as he gnawed his chapped lips, "but I won't beat around the bush." Bad Cop was a difficult role; she nipped a smile as it headed for her mouth. "You had the contacts. Tell me about the drug landings north of the lake."

"Hey, I'm no pilot. You really wanna know, I made my buys at the Bearden or at Yukon Jack's. If I'd spent more time at my camp and less in the bars..." He paused and chewed thoughtfully. "Lake drops? Maybe. Couple summers ago when we had those big winds for over a week, supplies got short. Bomber, that was my main man, said something about conditions being bad for delivery. I didn't think much about it. Come to think of it, I didn't think much period." He seemed pleased with the symmetry of his explanation and smoothed his greasy hair with a pudgy hand. Brilliantine or graphite, Belle wondered?

"Well, you haven't been much help, Derek, but maybe that's a good sign."

She paid her $45.00 tab with a roll of her eyes. "Are you sure you don't need me to put them on?" Derek asked helpfully. "Kinda hard in the cold. I mean…"

"Never mind, Derek. I think Ed will let me use his garage. And one more thing. You know people who ride the trail system. Anything unusual around the lake?"

He pondered, searched his elephantine brain until she expected a tortured grinding of gears. "Well, I'm probably screwing up my interests, so don't say nothing about this. Dan Brooks at the Beaverdam had me doing repairs there. Some old Arctic Cats. But guess what! I got curious about four funny shapes under tarps in the corner and took me a look. Wowee. Two new Mach Z's. First time I saw one up here. They's the 796cc liquid-cooled Rotax triple, R.A.V.E. and flat-slide TM-38 carbs. Big-o-mundo power revs with those ponies. Like to knock your socks off, especially on lakes. They say it's whip, blend and liquefy goin' through them gears." His eyes were glazing over like small, round hams; powerful machines came a close second behind his passion for food.

"You're a natural poet, Derek. Is that it?"

"No, ma'am. A Polaris XLT and a Ski-Doo Formula Z. You can run with the big dogs with those beasts. When Dan saw me, he blew up. Then he calmed down, talked about cashing in an old life insurance policy. Said he'd got to be ready to roll when that park opens. Figures he'll need at least ten to hire out. But that's nuts. Too good for rentals. 'Course he could be fencing them in a chop shop."

Belle tossed her sliders into the van and stopped at Poulton's for hot wings night. She packed up a few pounds, along with a container of potato salad, coleslaw and rolls. The Canada Food Guide had a special provision for Northern Ontarians: total grams of fat per day had to be double a person's age. If she were going to hell in a handbasket, let it be well-provisioned. The little liquor store in Garson sported a bottle of Wolf Blass cabernet, which cheered her, since usually Gallo tankcar #3333 was its sole concession to foreign wines.

When she got home and had reduced the wings to bones, American Movie Classics was featuring *Mutiny on the Bounty*. Laughton had been abandoned with his officers, promising to row thousands of miles in order to see justice done (and he did). In a more pleasant fate, Clark Gable leaned his handsome profile toward Morita's, and the crew of the Bounty was safe on Pitcairn Island, to interbreed and become tour guides by the nineties.

Belle flopped into her waterbed, reminding herself that she had not changed the sheets in about two weeks. Muscling the cumbersome rolling beast was a miasma. Though the process took only six minutes, she hated the chore so passionately that she spent a week on one side and a week on the other. As she drifted off to sleep, she heard the ice making prophetic groans, flexing its great shelf. While the cold still held, it would be interesting to visit the Beave.

SEVEN

S ix eyes beat two, so after Belle changed the plug, she drove down to Ed's place, a winterized cottage which the DesRosiers had expanded and modernized after selling their bungalow in town. Rusty, their chocolate-red mutt, chased out to meet her, a deflated soccer ball in her jaws, running crazed circles around Freya, who treated her as an undisciplined but harmless juvenile. The short trip to the lodge would help the dogs burn off some fat; regular walks were rare in winter, and like humans, dogs compensated by overeating or begging scraps.

"Hi, Trusty Rusty," she called. The bitch grovelled on her back in the snow and presented her pink belly in submission. Ed hated what he considered her feminine obsequiousness, but had been unable to break the friendly little creature of the habit. It was her nature to show this instinctive deference, Belle thought. To strangers, however, Rusty could present quite a performance of teeth and barks. Outside in the small oak trees Hélène had planted, bird feeders hosted a convention of colourful grosbeaks and a few robber jays. Freya jumped unsuccessfully for the suet ball and got a dirty look, so she ambled in innocence to her pal's food dish and tried a few snatches. At the kitchen window, Hélène, hearty as her own *tourtières* and running perpetually in first gear, hoisted a coffee in pantomime.

Belle entered, careful to remove her boots to spare her friends' new pride, a ceramic tile floor. Hélène was fiddling with a monstrous white apparatus that was humming and beeping. "Just taking this loaf out of the breadmaker. Bacon and cheese. Looks like it come fine." She carved a chunk, slathered it with soft butter and presented it along with a mug of creamy coffee. "Shortbread if you want it, too." Her hand tapped an industrial size pickle jar crammed with tiny pink, white and green trees decorated with silver balls and coloured sugar.

"My mother used to make these," Belle confided as she helped herself, noting with shame that she had to drop a few to suck her greedy hand from the jar. Melting under her tongue, they took her back thirty years and gave a sweet blessing to the coffee. "Are you two up for a run to Beaverdam Lodge?" she asked.

"What for? Got a lead on Jim's death?" Ed scratched his stomach thoughtfully, giving a self-conscious hitch to his pants.

"Sort of. Remember how we talked about Dan Brooks' business prospects once the park went through? Well, apparently those prospects are already materializing. Some pretty expensive new machines from God knows where. I want to look the place over. Check for renovations. Let's take the dogs. It's only five miles."

"We're glad to go with you, Belle," Hélène said. "I'm just sick about what happened to that boy." She paused and glanced at the latest family Christmas picture magneted on the fridge. "Raising kids is a chancy business, a tragedy like this always so close. A car, a bike, even a fall from a swing." Belle felt relief at her own single blessedness. Dogs were a heck of a lot smarter than kids, for the most part.

The ice was hard-packed with the recent traffic, and with

the unusual humidity, ethereal patches of fog enveloped the many tear-drop islands, a water colourist's dreamland recalling the Li River landscape. Periodically the trio stopped to admire the scenery and let the panting beasts catch up.

At Brooks' island, a decrepit dock jutted out onto the lake, surrounded by a couple of pickups with knobby tires, four-wheelers for hauling supplies to the mainland a half-mile away via an ice road. Near the juncture of three popular trails, the lodge saw a lot of traffic, especially beer traffic, and more especially after hours. Official closing times were relative for Dan as were limits on the number of drinks sold. Even during the day, Belle had seen more than one driver fall off his sled passing her house. One machine had hit a pressure ridge at high speed, executed a barrel roll and tossed its lucky rider into a snowdrift before crashing upside down.

They slid up the glazed boat ramps in front of the lodge. A satellite dish rose nearly thirty feet high on a steel pole bolstered by cables. Perhaps this was the landmark which the pilot pulling up to her dock had been seeking. Neatly lined up near a path which led to the cabins sat four Arctic Cats, their paint scuffed and chipped. "These aren't what Derek mentioned. In those sheds, maybe?" she suggested, pointing her mitt toward the back of the lodge.

Ed traced a fracture on one fibreglass hood. "Rentals are risky. I wouldn't want some idjit handling my baby for any price. Not even Hélène. That's why she has her own machine." His wife aimed a less than gentle kick toward his leg, but he continued with a grin. "Like to throw a cylinder or wreck the track on bad ground." He stepped aside as a large party of noisy snowmobilers walked past to the parking area.

One man yanked repeatedly on his starter in frustration. "'Course it won't start, you dumbass. You left the kill switch on!" his friend yelled while his buddies slapped the back of his head and guffawed.

Give me the Burians' little place any day, Belle thought. The Beaverdam was a circus. Old Pete Brooks had first built the lodge in the forties to cater to the fishing trade, but after the lakes suffered with acid rain, the trade had dropped off. Upon Pete's death ten years ago, his son Dan had taken over. More friendly than ambitious, Dan hoisted a few too many with his customers and had let the place rot. One visit had been enough to turn Belle away. Now the situation had changed. The lakes were reviving, and so was the Beaverdam. This was no cheap facelift, but a regular overhaul, complete with Pella windows, insulated French double-doors, new siding and shingles.

"You dogs behave now. No biting. Here's some jerky," Hélène ordered as the animals licked their lips and cocked their heads as if they understood. They were friendly and safe enough outside on their own. The idea of tying a dog in such a situation would make a Northerner laugh.

The trio tucked their helmets under their arms and entered the lodge, stamping their boots perfunctorily on the broad oak boards. A cheery fire burned in the fieldstone fireplace, Pete's pride, every rock lugged in his boat from the North River deposits. Stuffed pickerel and monster lake trout adorned the walls. Belle cast a glance at the additions which had tripled the size of the main room. Seating for an extra fifty at least. "Bucks" and "Does" were accommodated at the back, past a long, scarred bar stocking nothing fancier than Canadian Club. Most people drank beer anyway. Jars of pickled eggs and sausages sat by the cash along with chips and pretzels. It was quiet for late Saturday morning. The menu offered breakfast until eleven, so that was what they ordered. Very few places could screw up that simple meal.

"I miss Pete. Those days were the best. Plenty of fish in the lake, haul out five-pounders to fill our freezer. And no talk of that natural mercury stuff the Ministry keeps harping about now," Ed said, rolling his eyes. "Not that I worry. Tastes the same to me. Ozone layer blown up, chemicals in the food, radon in the basement, we're all goners."

"I wonder if Brooks is still taking Americans bear baiting," Hélène said, watching the waitress disappear into the kitchen. The common practice, disdained by purists, consisted of hanging rotten meat in a tree and bivouacking nearby, sipping a mickey of rye in a tree house until Bruno nosed out the gamey snack and went to heaven for his appetite.

"Salting deer and moose ain't legal, but baiting is. Laws don't make no sense. Bow hunting's another thing entirely, but this is fish in a barrel if you ask me. I knowed a guy used doughnuts. Red jelly kind did the trick," Ed said.

Hélène shook her head. "I hardly call that hunting. Murder more like. See any of that in our woods and I'll tear it right down. 'Course, if the animals come knocking, it's a different story." A fine black bear skin hung on their wall from one spring afternoon when a young boar, just awake and foraging after its long nap, had smelled fish cooking. It had ripped out a window on its way into the kitchen. A handy shotgun was never far from the cottagers' reach. The Ministry had fumed but admitted that 911 was of limited help against giant claws raking the cabin doors. Once in a while, for public relations, particularly if the offending bear were damaging property, officers from the Ministry of Natural Resources would trap one in a giant metal cylinder on wheels and relocate it a hundred miles north.

"There's been some money put in here," Belle said as she

scanned the room. "Those windows don't come cheap. That jukebox is new, so are the two video games and that big screen TV." She consulted a folded card on the table. "Karaoke Night? We are getting very fancy here, folks."

The waitress brought their eggs, bacon and thick homemade toast. Hélène's eyes followed her as she moved around the booth, and Belle wondered at her interest, chalking it up to motherly concern. The girl's skin was nearly transparent over her prominent cheekbones, her eyes ringed with dark shadow. Hélène touched her arm gently as she turned to leave. "Brenda?"

The girl's face brightened. "Mrs. DesRosiers. I didn't see you."

"Working for your dad this winter?"

She nodded, pushing back her limp hair as if suddenly embarrassed at her appearance.

"Are you still writing stories about those Puddingstone kids? You were on to something there," Hélène said.

The girl's wan smile brightened her face. "Sometimes. Dad said I could take a course at the college next fall in between our seasons."

"Brenda!" An irritated voice yelled from the kitchen.

"Nice seeing you." She moved off, pausing to clear the next table quickly, the dishes clattering on the tray.

"Brooks' daughter?" Belle asked.

"Slave," Ed said. "He couldn't run the place without her and the wife working like navvies."

"How did you meet her?"

Hélène looked at her husband. "She went to school with our youngest son. Came to his graduation party must be three years ago and spent most of the time helping me in the kitchen, poor shy thing. Had a fancy to write a book about the

77

Puddingstone kids, she called them. On St. Joseph Island where she used to visit her grandfather."

Belle tapped her knife on the placemat with a map of Ontario. "On the way to the Sault. Now I remember. That pretty rock. Kind of a pink with dots of green and red like a steamed pudding."

"It was a cute idea. It might have given her an escape from here and from her father. Doesn't look like she'll get the gumption to leave on her own. Best thing she can do is look for a husband." She noticed Belle's sniff and explained. "It's quick and easy, and it often works. Sometimes a woman needs a knight."

Coffees finished and the tab paid, they strolled the yard like confident, overfed American tourists. "Let's find the septic system," Belle suggested. "That's where big money has gone. I count ten cabins, and the lodge, of course." Over a small hill near a barn lay an expanse of undisturbed snow. A humming motor inside an open shed nearby caught their attention.

Ed rubbed his mitts together. "Big 'un all right. Listen to her purr. Sent all the way to Toronto, I'll bet." Behind hockey and fishing, septic systems were the third most popular topic on Edgewater Road. Requirements for a permit were stricter than the bar exam. People drank out of Wapiti, and no one wanted the water tainted by ancient cracked tubes to nowhere, well chambers made of rusted oil furnace drums and field beds flooded by bad drainage. The Boreal forest, with its thin veneer of peat over rock, made a good system costly. Building one required large excavations and tons of backfill. The tab for Belle's house had run over eight thousand dollars. On the Beaverdam's rocky island, the only option would be a so-called Cadillac installation where electrical power heated the effluent for more rapid breakdown and allowed a smaller bed.

Belle looked around furtively. "I'm going to check the barn. You two keep an eye out."

She slipped into the weathered frame building while Hélène and Ed talked outside. In the back, under tarps as Derek had discovered, was a steroid brigade of powerful gleaming new sleds. Suddenly a whistle caught Belle's ear and she slipped out a back door, just as a lean man in work clothes, a heavy red-checked shirt and insulated vest came towards them from the lodge. He was carrying an ice auger. "Help you folks with something? Need to rent a machine? Come in from one of the huts?" He motioned to the ice village off the point half a mile and lit a cigarette as the collies nipping at his heels exchanged canine courtesies with Freya and Rusty.

He gazed with interest at Belle's tracks alongside the barn. "You don't want to be walking off the paths. There's all sorts of machinery and old metal parts under the snow."

Belle answered with a sheepish smile, though she felt her pulse throb against her neck. "I was looking for that big yellow birch. Carved my name on it when my uncle brought me up here as a kid. You must be Dan. I'm Belle Palmer, and this is Ed and Hélène DesRosiers." The men shook hands.

"I couldn't help admiring the job you've done with this place. Looks like a million," Belle added.

He drew slowly on his cigarette, then flipped it into the snow and grinned broadly, the proud proprietor. "Well, not really. Needed some fixing up for a long time. You folks from around here?"

"We live down the lake. Out this morning to exercise the dogs. Saw you had some rentals and wanted to tell our friends in town. How do you like the Cats?" Ed asked, winking at Belle as Brooks turned away to cough.

The lodge owner waved his hand in dismissal. "Oh, picked

them up at auction down south. Nothing special. Good enough for the tourists, though, if you take my meaning. Don't want to give them anything too new or fancy or it'll be junk quick enough."

"What do you charge?" grinned Ed.

He snorted. "Well, you know city folks. Sounds like a lot to them, seventy-five an hour. But five hunnert wouldn't pay if they can't handle 'em. How many times I've had to go carve those suckers outta the slush. Not supposed to go into the bush neither. Two Toronto fellas ridin' double on the cheap broke down north of the lake last year. -25° that day. And they's none of them had the sense ta carry even a match. Some old trapper saved their dumb hides. Make 'em take survival gear now, tarp, lighter, extra gas."

Ed gave a hearty laugh. "Have to show them how to use it!"

Hélène had been checking her watch. She pulled on Ed's jacket. "Come on. Someone has to get to town for groceries." They left Brooks patting his dogs and casting an eye over his property.

While they rested at the half-way point, Belle pushed up her visor. "Somehow I don't think he bought the story about the yellow birch," she said.

"Maybe not, but you can bet he'll get rid of those beauties you saw in the barn. Big business now. *Star* said yesterday there's been over 230 stolen each of the last three years. Ship 'em off fast, though. Can't ride a hot machine anywhere on the trail plan where there are wardens to check your permit. And a Mach Z'd stick out like a sore thumb," Ed said, gunning his motor with his own digit.

That afternoon Belle called Mike Minor, the health inspector for the region, who stamped approval on every new septic bed. "Mike, I need some information about aerobic systems, like at the Beaverdam," she said.

"Anaerobic, you mean," he responded with a laugh. "What do you need to know?"

"How big a system would Brooks need with all those cabins? What would it cost, including backfill?"

"Pay attention now. I might ask questions later," he replied. "I certified the whole shebang just before the winter. Must have struck it rich with the Super Seven lottery. Cost of the fill means nothing. Hauling it in by barge is the problem. 'Course, he has a Bobcat backhoe, so he does his own work. Still, you're talking forty grand minimum with the ten cabins."

"Where do you think he came by that money these days? Cashed in some insurance?"

"A lottery ticket's his only insurance. I've had my eyes on violations ever since he took over from Pete and let the place go to hell. Nearly shut him down five times. Sharp-eyed boaters reported raw sewage was pouring into the lake one Labour Day weekend. An accident, of course. Nothing would surprise me about that fellow, but he'll be as hard to catch as a century sturgeon. What are you getting at?"

"Not sure yet, Mike, but we'll have a smasher when I get in a supply of Wild Turkey for you."

Fresh with the information about Brooks, Belle tried calling Steve, but his answering machine took his place. She left a brief message, glad to avoid another lecture.

Come to think of it, Belle recalled, the lodge owner did look like a sturgeon, lean and mean and shrewd and primitive. Likely to bite off innocent toes dangling from a dock.

EIGHT

B elle slept late, squirrelled away under a goosedown duvet, having slapped off her radio wake-up station when it blasted out a song about Bubba shooting a jukebox. The warm undulations of the waterbed, so forgiving of bones and sinews and muscles, undermined good intentions about early rising. I spend too much time in bed, she decided, trying to rouse herself with thoughts of a postcard sunrise and the Toronto Stock Market quotes.

Out of luck on the first count at least, the warmer temperatures having painted a steel-blue sky, overcast with a threat of snow. What had happened to the greenhouse effect? It had been the coldest winter in 140 years, the paper said. The frost had reached an incredible eight feet into the ground; so many town water mains had ruptured that people were being asked to run one tap at a pencil width until the end of April! Steam jet outfits were making three hundred dollars a trip, blasting frozen septic lines. Belle thought ruefully of her perennials under their blanket of snow. Would she ever touch the bronze irises again, the Oriental lilies, the Jacob's ladder, monkshood, peonies? Had she been crazy to plant a kiwi in Northern Ontario, though the forever optimistic spring catalogue had dubbed it hardy through Siberian zone 3?

She shivered as she inserted her feet into a pair of sheepskin-lined house slippers and put on her fleece robe.

Downstairs, only a bed of coals remained in the stove. She went onto the deck and down the stairs to a wood supply under a tarp, bringing back two pieces of maple.

From the feeder tank in the basement, she collected six victims in a juice pitcher and bore them upstairs. First she tossed Big Mac a handful of chopped sole. His twenty inches of lithe gray muscle vacuumed the tank, gulping large frozen chunks with a piscine sang-froid. The "dickeybird" discus, soft blue and brown stripes and delicate mouths (tossed out of the piranha family for good behaviour) picked demurely at a few shreds. Then when Mac slowed down, Belle dumped some flakes and the live sacrifice. The goldfish, shocked by the warmer water, dropped to pant on the bottom, hiding confidently beside Mac's battleship bulk, which they interpreted as cover. He merely opened his mouth and swallowed them along with a few small rocks, bits of scales spewing out along with the pebbles. What was keeping Hannibal? Finally the needlefish's radar located a moving target. His tiny propellers fanning, he zeroed his torpedo body, long ball-tipped snout pointed at his prey. Then with a z-kink from the Permian programme in his old reptilian brain, he zapped forward, snatching the fish in the middle, working it gently to slide head first down his gullet. "Good for you," Belle said with a maternal nod.

So much for finding any leads at the Beaverdam, Belle thought. Maybe a chat with the local coroner would be more fruitful. She paged through the phone book to find Dr. Patrick Monroe's practice. A personal visit would tell more in body language than in words, not that she expected a doctor would take a phone call anyway. The Ontario Health Insurance Plan had delisted that luxury.

Downtown Sudbury hadn't changed much in the years

since Belle had arrived. Businesses had suffered in the boom-bust mining town, and multiplying suburban malls had dealt the downtown area a further blow. Why pay parking fees only to run a gauntlet of winos and annoying teenage panhandlers in their shiny Doc Martens? Even the icon Canadian Tire had moved to the south end. Aside from a theatre, the YMCA complex, a chain store or two and some established shops with a loyal clientele, only a new seniors' apartment along with the city and provincial government building porkbarrels kept the core on artificial respiration. And not all the fancy brick sidewalks or tree plantings could revitalize it. The only good news lately was the rumour about a giant call centre taking over the old Eaton's complex.

Parking at one of the meters, she dropped in a loonie, narrowing her eyes as a young man sidled up. He wore a heavy hydro parka and carried a worn plastic bag. A red toque covered his head, mashing his long hair well down his neck. Stubble covered his chin as he gave her a lopsided grin, exposing a dark tooth. "Spare a dollar-fifteen?"

A dollar-fifteen. That was a novel approach, she thought. "Sure, but that won't buy a beer," she said.

"Huh, I want a coffee, that's all. It's cold." He blew out his breath for effect, and Belle retreated a step.

"Well, that sounds reasonable. Tell you what. I'm going down the street to pick up some heavy cartons at the bookstore. Give me a hand, and the money's yours."

He leaned against the meter, placing it under his arm like a crutch. "Ah, get away with you."

"I'm serious. Do you want the job or not?"

"Get away with you," he repeated in a cheerful tone that implied that he found her as much a character as he was and turned to consider the saner prospects leaving the bank teller machine down the street.

The Maley Building, circa 1922, tall for its time at five storeys and once a decent professional address, reeked of musty paper, cigar smoke and antiseptic as Belle walked down the dark hall to an old-fashioned frosted door which bore Monroe's name, General Practitioner. In the tiny waiting room sat, or rather perched, a gigantic woman, shifting buttocks in polite discomfort, while she read from Max Haines' *Doctors Who Kill*. She smiled a Rita MacNeil greeting, and Belle nodded back, looking in vain for a secretary. Shrugging, she picked up an ancient *Newsweek* with Reagan, the Great Communicator, on the cover. The world had turned over many spins since then, and his descent into Alzheimer's was depressing for someone with an aging father, so she opted for a pamphlet on smoking. Maybe it was time to convert to the patch. Her arm itched already.

For a few minutes, the only sounds were the flipping of pages and Rita's laboured breathing. Finally, a young man in work clothes emerged from the inside office with a limp characteristic of industrial back injuries, lit up a cigarette and walked out whistling "Country Roads". When the door opened again, an attractive man in his late fifties, silver hair carefully brushed, a pressed lab coat and Windsor knot in his red striped tie over a pale blue oxford shirt, announced, "Judith Ann Harrison." Rita beamed and twiddled a goodbye.

By five o'clock, the office had cleared. "I don't have an appointment, Doctor. My business is personal. Could you spare five minutes?" she asked at his puzzled stare.

"Medicine is always personal. If I can help you, my dear," he eyed her appraisingly, "come into my office."

Seated in the chair in front of his desk, Belle could see framed certificates on the wall attesting to his degrees. Golf trophies and tournament photographs lined the shelves behind him. There was a moment of silence while he looked at her expectantly. "I understand that you acted as the coroner in the Burian drowning," she said abruptly.

He stiffened and shifted to a cold, official tone. "We don't have a full-time coroner. I was on call that month. Is this a police matter? You didn't show me any identification."

Belle gave him a worried smile that spelled naïveté. "I'm a realtor, Doctor, not even a private investigator. But I was Jim Burian's friend, and I was the one who found his body. I still see his face in my dreams. And that hand." Her voice trembled and she looked at the floor, a human version of Rusty's deferential belly presentation.

Monroe sat back in his chair, his voice mellowing sympathetically. "Well, now I understand. That must have been quite a shock. The hand protruding from the ice was unusual. Apparently a branch worked under the coat. Shallow lake full of deadwood, the officers said. Now, normally a body floats head down, bent over from the waist." He passed her a box of tissues, which she accepted with a grateful nod. Then he flexed his hands, patrician fingers curving gently around a Mont Blanc pen. "As for what I found, there's a copy of my report at the police department. These deaths are tragic but getting all too common with the popularity of snowmobiles. And 90 percent of the accidents occur to young men between 18 and 30. A dangerous cocktail of alcohol, drugs and hormones."

"I knew Jim since he was a kid. And that rationale just doesn't fit. Jim never drank when he drove, not car, snow machine or boat. Drugs would be out of the question. Most of all, he was cautious and experienced. Riding was second nature to him, never had even a minor accident."

"Nonetheless…" He lowered his gaze in professional resignation.

"What can you tell me? It would be more helpful than reading the report since I could ask questions."

He sighed but seemed flattered to display his expertise. "Drowned, of course. Water in the lungs clearly showed that. But even without that, it might have been what we call a dry drowning, especially with the shock of the cold."

Belle leaned forward on her chair. "A dry drowning! You mean it wasn't an accident?"

"No, my dear. I don't mean that. A dry drowning is simply the term for what happens in a sudden laryngospasm. The esophagus shuts off, you see." He made a *coup de gorge* gesture, shooting his gold cufflinks.

"Now I understand. Forgive my ignorance. Is this common?"

"Not really. Fewer than 15 percent of drownings. The autopsy would reveal no physical evidence, nothing more than a lack of water in the lungs. 'Suffocation' is a more exact term here, suffocation caused by shock."

"Sounds grim." She shuddered. "What else did you notice?"

He plumped up at the compliment and went to his files, returning with a manila folder. "You're so persistent, Miss or is it Mrs. Palmer, that I might as well be exact." He put on a pair of oval tortoise-shell reading glasses and selected a sheet. "Ummmm. Let me simplify the technical language. No sign of any contusions or bruising. No drugs or alcohol, as you tell me."

"I guess it's hard to determine the time of death."

"I should say so. With the body preserved in such cold water, we have to weigh other factors. When had he last been seen? What were the temperature and conditions for refreezing the ice? The best guess is that he died within twelve hours of your finding him. The officers said that the lake had refrozen several inches. Swamp lakes with their vegetation and gasses are always warmer, always dangerous. Then again, if only he had been going slower or faster."

"Yes, he might have stopped, or more speed might have carried him over. I've seen those silly summer runs over water, too. But Jim's Ovation was so underpowered that he would never have counted on speed to get him out of trouble. I own the next size down, and believe me, it's fine for plugging along, nothing more. He had no reason to be within miles of that lake. And even so, not even to try to struggle to safety? A strong young man like that?"

"There was a storm, I understand. A moment of confusion. A big price." Monroe grew philosophic. "He was fifty feet from shore, wearing a heavy suit and full-face helmet, which evidently he was unable to remove. Shock hits like a hammer. In a matter of seconds the whole nervous system, breathing, everything, is nearly paralyzed. Maybe if he'd had one of those flotation suits…"

Belle gave him a sad nod. "Wish I could afford one." She'd had personal experience with cold water shock thanks to a stupid experiment. One early May when a few shards of ice still drifted on Wapiti, she had climbed out onto the rock wall to break her record for first dip of the year. The water felt numbingly tolerable up to the knees, but when she dropped to her neck, her breathing failed. With a supreme effort of will against paralyzed lungs, Belle had crawled back to the rocks and collapsed, gasping with relief.

"And the stomach contents? They always ask that on TV." Belle was warming to her role.

Composed as he was, this made Monroe smother a laugh,

a smile teasing his handsome mouth. "You are so very scientific. His stomach was empty, which was odd since I did find shreds of fish and vegetables between his back teeth." His voice grew pensive and she leaned forward. "It didn't seem significant at the time. I thought that perhaps he had vomited. Perhaps he had been ill earlier, or the shock from the accident." He drew circles on a notepad. "The flu, a fever, that might account for some disorientation, but after all, we don't conduct autopsies searching for the common cold." He sighed and consulted his watch, a splendid Rolex. "I expect one late patient. But I could meet you for a drink at the Camelback Road, say, if you have any other questions. They make a superb vodka martini." He removed the glasses and leaned closer, raising an expressive eyebrow which reminded her of Francis X. Bushman in the original *Ben Hur*. Charming, knowledgeable and the slightest bit dangerous. Always more interesting than the nice ones.

Belle extended her hand and enjoyed the warm smoothness of his skin when he pressed it a moment longer than necessary. "Unfortunately, I have an appointment in half an hour to show a house. You know real estate." She flashed a bright and earnest smile. "You've been helpful in addressing my concerns. I just had to check. Jim was a good friend."

She hummed tunelessly as she left the office and headed straight to the nearest Tim Horton's for sustenance. "No, no, no, dear Doctor. I still don't buy this convenient scenario. Even you were starting to question your findings. If those drunks who went down on Matagamasi last year had the wits to swim for it, a sober Jim would have tried and made it too. He knew how to build a fire, always had a lighter or wet-safe matches in his suit."

Fresh-baked aromas wafted under her nose as she ordered

her brew. Despite the imminence of dinner, she found herself pointing shamelessly at a giant croissant dripping with white chocolate and sprinkled with almonds. Detective work definitely sharpened the appetite.

She moved the sugar container pensively, as she alternately munched and sipped, pondering the unsettling details of the autopsy. Had Jim had the flu? Had he been on any medication? Sometimes cold pills caused drowsiness, especially combined with a fever.

The information she had so far left three probable causes for Jim's death. An accident, a planned murder, or an opportunistic killing. But only a fool would count on meeting his victim in a blizzard. Even if Jim had been attacked, why weren't there any traces of injuries? Why no signs of another sled? Maybe she was looking without seeing. Her mother's time-honoured theory was that lost objects often were exactly where they were supposed to be, so what was she missing? Suddenly Belle noticed that she had poured half the sugar bowl into her coffee.

"Go for it, darlin'. Sweets for the sweet," an oily voice drawled. Tony Telfer sat down without an invitation. In a bizarre combination of Yellowknife, Calgary and Toronto, he wore a snappy beaver hat and a pair of snakeskin boots with his woollen trenchcoat. A builder just on the lucky side of crooked, he was always trolling. Once the hook was taken, he coaxed the client into expensive features like designer closets, Jacuzzis and gigantic Malibu foyers. King of short-term corner-cutting, he substituted utility grade for number one wood, spruce for pine, half-inch for five-eighths-inch plywood, and supplied shingles which shed their grit faster than the perch of a hyperactive budgie.

"Moving any insulation these days, Tony?" asked Belle. His

brother Charlie had made front page news a decade ago by constructing an entire subdivision with the same batts of insulation, ferrying it on to the next house after each inspection. By the time buyers turned on their thermostats in September, Good Time Charlie was long gone to warmer points unknown with a sizable profit from each home.

"Come on, Belle. Charlie's the black sheep of the family." He flashed an army of gleaming white caps from Sudbury's best dentists.

"And you're the wolf?" she laughed, snapping her teeth. "So how's your business, to speak in the loosest possible terms?"

"Grrrrrreat. Tony the Tiger knows. Heard about that new park on Wapiti? I have an angel who's going to put up a block of condos, no expenses spared. St. Pete style, only tasteful, you know? The old doll wants to remember hubby by bringing over all his relatives from the old country or something. I think my proverbial ship is coming in. There might be a little dinghy in it for you, Belle." He drummed his fingers near her coffee cup as she smothered a laugh.

By now the courts should have frozen Julia Kraav's assets. Tony had a big surprise coming, but Belle wouldn't spoil his pleasure today. "You'll never get the zoning, my friend. No way."

"Oh no? Just watch me once the park goes in. It's long overdue. That whole lake is crying out, 'Tony, develop me, develop me.'" He chuckled wickedly, twirling an imaginary mustache like a *Perils of Pauline* villain. "And I'll tell you something else, dearie. This is going to be so sweet that I think I'd kill anyone who got in my way. Figuratively speaking, of course."

Berlin of the twenties, Canada of the nineties. Money makes the world go around. That clinking, clanking sound. No matter where or when you lived, commerce trotted along like a hungry puppy which would grow up into the Hound of the Baskervilles. Belle left a fifty cent tip on the table and glanced over her shoulder as she left to see whether Tony grabbed it.

On her way to the DesRosiers, Belle picked up a bottle of Glenlivet as her contribution to the evening. A good guest always came with a thank-you present, her mother had said. Their ice hut had provided several small lake trout that week. She knocked and entered simultaneously, twirling the bottle on the kitchen table. "Crank up that hot fat. I feel a chill," she said. A hiss of oil, and the race was on. The deep-fried fillets revved up her taste buds with their mustard and corn meal batter doused with New Orleans hot sauce. Hélène had shaved a cabbage for cole slaw and sliced potatoes. The fry-for-all was doing no favours for anyone, but who cared? Remembering Jim laughing as he grilled her a fresh pickerel over a crackling campfire, Belle savoured every bite. They'd all be thinking of that senseless death until the Scotch ran out.

Belle described her meeting with the good doctor. "Monroe looks like a charlatan." She sprinkled vinegar over everything not moving. "Never missed a chance, though. Wanted to have a drink at the Camelback. No doubt rent a room nearby, too."

Hélène agreed. "I'm no fan. He used to be our family doctor. I've known some gets tranquilizers like candy from him. My sister, for one, floats around in a blue fog when it's that no-good husband she oughta get rid of. Darn near killed herself and her daughter hitting a slurry truck last year."

"Thought we were here to cheer up. Where's that dessert?" Ed poured another slug into his coffee royale while Hélène brought in the sugar pie. Belle moaned in anticipation. Was there any greater invitation to gratuitous gluttony than this sinful French Canadian concoction? As if the marathon meal hadn't been enough, Hélène sent Belle home with a three-pound chunk of moose meat and a recipe for jerky. "Réjean, my cousin from up near Bisco, got lucky this year and remembered his old aunt. It's been in the freezer since the season was over, but good for drying. Let me know if you like the garlic flavour. I got sweet and sour, too."

When Belle got home, Freya seemed unusually yappy, as if something had disturbed her routine. To the Purina, Belle added milk. "You have the best diet of us all. Sometimes I think that I should try a bowl. Cheap, quick, maybe no worse than those vegetarian mushburgers I brought home last week."

They moved into the video room, Belle into her recliner, Freya with three chile babies. A frustrated mother, the dog was forever assembling them, squeaking and licking the toys, and dragging them to bed.

TNT's choice was *The Great Lie* with Bette Davis and Mary Astor, two classic bitches in the archetypal woman's picture. Hollywood was ripe for a return to the heyday of strong female leads, *Thelma and Louise* having been at the cutting edge of nothing.

Before turning out the lights, Belle selected an exotic new cream: orange, lanolin and witch hazel. The costly treat had been initially disappointing, but out of cheapness she decided to give it another try. The lights went out to mutual sighs and scrabbles. She hoped the dog would not snore. Instead of sheep, Belle counted snowmobiles.

A few hours later, as the full moon poured through the bathroom window, the phone rang. She glanced blearily at the clock. 3:30. Picking up the receiver, she heard a click. And then silence. Freya sat up and shook her head as if to wake up, ears pricked for sounds. Nuisance callers. Belle unplugged the phone and looked out for a moment as the Northern Lights dazzled the lake like a hyperactive rainbow, drowning out Orion and Betelgeuse. In the uneasy dimension between disturbing dreams and a pleasant reality, Belle saw Freya chasing a rabbit across tracks in front of a never-ending train. She heard the muffled drone of snowmobiles outside which mimicked the roar of the engine in her dream. Freya barked once. "Calm down, girl. Wait for me." And Belle fell asleep, the chimney smoke gently curling into the night.

NINE

On Tuesday, the famous shrimp dinner day, Belle left herself plenty of time to reach the nursing home. When he had lived in Florida in his own house with his own dog and own cat, time had been a joke with her father: "I get up at ten to six every day, not a quarter to six, not five to six, but exactly ten to six." Now lagging hours and minutes measured only intervals between mealtimes. Belle knew he didn't realize her difficulties in maintaining a schedule given long distances and the vicissitudes of winter.

A mile past her house, a spectacle had occurred, a rural version of Canada's Funniest Home Videos. The plow had sloughed off the road at a wickedly banked corner. Looking like a metal mantis conceived by an idiot, the gigantic apparatus was flailing its legs and flexing its lifts, trying to free itself, but only sinking perilously closer to the hydro pole. Belle held her breath at the possibility of the pole snapping like a matchstick, stranding most people in a cold, dark and waterless hell. The sheepish operator assured her that he had radioed for help.

Across the road from Carlo's place, a large red fox, its tail bushy and bold, stood fearlessly watching her car. As she drew abreast, it bounded easily up the hill through heavy snow. Belle hoped that the creature had been supping on Carlo's cats, a wish probably shared by all his neighbours. An electrical engineer from Brownsville, Texas, Carlo lived a hermit's life in a ramshackle cottage. When the septic system clogged, and when pump repair and frozen waterline bills became too onerous, he did without plumbing, to the dismay of adjoining home owners. Once in a blizzard he had knocked timidly at Belle's back door with a small bottle in his hand, seeking drinking water. Although he had a woodstove, he holed up in his triple-insulated bedroom with only a tiny space heater, he said. He bathed at work and ate out, yet he looked strangely debonair on the rare occasions he did appear in a three-piece suit and fedora, as if he had stepped out of a film noir.

A few years ago, somebody dumped two cats secretly into his trunk at a gas station in Point au Baril. This accidental conjoining had relieved his conscience from all responsibility, so he had let them multiply until they had decimated the bird and squirrel population for a mile in each direction. Feral survivalists, the Darwinian remainders terrorized little children in the summer and ransacked garbage more ruthlessly than the bears. With no vet care, they likely carried rabies as well. Wrenches sticking out of his overalls, Carlo was bending over the rusted helm of an ancient Mustang, one of the seven or eight in his personal inventory. An enterprising cannibal, he juggled batteries, tires, and licenses routinely to stay mobile. "How many cats left now, Carlo?" Belle asked as she stopped and rolled down the window.

A cloud of garlic, his universal panacea, drifted into the car. "Oh, come on, do not tell me you are still mad about that," he grinned, wiping a greasy hand on his overalls, then pulling a comb from somewhere to rake his thick black hair. "Say, when can I come and rent a room with the most beautiful woman in Canada? Hot water would be fantastic, not to mention your company." He gave a theatrical leer to emphasize their ongoing joke.

"Don't be so cheap, Carlo. You make enough to equip your cottage quite nicely. You have another twenty years to retirement with Ontario Hydro. Why not enjoy them in the twentieth century?" She grinned. "And as for your social life, take out an ad. Men, especially ones with bucks, are at a premium, or didn't you know?"

He cocked his head like a whimsical jay. "Perhaps they would be interested in me only for my cars. I'm going to Windsor to buy another Mustang. A red fastback 1970 V-8. You must come for a ride. You will look like a queen. And I will treat you to dinner at the airport."

The airport? Carlo ate there regularly and chatted with the staff. "Seen any strange plane landings on the lake, Carlo? After dark?" she asked.

"That's not allowed, you know."

"Don't be naïve. I'm talking about drug landings."

"Oh ho!" he chuckled, sticking out his lower lip and paddling it thoughtfully. "It could be true. There is a lot of money to be made that way. I travel back to Texas three times a year to see my family. Lucky for me I am honest." He patted his chest in appreciation of his ethics.

"What about suspicious characters at the airport? I know you're one, but anybody new?"

He mugged shamelessly, clearly enjoying the spotlight. "I talk to everyone, the pilots, the mechanics, and especially the beautiful flight attendants. But there is one flyer I never trusted who comes through once in a while with a Beechcraft. Very unfriendly. He has been in the restaurant, but he refuses to enter into friendly conversation. I don't like the looks of him."

Wishing Carlo well, Belle drove off, keeping the window open to air out the garlic. Medical science might prove him right. Garlic cloves were being touted as cures for any ailment from colds to cancer.

Before that shrimp lunch with Father, she had allotted an hour to the unsavoury task of a chat with Ian MacKenzie, Melanie's estranged boyfriend. According to her, he lived in a townhouse complex near the New Sudbury Shopping Centre. Perhaps he would be home, perhaps not. Perhaps he had a helpful roommate, perhaps not. So many unknowns. Belle was grateful not to be a genuine private investigator. Selling real estate put more kibble in the bowl. As she reached the first set of traffic lights which spelled city, she noticed that the town was in the grip of an icefog, a strange meteorological combination of cold, vehicle exhausts and moisture. Like a London pea-souper, but marginally healthier. A surreal gleam surrounded streetlights, and people drove with unusual caution, hoping the late morning winds would clear the air.

The covey of older townhouses, three stories and garage apiece, was beginning to fray at the edges. 1245 Nottingham had a skitter of snow in the driveway and no signs of feet or tires. She rang the bell. No answer, but a face peeked from the third floor. She rang again, and again. Finally the door opened, and a head peered around with half a body exposed, state-of-the-art biceps a definite plus. "Who are you, who were you, and who do you hope to be? I was working out." His blonde crew cut was wholesome enough, but a sullen curl to his lip reminded Belle of a musclebound weasel.

"I'm Belle Palmer. Are you Ian MacKenzie?" she asked.

"We're both doing well so far. What's the story? Where are your brushes or encyclopedias?"

"I was a friend of Jim Burian's, and I—" A slam of the door cut her sentence in two.

"I only want to ask a few questions," she called against the traffic noise behind her.

"It must be our little Mel put you on to me. This is a joke, right? You can't be a police investigator or you would have shown me your ID." A loud cheer followed.

Belle took a stiffer tack. "There may be things the police don't know yet, and you may find yourself involved. Make it easy for both of us." There was definitely something in his defensiveness, she imagined as her heartbeat quickened. Perhaps it had been unwise to come alone.

The cheers turned to roars, and a thumping began. Was he pounding the wall in mirth or rage? Mel had said that he got violent. She hadn't smelled liquor, though. Vodka?

"OK, OK, I confess. I did it. I creamed the little bastard with that pretty scar. He took my girl. I took him. 'Mother of God, is this the end of Rico?'"

Hardly had Belle time to correct him with, "'Mother of Mercy.' The censors were picky that year," when the door opened again. She locked eyes with a wild-eyed blond man, then looked at his clothes. Pyjama bottoms on...one leg, the other in a heavy plaster cast.

"Heeeeeeeere's Ian!" he yelled. "And don't ask, honey, 'cause I cracked the sucker in Mattawa the week before Jim bought it. Check the hospital if you don't believe me, and now, if you'll forgive me, my jammies are beginning to ice up."

Well, at least he's a film buff, Belle thought. I could write *Investigations for Dummies*. Despite his animosity to Jim, she couldn't convince herself that it might be possible to drive a snow machine and orchestrate the accident. Ian was a jerkwater, to use her father's old term, but he was off the list.

She started the van and navigated through the fog across town. The last fifteen years of massive early retirements in the nickel industry had left Sudbury with a critical shortage of geriatric care. One huge highrise nursing home overlooked the million dollar mansions on Lake Ramsey, its twin building stood in New Sudbury, but their waiting list was longer than the Monica Lewinsky impeachment proceedings. When her father had fallen ill in Florida, the only spot available was in Rainbow Country, a converted two storey apartment building. Rainbow was older, smaller and a little shop-worn, but it was immaculate and gave excellent care. She knew most of the staff by name, and they knew her. Every rash and cough was chronicled, and when necessary, nurses had called to report her father's falls or the doctor's advice. Best of all, given her father's healthy appetite, the meals were tasty and generous. Quiches, stews, roast beef, even pie and ice cream appeared on the menu. In the winter, though, without the brief pink of the flowering crabs out front, the building was depressing. The Rainbow nurses and staff put up holiday decorations and dressed festively, but still… Belle had thought about ordering *Final Exit*, a self-help manual for suicide with dignity as an alternative should she ever see the end of independence.

Belle stopped across the street at the restaurant which they had frequented when he could still walk: Granny's Kitchen. It was run by a voluble fat Italian woman who was her own best marketing device. Belle had appreciated the owner's kindness and patience when listening to Father's order (always the same), cleaning the littered floor or scouring the bathroom after his visit to the facilities. "How you doing, Maria?" she asked. "The usual: shrimp dinner, easy on the fries, hold the seafood sauce but lots of coleslaw; cherry pie and ice cream." She gazed at the menu she knew by heart. "And a foot-long chili dog for me, I guess." Meanwhile, she went next door to the confectionary for his *National Enquirer*, pausing at the bank machine to call up $100.00.

Loaded with bags of steaming styrofoam boxes, Belle climbed the ramp to the home and discarded her icy boots as a sign suggested. A tiny bichon frisé trotted up warily, pet of the activity director. "Hi, Puffball," she said, giving his well-clipped white fur a pat. "Watch those feet." Stray shoes shuffling his way had taught the dog to be wary of life at ground level. At the front desk, Cherie smiled at her. One of the friendliest nurses, this curly blonde powerplant never seemed tired.

"Lunch day? Aren't you a sweetheart," she said as she filed some charts.

"So how's he doing?" Belle asked, a prayer on her lips.

Cherie shrugged a smile. "The same. Asking for you since breakfast. Knows when it's Tuesday, but always thinks you won't come."

"And I've never missed in two years. Are his feet still swollen?"

"I'm afraid so. The doctor increased the Lasix dosage. Could be his heart. No other problems. He likes his food as well as ever. Do you want a follow-up call next visit?"

"Might be a good idea. Thanks, Cherie." In search of a fork and bib, Belle toured the small dining room where several patients waited for lunch, exchanging a few words with Billy Kidd, a blind man dressed to dapper perfection, and waving at familiar ladies (always so many more ladies). The saddest group sat docile in gerry chairs, heads lolling. They were fed by the staff, one of the time-consuming attentions which accounted for the monstrous monthly sum per patient. Even so, over a ward fee of $900.00 to her father's private rate of $1,700, the government added a similar contribution. Staggering numbers, but a friend of Belle's had reported in tears that her father might have to pay $60,000 a year to put

101

her mother in a nursing home in Vermont. Maybe overtaxed Canucks should *"se taire,"* or keep quiet.

Down the hall she could hear his television reporting the local news. Sudbury's first murder of the year had occurred: a ninth grader had left her newborn in a cardboard box. She had wrapped the child in a flowered nightie and pinned on a note, "I love you, precious" when she placed the box beside a dumpster in a -25° night. "Precious" had been found by two schoolboys the next day. The mother waited under the protection of the Children's Aid until a court decided if charges should be laid. Children having children, Belle sighed.

As she entered his room, her father pointed at her from his gerry chair. Its locking table prevented him from falling, a necessary but cruel protection against the danger of a broken hip, but he hated it. "I thought you weren't coming," he said. His thick white hair was fresh-cut and his clothes clean, matching blue shirt and practical navy work pants good for one thousand washes. She arranged the bib and set out his meal, filling a plastic glass with water from the narrow bathroom. The builders hadn't anticipated the problems of the elderly. How the attendants manoeuvered him attested to their logistical wizardry with a Hoyer lift.

While he enjoyed his shrimp and she made messy inroads on the chili dog, Belle leafed through the *Enquirer*. Jackie O was still getting headlines even after answering the last trumpet. If it could happen to her... Belle probed behind her right ear where she had been having some discomfort. No lump yet. She checked discreetly to see how her father was faring since it wasn't wise to chat with him while he ate. Coordinating breathing, chewing and swallowing became difficult after a series of small strokes; aspirated food was a geriatric nightmare. He cooperated with her, but with the nurses he was bossy and demanding, reverting to the "bad boy" of his childhood. However, he seemed more "with it" today. "Good shrimp. Good shrimp," he nodded. "Pie and ice cream?" His eyes darted back and forth to the box on the dresser.

"Sure, as soon as you're finished," she agreed. Shortly after, she replaced the remains of the meal with the dessert. "Hey, you're in luck. Cherry pie. Remember how Mother used to make it? What a dope I was to lose her pastry recipe." Then she went to the dining room and returned with his tea.

"How are your feet?" She looked sadly at the swollen pair.

"OK, OK," he insisted. "Can we go out for lunch next week?"

She didn't like to believe that he would not walk again. Just getting him to medical tests was a bitter challenge, weather aside. A recent chest x-ray had been a logistical horror story, though he had tried his best. "Well, there's still lots of snow left. And you would have to walk to the van."

"I can walk. I've never let you down yet, have I?" he asked. And she felt her eyes tear and pretended to look out the window at a chickadee.

"No, you certainly haven't." She shifted topics. "Do you know that this has been the worst winter in the last century and a half? That means that no other Palmer ever in Canada has seen one as bad." He liked to boast about his family emigrating from Yorkshire in 1840. In Toronto she had taken him to Prospect Cemetery to find the grave of his grandfather, a corporal in the New York 22nd Cavalry during the Civil War. Many Canadians had gone south to fight for glory or purpose or something absent in the peace-loving North. When her father had first arrived at the nursing home, he had had a black roommate, to whom he had proudly related his grandfather's service.

"Oh, I saw *Love on the Dole* last night. Remember that one?" She knew he loved talking about his working days.

He brightened, sipping his tea, which she had cooled first with an ice cube from his bedside pitcher. "That's an old one. Deborah Kerr. Before the war, right?" He scratched his head. "No, 1941. Brits were at war, maybe not the Yanks yet. I saw every picture ever made back then." When the television news ended, Belle rounded up the detritus and left him anticipating his afternoon soaps and after-dinner favourites, *Wheel of Fortune* and *Jeopardy*. He had been interested to learn that Alex Trebek had come from Sudbury.

On her way out, she leaned over the high desk at the nursing station. "You know most of the doctors in town, Cherie. What can you tell me about Dr. Monroe?"

"Are you taking your father *there*?" She emphasized the last word with a gasp.

"No, it's a business matter. I met him the other day and had a few questions."

Cherie leaned over the desk and glanced around. "A woman in my nursing class dated him, if that's a polite word. After they broke up, she had some pretty harsh words. Hypocrite, liar, that kind of tone. His qualifications maybe?" She paused and looked sceptical. "Could be spite, though. She went to Victoria after that. Wanted a change." She snorted, pointing at the snowdrifts outside. "Guess she got it."

"Wouldn't his credentials have been checked?"

"In those days? He came here back when the place was desperate for doctors. You know the North. Always on the short end. Glad to get what we could." She lowered her voice until Belle had to lean perilously. "But don't mention this, will you? Not too ethical of me to blab."

"Of course not. And thanks for keeping an eye on the old

man." Belle went out into the sunlight that had replaced the morning fog. Behind her in the nursing home, every day was the same, just like in her fish tank. They did their best, God bless them, she thought, getting into the van and turning on the radio as Oprah's voice beamed out, greeting her fans in Northern Ontario in connection with a contest to win a trip to her show in Chicago. The country station plunged on. "Last time I saw him, he was Greyhound bound," Dottie West sang as Belle blinked into the brightness.

As she returned home, the plow sat in the same spot. This time the driver had been joined by a front end loader large enough to shift the Skydome. Likely laughing at his friend's poor driving, the loader man had ignored the banking and slipped off at the same spot. Megalon sent to rescue Godzilla and not a brain cell between them. Strolling neighbours were pointing and laughing, while the men hunched morosely in their cabs. What kind of unimaginable bigger brother would have to be summoned now? The churned-up land looked like Guadalcanal.

TEN

It was time, past time really, to search Jim's camp. Belle checked her calendar. Clear for tomorrow. Perhaps if the weather held, she could go. She filed some papers, made a list of places to visit which included the land registry office, and sent two new bills. And three reminders. And one downright threatening, well, sort of, letter to a man who owed her over two thousand dollars for her appraisal of his twenty-unit apartment. Her "1001 Letters for All Occasions" software had seven inventive sequences of seven dunning letters, like the biblical seventy times seven. At first, assume that the person had merely overlooked the bill (reminder stage); then get the facts about why payment had not been forthcoming (problems stage); in the crisis stage, hint gently that it was to the miscreant's credit rating that he pay, suggesting legal intervention only if all else failed. In Belle's experience, professionals who baked in Jamaica over the winter and paved their double-wide drives in salmon stones were the worst. She typed "Dear Mr. Bowman: It has been ninety days since we..." Too bad she couldn't hire Jimmy Cagney as a collection agent, someone to rub a grapefruit into the client's face, or maybe a rutabaga.

Bored by her prosaic prose, she turned up the news on the radio and flipped off the computer. A bad storm was blowing down from the northwest, the worst direction. Thunder Bay had two feet of snow, and the blizzard was charging through the Sault, closing the Trans-Canada route. She tapped Miriam on the shoulder. "Bad storm. Better get home while you can."

They trundled out together, pulling scarves up and wool hats down against the gusting white swirls. Five quick inches had fallen by the time Belle hit the Jem Mart for the obligatory cream, bread and eggs, along with a couple of packages of Kraft Dinner (50 cents—bargoon!). A Score bar jumped into her basket, then another. Her university roommate Pamela had always said that every now and then, everyone needed a score. True then, true today, she thought, crunching one for solace as the snow began to cover the vehicles outside. "Another bloody dump of snow," a grizzled man in a snowmobile suit grumbled, tearing Nevada tickets in a mindless routine as he stuffed the unlucky remainders into the trash. "This winter's the limit. I've been here sixty years and never seen the like. Can't even afford Ft. Myers with the dollar in the toilet." Then Belle remembered her fish. If they really were in for it, she had better stockpile feeders for Hannibal.

She reached the pet store at the mall just as "Mrs. Popeye" was turning the closed sign. The old girl was a living Victorian etching, impervious to medical advances; forever wheezing, with lively brown eyes pressed into her face like raisins into a cookie, she bullied her teenage clerks like an old pirate. "Do you want some feeders, my girl? You're just in time. We are closing early with this terrible storm. The usual dozen?" She stroked an overstuffed Siamese which homesteaded by the cash register, then rocked on her swollen legs as a coughing fit shook her. A few whiffs from the oxygen bottle clipped to her hip stopped the spasms. "Mother's milk," she snuffed.

Belle paused to calculate. "Make it two. I probably won't be back in town for a few days."

"That's a good idea. We are running low, and no shipment will leave Toronto in this weather," the old woman added as she netted the merry victims, all anticipating a private bowl, a modest sprinkle of gravel, plenty of tasty pellets and a little porcelain "No Fishing" sign. Poor babies, Belle thought, if only you knew. She accepted the bag and couldn't believe that she asked if they had any new Orandas.

"Some beauties. Golden pom poms." Mrs. P pointed to a small tank.

Belle choked back a sob. They were tempting, even at $39.99. Words like "grotesque" and "bizarre" did them pale justice. Huge, porcine goldfish with bulging sides and gaping mouths, scales of a gleaming copper rare to the aquarium, they sported a floppy pom pom over each eye, like chubby cheerleaders who had plastered their decorations to their faces. Just in time, Belle recalled the tortuous deaths of her own Orandas, Beanbag and Ochi, hellish red streaks eating them alive. Her PH balance mastery was still in question. Orandaless but proud of her self-discipline, she returned to the parking lot, trying to remember where she had left the van. When she saw it, her attention fell on the wheelwells, clogged with crusted ice and grit jamming the tires and inviting steering problems. A few tentative pokes with her boot toe did nothing. The ice was too hard. So she backed up to the wells and aimed strong heel kicks karate fashion. At last the mess fell free, but at a painful cost. She winced as she tried the key. Was the lock frozen again? Then a thin voice screeched through the wind. "What are you doing to my van? I'm calling security." Belle spotted a tall figure in a embroidered parka turn and trudge back to the mall. In her embarrassment, she recognized that her own van was one row farther down.

Her foot throbbing to the sounds of "Heat Wave" on the radio (very funny, guys), she wheeled out onto Lasalle Blvd, skidding on the greasy surface. How many words did the Inuit have for snow? How many for the sounds of a storm, the shriek of a wind which would freeze skin in thirty seconds and send weak branches crashing onto roofs, slicing off shingles? Just before the airport hill, Belle saw flashing blue lights, a comforting sight, and nestled herself in behind the plow, its mammoth wings clearing the way like the arm of a merciful God. For once she didn't mind turtling behind since the flat, open stretch past the airport was famous for blinding whiteouts and head-on collisions. The radio reported that a ten-car pile-up near Whitefish had closed 17 East. Three were dead and many injured. When the plow detoured into the airport, Belle floundered along until she reached her own road. She stopped at the mailboxes to sight down the most dangerous hill, covered a good eight inches deep, pristine and untouched by tread. Turning off the radio to concentrate, Belle steered down the steep slope, wary of the treacherous ditching on either side. It was important to take the big dip by Philosopher's Pond at top speed to make the grade up the other side. Anyone stuck at the bottom, at the bend of a paper clip, would stay there until the next thaw. As for the rest of the trip, Belle's strategy was to hug the right and pray that no one would be coming around the tight and often obscured turns.

This time fortune had been with her. Belle whispered a special hosanna as she glided into the driveway, then tensed at the confusing sight of a dark form against a snowbank near the propane tank. It was Freya, still and limp, a bright stain beneath her head. How had she got out? Belle knelt in the swirling snow, smoothing the soft fur, following the shallow rise of the chest. One eye was barely open as the dog tried to lift her head, a torn ear pricking up feebly in response. A quick assessment showed the head wound as the only apparent damage. Nearby lay a shovel used for tossing ashes on the drive, its metal edge darkened. Back inside the house, Belle grabbed a sheet which she used to drag the dog to the van. No way could she lift nearly ninety pounds. A piece of plywood from the junk pile served as a ramp. The driveway was badly drifted, and there was no sign of Ed's plow truck. He had probably come to fetch it home for a quick morning start. As for the road back, Belle didn't allow herself to imagine its condition. All she knew was that Freya needed help.

After tucking several blankets around the dog, Belle dialed from her cellular phone, glad that Shana lived on the clinic premises. On the tenth ring, a tired voice answered, "Petville Animal Clinic."

"It's Belle. Freya's been hit on the head. I'm bringing her," she gasped, glancing at the quiet form in the back.

Shana had no patience for useless questions. "Is she conscious?"

"Barely. Slipping in and out."

"Keep her warm. And for God's sake, be careful. It's pure hell on the roads. What if you have an accident in the middle of nowhere?"

"Don't jinx me. See you in an hour with luck."

Back down the road Belle drove, side-slipping, glad to have her own grooves to follow, taking the hills at crazy speeds, hardly caring if she were in the middle or not. "Hang on, pal," she called. "You did your job. I'll do mine."

Battling thick gusts of whiteouts through unprotected spots, Belle inched along the flats. Night vision problems had been plaguing her lately. Ten or fifteen feet of road at a time emerged as she rounded corners, skewing dangerously. At a particularly bad stretch across the swamp, she forgot the icy patches beneath. The van tried valiantly to correct, but the steering was too tight for Indianapolis 500 hairpins. Pivoting 180 degrees, it skidded fifty feet, and brushed through alders at the edge of the road, back wheels miring in the soft muck several yards from a culvert. The jolt was kind. Belle wasn't hurt, but it wasn't likely anyone would be along for hours, not until the plow had passed. The machine near the airport belonged to the city; a separate provider took care of Edgewater Road and might not arrive until morning. She touched the cellular phone. What good would that do? The police wouldn't put an injured pet at the top of the priority list with serious accidents all over town. Oh, she would be safe. Every Northerner carried an emergency kit: blanket, matches, chocolate and candles. But that wouldn't help Freya. Belle crawled back to stroke the dog, noticing that her eyes were closed and her breathing fast and noisy.

She struggled out of the vehicle and squinted painfully into the whitelash, tears freezing on her cheeks, her fists pounding the top of the van. Then, even over the rush of the storm, the shrill cry of the wind through the dry reeds, the purr of a motor met her ears. Standing in the middle of the road, waving her arms, she hoped it was travelling slow enough to stop. A green Jimmy materialized out of snow and skidded to the side. The door slammed, and a man in a huge sheepskin coat approached her, shielding his face against the gusts. His voice was calm and familiar. "You look like you can use some help. How long have you been here?"

Belle peered in astonishment. "Franz, is it?" she said. "Whatever angel brought you?" She pulled him over to the van.

What a miracle to have the strength of a man, Belle thought as she watched him pat the dog, whisper to Freya to gain her confidence and then effortlessly lift her into the back of the Jimmy, covering her gently with a red Trapper point blanket. The four-wheeler, with its high clearance, made an effortless path through the snow, cruising up the final killer hill as if it were a parking lot. Franz turned up the heater and glanced back at the dog. "You'll soon warm up. What happened?"

"Jesus. I don't have any idea. I got home and found her bleeding. Somebody had been in the yard. Maybe a break-in. Then I took the hills too fast." She shivered in damp clothes in spite of the heater's blasts. "I'm surprised to see you out. Doesn't Shield ever cancel classes?"

"Wednesday is my big lab day in physical anthropology. I'm usually there from nine to six. When I saw the weather, I gave my last group a take-home assignment." He paused. "I forgot to ask where you were taking her."

"Petville on Garfield Road. Do you know it?"

"Shana, of course. She's been treating my dog Blondi for years for a serious eye problem. Don't worry, Belle. She'll know what to do."

The plows had just begun cleaning the main routes in town, so a few brave or foolish cars were already plying the slippery streets against radio advice. At the clinic, Shana answered the door in a sweat suit, dark circles under her eyes, and her raven hair, usually neatly arranged in a chignon, spilling over her face. Thin but incredibly strong for her fifty-five years, she touched Franz's burden with a sympathetic murmur. "Took a bad hit, did you, girl? Hoist her up. But careful, careful," she cautioned as she directed them to the examining room. "First I have to treat for shock." She set up an IV quickly, rolling it into place, then reached for a muzzle. Belle tried to move it away. "For God's sake, she wouldn't hurt—"

Shana grabbed her arm firmly. "No, Belle. It's just a precaution. You can see that she's conscious, so I can't inject pain killers until I rule out swelling of the brain. Freya might lash out in confusion, hurt herself or us."

She slipped on the muzzle, and Freya's eyes followed her, raising Belle's hopes. "Now to debride the wound." Shana flushed the injury with warm water, cut away the nearby hair, then dabbed on some peroxide. After taking the dog's blood pressure, she flashed a light into Freya's eyes and smiled broadly. All Belle could hear was the pounding of her own pulse as she waited for the vet's opinion. "So far so good. You two wait in my suite and relax. Put the kettle on. I shouldn't be long."

An hour later, the x-ray indicated no broken bones, perhaps a slight concussion. "Lucky old hardhead. Just some bad bruises, maybe kicks. Of course we'll keep her for a few days to make sure there's no internal bleeding or other surprises. This mild sedative," she explained as she gave the dog a shot, "should let her sleep for awhile."

In Shana's living area, mugs of strong tea, well-laced with honey, were passed around. "Drink it, Belle. You've had a shock, too. It's herbal. Ginseng. I had a terrific sinus headache with the storm and went to bed early. Didn't figure anyone would be in," the vet said. Six cats of six colours and sizes prowled around, and a Jack Russell terrier showed interest in Franz's crotch. Shana called the little fellow into her lap. "They're not all mine. Just some patients who benefit more from being free in the house rather than in a cage. Frisco's getting picked up tomorrow," she added as she petted a miniature Doberman twining around her knees. "Love that short hair."

"I'll vacuum ten times a day to get Freya back," Belle said, limp after the trauma. "I'm just glad you were here. When can she come home?"

"Give you a call," Shana promised. "She'll be running around depositing pounds of hair by tomorrow night. Oh, and Franz, how is Blondi? Is the Neocortif doing its job?"

"Seems to be. We keep her out of bright sun as much as possible, but the snow reflection is cruel. You know, I'm inventing a pair of dog sunglasses!"

"Now that's an idea," Shana responded with obvious interest. "Those Shepherds in avalanche rescue training need eye drops every two hours against the glare. Maybe you could patent your discovery."

Franz dropped Belle off at Bruno's Towing, where she was beginning to feel at home. Perhaps they were listed on the Toronto Stock Exchange; she might as well buy shares. "Sure you can make it alone? It's stopped snowing, and they'll get you out, but the road will still be bad. I could follow you back." She gave him a thumbs-up sign, making a mental note to thank him with something more substantial. The driver, a friendly, red-faced man with a shredded cigar dangling from his lips and "Irv" painted on his door said, "Fasten your seat belt. We're in for a bumpy night." He didn't look anything like Bette Davis. As they made their way out the road, plowed at last, Belle knew that the spot where she had bogged would join other sites of fabled blunders, pointed out to children as warnings against speed and carelessness.

How ignominious, she thought drowsily, to be cocooned in a perfectly gigantic truck that could haul anything out of anywhere. She was headed for a warm bath with a warm Scotch and warm food and Freya was fine and… She barely heard Irv attach a tow rope to the van at the swamp.

ELEVEN

B elle should have had enough sleep since she'd had fallen into bed directly after three whopping drinks and a can of tasty, never-fail Chef Boy-ar-Dee ravioli, her comfort food since the age of six. But when the phone rang, she answered with a tempered testiness.

"It's Steve. I got your message. Against my better judgment, I trumped up some reasons to question Brooks. Seems he has an alibi, a poor one, but his wife and one of his sleazy friends will testify that he was home preparing his tax returns the night of Jim's death. Feeble, but you can't fight it."

"Taxes, right. What a concept. Why don't you take him in and grill him?" Belle rubbed at her eyes, gritty from sleep.

"You've been watching too many old movies. Anyway, we've had our eyes on him in our ongoing drug investigations, so leave him to us. Go sell some houses; I could use another lunch."

"So he could have had a henchman."

He snorted. "At least bring your crime slang up to speed. And in less than polite terms, Madame, butt out. Monroe's autopsy showed nothing surprising. Jim got off the trail in the storm, went through the ice, and that's all she wrote."

"Now you're talking country songs." Belle snapped down her ace in the hole card. "What about my dog, then?"

"Freya? What about her?"

"Oh, no big deal. I just got home last night to find her

whacked over the head. She's at Shana's. Should be all right."

"You should have called me! Did you see anyone? What about the tracks? Was there a break-in?"

Belle nearly dropped the receiver. "I had to get to the vet! Sorry that I didn't have time to check my entire acre with a magnifying glass after dark when I finally got home. And that was after I bottomed out in the swamp. No, Steve, nothing in the house was touched. I doubt that they even got in. As soon as they opened the door, out ran the dog and they clobbered her with a shovel. Looks like they heard the car and took off just before I turned down the driveway. I didn't see them, so they probably came by snow machine. As for tracks, forget it with the new snow."

His voice relaxed. "Hmmm. Sounds like a simple break and enter. It wouldn't be the first time on your road. Dubois had two chain saws taken in February, and Landry lost his snowmobile last week. That's the thirtieth one this month in the region. The insurance companies are crying."

Keeping her probes about Brooks to herself, Belle hung up after agreeing to meet soon at a new Indian restaurant, the Bengali. It sounded a bit vegetarian, but anything magma hot was welcome.

Belle sliced a blueberry bagel and popped it into her beloved coolwall oversize toaster. With all the charitable largesse from Hélène's breadmaker, English muffins and other large pastries, she needed an appliance that could toast anything. Bypassing Meg's jam with a flash of guilt, she lathered on cream cheese and added a dot of marmalade, remembering her mother's corny joke about a baby chicken talking about the orange that "marma laid." The juicy blueberries reminded her of that four-week phenomenon, summer. How long before she and Freya would again revel in the hot sun, picking and eating those cobalt jewels? The dog loved to strip the branches, nose out the berries, cool and tart in the shade of pines and birch, honey sweet and hot in the sun.

The sun through the windows was so bright, and the sky so achingly blue, the firs and cedars frozen in a picture of benign beauty, that she forgot how fierce the storm had been the night before. Time to clear all paths again, especially to the woodpile. Knowing that she would be working up a sweat, she threw on a medium weight jacket and went out to assemble an arsenal of shovels. If they knew anything about winter, Canadians knew its implements. First there was the broom for light attacks, especially on cars, then the snow scraper, good for the deck, several sizes of shovels for lifting deep snow, and the famous snow scoop, which floated massive chunks downhill. A growl, a scraping in the driveway and a few backfires sent her over to greet Ed. He leaned out of the cab of the plow truck, a 1957 Ford model with the bed rusted off and no windows. His dog sat beside him as supervisor, nosing a dab on the windshield. "Hi, pal. You must have come and fetched the truck last night," she said, wondering if the presence of even a handicapped vehicle might have dissuaded the thieves.

"Yup, she needed an oil change and more anti-freeze, so I took her back to my garage when I heard the storm was on the way. Figgered we'd need the old gal in tip-top shape today." He listened with interest as she told about the attempted break-in and the rescue. "Freya's OK, though, eh?" he wanted to know. "I'll have Hélène run you out some cabbage rolls. Look like you could use them. Oh, and you'll have to show me where you got stuck in the swamp. Maybe I'll put up a plaque." With a wink, he turned the country station up to "deafen" and began his artful rearrangement of the snow in her large parking area.

As she dropped some dried shrimp into the tank for the discus, Belle's heart skipped several beats with horror. The goldfish were still in the van, forgotten in the rush of the night. "My apologies, little friends," she muttered as she retrieved the colourful chunk and set it to thaw in a soup plate. "It was you or me."

Belle wasn't surprised to find no telephone listing for Franz on the island. Would he be offended if she dropped off some thank-you gifts? Perhaps she could pretend that she was "driving by" anyway since his property overlooked the North River entrance to the trails. A trip to town took her to the newest chichi *chocolaterie*, Lady G, for a pound of butter-smooth hazelnut truffles, an experience which the clerk assured her left sex far behind, and, even at $30.00, was a better investment. At the liquor store, she added a bottle of an old favourite, German May wine with woodruff. Roses would be a classic European gift, but how could she carry them on the snowmobile?

Belle returned home to gas up the machine. The sliders could wait. Although Franz's Jimmy navigated the ice road from the marina along with other trucks headed for the fishing hut villages, the van's shallow clearance was not suited to deep slush. As she took the cover off her snowmobile and broomed away the drifted snow, she noticed a small piece of torn red checkered wool under the track. Brooks wore a shirt like that, but so did every other male in Northern Ontario and half of the females, including herself. DNA tests for dead skin flakes? OJ overdose. Steve would laugh in her face.

After tucking the shred into her pocket and stashing the gifts, she started across to the island, which jutted like an upturned egg from the lake bed. Belle was intrigued to be visiting Franz's home. In the summer, training her binoculars on it while pickerel fishing at the North River, she had made out a paradise of pink and purple phlox dripping from rock gardens, while bronze or slender blue irises waved in the soft wind over silver mounds of artemisia. As she drew near, all was blanketed by snow. The main building, a two-storey log cabin, had three wings, melded so well it was hard to determine the history of the additions. Over the island loomed a large wind generator, its wings patiently humming.

She neared the docking area where the Jimmy was packed with garbage bags likely destined for the dump. Two tarped snowmobiles sat alongside. When a black and tan female shepherd trotted down the steps warily, Belle did a double-take at its Flash Gordon headgear. The animal gave warning barks but responded to a deep voice from the cabin door. *"Blondi, hör auf mit dem Bellen! Das ist eine Freundin."* A wagging tail propelled the dog toward Belle, head low in deference while Franz came down the stairs to remove the dog's strange headgear. Blondi's eyes seemed full and dark, but Franz's were sad and thoughtful as he rubbed the dog's ears. "It's Panus, an auto-immune disorder. She sees well enough to get around. Can't be cured, but maybe slowed long enough so she can live out her life with normal activity." He presented the glasses to Belle. "What do you think? I worked on these all fall. Sun hurts her desperately, though she lives to be outside."

Squinting through the glasses and fingering the triple straps cleverly arranged to retrofit the apparatus to an animal, Belle said, "It works! So how come your side lost the war?" She stroked Blondi's massive head, so much like Freya's. "Dogs don't need perfect vision. Smell and hearing are their greatest powers."

"Are you on your way to the north trails? It's good fortune to see you again so soon. You must come in."

With a low bow, Belle offered her booty. "I come bearing gifts to my true knight of the road." As she looked up, a shadow passed one of the windows.

Trying to suppress a shiver since he had left his coat behind, Franz acknowledged her tribute with a snap of his boot heels. "Knight? *Ein Ritter!* But of course, *Fräulein*. We have few visitors, but we haven't forgotten our hospitality. I think Mother has a fresh apple strudel."

As they climbed, Belle admired the sets of tiered stairs snaking upwards like an Escher perspective, glad that Franz had a firm grip on her arm. "The turns are more practical than you might think. Fewer stairs would be needed to go straight up, but the grade would be too steep. Still, it's a task to keep them all clear," he explained. Salt was forbidden because of the run-off to the flower beds and into the lake. Up close, the cabin complex which capped the rocky island blended early Canadian with classic Black Forest. Carved shutters decorated every window, empty flower boxes begged spring's return, and cedar bird feeders on long poles poked through the snow, spilling brown seeds below, which attracted noisy chickadees tossing their food in delight. Opening the door, Franz called out loudly, *"Mutti*, we have a visitor."

Inside, Heidi's chalet had been reborn. Instead of drywall, tongue and groove boards lined the walls. And the woodwork continued in copious pine and oak cupboards, carved stairs with newel posts, and an ornate Victorian sideboard sprinkled with porcelain figures. Three doors led from the great room to bedrooms or a den, perhaps. Over an easy chair spread with what Belle's Aunt Marian called an antimacassar, stood a large and unfamiliar tree. "How unusual, Franz. What is it?" she asked, touching its tender leaves with care.

"From the homeland. A linden, dwarfed to keep inside,

safe from your Canadian winters. A German version of bonsai. You have heard of our famous street, Unter den Linden?"

"I've seen it in pictures." Belle admired the delicate hues of a table of violets, artfully arranged to graduate from white to pink to dark purple. "And what heavy blooms in the middle of winter. Your mother must have a true green thumb. Violets are too tricky for me. My pathetic plants either dry up or rot."

A spicy smell of baking met Belle's nose as a Dresden statue of a woman glided in, blonde hair turned to silver. In her youth, perhaps, the Teutonic ideal of Leni Riefenstahl's films, a terribly innocent beauty. There was a paleness to her skin, a translucency which suggested vulnerability under strength.

The woman extended her hand and held Belle's warmly, as if welcoming feminine contact. Her gentle, reassuring voice made Belle instantly regret the tactless stereotype. "A visitor. We are honoured. Please call me Marta." She smoothed the creases of a spotless dirndl apron, and a small, dry cough punctuated her conversation.

"This is Belle Palmer, *Mutti*, from the other side of our lake. I told you about the attack on her dog."

Marta shook her head and gestured toward the wall at several black and white pictures of German shepherds. "We love our dogs as our family. I was so glad that Franz could help you." As she spoke, her light accent gave a rich European charm to the room.

"Look what Belle has brought us," Franz said, unwrapping the gifts.

Marta clapped her hands in a gesture touching in its total spontaneity. *"Schokolade und Wein. Danke."* She examined the bottle. "Woodruff. A delicate white flower. I have tried to grow it in my herb garden."

Belle said, "I have a chive patch which thrives on neglect.

That's it. What are your specialties?"

"Natural medicines are my hobby," she explained, a glow brightening her face. "You have probably seen the bitters, the essences at the health food store. My mother taught me the healing properties of common plants, but she taught me even better the deadly properties. Pokeweed, for example, the tender fresh shoots in the spring have a tonic effect, but any leaf, root or berry from older growth can cause death. Our ancestors learned to be very careful."

Belle waved her arm at the violets. "And your flowers are so cheerful in the winter. I thought of bringing roses, but I didn't think they'd weather the trip."

"The roses are my greatest challenge. Of them all, it is the Maria Stern variety that pleases me the most. Her colour is like a ripe peach. And very hardy in winter. Sadly, some of the most lovely varieties I knew in the old country will not thrive." For a moment her eyes glistened. "But you must have some coffee and strudel. *Franz, bitte, hilf mir.*"

He followed her through a wide doorway into the kitchen, where shiny copper pots hung over a mammoth wood cookstove. Belle strolled around the room, conscious of the Old World flavour in the paintings: King Ludwig's castle and some dark nineteenth-century Flemish works, their varnish spiderwebbed with age. In the only modern note, a Böse stereo system and radio. No television. Despite the dry winter air, a croton spread riotously in a large pot by the picture window, its leaves a rich tapestry of burgundy, green, and yellow. She moved over to the mantel above the massive stone fireplace. A picture of Franz, compelling even as a youngster. Who was that actor in *The Blue Max*? George Peppard? Several others depicted a balding man displaying fish catches. The father? But a photo of a young girl on a diving dock puzzled her. Who could that be?

Over the coffee, as they sat in front of crackling birch logs behind a brass fire screen, Belle petted Blondi and praised her obedience. With a flicker at the corner of her mouth, Marta slipped the dog a morsel of cake. *"Mit Blondi hier*, I fear nothing. We don't have many guests, but the snow machines, what a nuisance."

Belle sat back on the soft couch. "It's so comfortable. How old is the original building?"

Franz answered with pride in his voice. "Older than anything in the region. In 1820 a Hudson Bay factor had the first cabin raised in an effort to regulate the fur trade, decades before any mineral exploration or logging. This room would have been the original shelter. Look at the darkened beams above the fireplace. What a desolate and fearful place it must have been in those days, almost like a fort. Of course everything has been redone with each new owner. We are always discovering small evidences of their lives every time we dig the gardens. Bits of crockery, clay pipes, coins and the rare shard of glass."

"Like living in a fine museum, but with all the conveniences."

Marta gave her son a wink. "Not as many conveniences as I would like. Wolf and I, Franz's father, who is gone from us now," (she crossed herself) "was not only a master carpenter, but an electrician and a plumber. For power, you saw the wind generator."

Belle nodded. "Enough to run your appliances?"

"It's the heating devices that drain the batteries. And as you can see, we have the fireplace and a cooking stove. We can store from the wind for only so long until we must start that awful gas generator. So loud that I hate to have Franz pull the cord. But my radio can use batteries."

"Do you enjoy classical music? It's frustrating up here," Belle said, "Only the satellite can pull in those selections."

Marta reached forward and touched Belle's arm gently, looking deeply into her eyes. "It doesn't matter to me, *Liebchen*. You see, the radio is the voice of freedom. During the war, we were forbidden to listen to the BBC. *Mutti* would turn it on so very quietly that we would sit with our ears on it. Once a nosey neighbour came and she had to switch it off quickly. *Mutti* was so frightened, but she laughed as if it had been a mistake. And we children laughed, too."

No one spoke for a minute, until Franz asked, "How are the Burians, Belle?" He turned to his mother. "I haven't seen them since the funeral. Sometimes there is smoke at their lodge when I pass, but I don't want to intrude." Marta excused herself and went into the kitchen.

"As well as you'd expect. They're strong people. Probably won't be at their lodge much anymore, Ben said. How long have you known them?"

"Oh, only to say hello. Jim was a good deal younger, but I got to know him when we organized the rally against the park. As the representative from the Forestry Management program, he was covering the impact to the woodland."

"I'll try to be there. None of us wants this development. It's going to bring chaos to the lake."

"And besides the destruction, the new access roads bulldozed across the forest will be even more of a problem. There is a First Nations burial ground not one hundred feet from the proposed shower site. And of course the pictographs on the canoe routes. Just imagine what will happen when those become accessible from the main entrance. They cut the timber a hundred years ago, and now they want to rape the land again. We must take a stand or explain our cowardice to the next generation."

"There was something else I wanted to ask you, Franz. It's about Jim's death. I'm still trying to gather information in case he stumbled upon something in the bush. A drug transfer, perhaps. I can't imagine what else. Melanie said that you had heard small planes recently, just like he had reported."

"Yes, at my camp near Cott Lake, but I've never pinpointed any landings. It's always dark when the sounds come, which drew my suspicions. One of these days when I finish my projects, I'll put on my snowshoes and have a good look around."

Belle nodded her agreement as Marta returned to pass around a plate of strudel. A leather-bound volume of poems on a side table caught Belle's eye. "May I?" she asked, lifting it with reverence.

"Of course. Not too many people appreciate the old things," Marta said. "Franz tells me that one day no one reads books anymore. Only computer screens."

"Now really," he chided gently, "that is an oversimplification of my ideas."

Belle ran her finger over the page as they watched in polite amusement. *"Fraktur.* Can't read this Gothic very well, although I studied German in university." She closed her eyes. *"Möwen, Möwen, sagst du, wir haben Möwen in dem Haus?"*

They both stared at her as if she'd suddenly gone mad.

Belle couldn't suppress a grin. "Oh, I know. 'Seagulls, seagulls, do you say that we have seagulls in the house?' Useless, those silly sentences which we had to memorize. Better if I could order schnitzel." As they both joined her in laughter, she sipped the last of the coffee. Strong and rich, oddly aromatic, she told Marta.

The older woman's face lifted at the praise, her eyes sparkling. "We make it with the bitter chicory, in the continental style. You can buy the essence at the Health Food Store, but I grow and dry the plants myself. It has a lovely blue flower. And the blue flower, now, was a concept of the book you hold by Novalis. It represented the romantic ideal, a symbol of eternal search much like the Holy Grail."

"Knights, quests, you're inspiring me. I'm going to have to get out my German grammar books and start from scratch." Belle said as she stood. "But now I must be going. Thank you so much for your hospitality. I have admired your gardens from afar in the summer."

Marta took Belle's hand and broke into a smile more dazzling than Dietrich's Blue Angel's. "Then you must surely come back and see them in their glory." She gathered the dishes and went into the kitchen.

"And thanks again for your heroic efforts, Franz."

"*Der Ritter* is at your service."

Belle stopped at another picture of the young girl, fair-haired, vital and energetic, pointing up in childish delight at a ten-foot sunflower. "An old girlfriend, Franz?" she asked on a whim.

His voice grew soft. "My sister."

"I didn't know you had any brothers or sisters."

"She moved to the States. Lives in Boston. She wanted to get to the big city, never liked the bush."

"Lucky her," Belle said, summoning a joke to cover the awkwardness she suddenly felt. "This wretched winter, I feel like driving non-stop to Florida and throwing myself on the mercy of the welfare system just to enjoy the sunshine."

"Better not," he advised, his tone lightening. "They don't pay as well as Ontario."

Franz showed her to the washroom before she left. A very expensive electrical composting toilet system she had read about in *Cottage Life*, but what else would work on that rock? A faded embroidery on the wall read, *"Ein gutes Gewissen ist ein sanftes Kissen."* A good something is a soft something else? Too rude to ask for a translation of their bathroom art.

Marta stood by the door and pressed a warm, fragrant package into her hand. "Strudel for you to take home. Give a little bit to your dog, too. Soon you come again."

On the way down, Belle noticed a small grotto of cemented stones surrounding a female statue. "Mary? Aren't most Germans Lutherans?" she asked. Around the region, in French areas especially, she had seen many similar shrines, some even illuminated. This one was carefully swept with a small bunch of frozen carnations at its feet.

"My father's family were Junkers, a landowner class, who took part in the *Kulturkampf,* the nineteenth century struggle between the Roman Catholic church and the German government," Franz explained. "Mother keeps the traditions. Since we don't go to church here, she has her own way of worshipping. This isn't Mary, but Dymphna, an old Belgian saint from where my grandmother lived. I built it to practice stone masoning." He shrugged. "Me, I'm just a garden variety agnostic like most scientists."

Blondi had followed them down to sit dutifully at her master's boots. "From her looks and her comportment, her pedigree must be excellent," Belle remarked.

"Her parents were Schutzhund Threes. We can trace her lineage to Axel von der Deininghauser Heide, a legendary sire," Franz recited with clear pride, "but then so can most people who own purebreds. Axel's there somewhere on the chart. Perhaps Blondi and Freya are related very, very far back, do you think? As for her training, we didn't see the necessity of putting her through such severe paces since she is a family pet."

"I know what you mean. She's a friend first. And please thank your mother again. It was a privilege to meet her. You must love her very much."

"Her heart is not good, I fear," he said, tightening his lips in a resigned gesture. "You heard the cough. And of course we run a risk out here on the island, though there is the air rescue."

"You're in the right town for heart and cancer specialists, Franz. Anything else and it's Toronto. I wish her well."

Belle waved as she headed off across the frozen wasteland. How did they manage to live here all year? Franz must have to stay in town at freeze-up and ice-out. As she throttled up, behind her the island got smaller and smaller. Knowing how disorienting distances could be, she aimed directly across the lake, sighting off a bare hill near her house, watching the landscape enlarge at warp speed. Whether from her canoe or from her Bravo, the sight always thrilled her, the sun gleaming off her windows and the russet siding glowing in sunlight. Xanadu, a golden pleasure dome, even without Alf.

Later that night with the help of her German dictionary, Belle translated the motto from the embroidery in the bathroom: "A good conscience is a soft pillow." She hoisted her glass with a grin. "'Malt does more than Milton can to justify God's ways to man.' And single malt, now that can justify anything."

TWELVE

The *Sudbury Star* reported that the rally was scheduled for noon at Shield University. The crowd would hear speeches and then march downtown to the provincial government buildings where Franz would present a petition to a Ministry representative. Concerned citizens from the community were urged to join the assembly.

By nine, Belle was climbing the stairs to the university library, a place of monastic peace overlooking Lake Ramsey. Once the elitist haunt of the nickel barons with their stout brick and fieldstone homes from the twenties and thirties, the lake was now home to doctors, lawyers, politicians, academic upper management and business magnates. Happy pensioners whose tiny cottages had sat there for decades traded their lots at $100,000 or more as the newcomers cantilevered their modern stone and cedar structures over the water. The futuristic complexes of nearby Science North, the Northeastern Ontario Regional Cancer Treatment Centre and the new Superhospital complemented the lake on postcards, along with the ever present stack in the far background, reminding the city of its roots.

In the companionable silence of the tower, Belle recalled the first time she had driven up from Toronto with Uncle Harold at the wheel of his Packard, chrome-heavy and as comfortable as a galleon. She had yawned at the farm fields reaching toward Barrie, then perked up as they crossed the

Severn River. "Entering the Grenville Province now, girl," he had said. "You're going to see the rocks at the very centre of the world." And she did, massive outcrops for the next 150 miles which explained why people shuddered at the reports of a driver "hitting a rock cut". Three hours of bush later and Sudbury had appeared to her like the city of Oz. Returning to smoggy Toronto at the end of every summer always depressed her, especially as those cliffs and boulders flattened into the boring plains of Southern Ontario.

To kill an hour before the rally, Belle paged through bound volumes of century-old *Canadian Mercury* magazines and browsed in the excellent fiction collection. Then she hit the periodical rack for current computer information, copying pages of printer reviews and scanners so that she and Miriam could upgrade their system before tax time.

Belle yawned, checked her watch and hunted down a restorative coffee in the little refectory in the basement. One rock wall remained, a common basement decor in older homes built when blasting had been prohibitively expensive. The effect was medieval, short a few sets of iron handcuffs as a backdrop for the *Prisoner of Zenda*. Too bad about the melamine, though, Belle thought as she looked at the modern tables. In the corner, Melanie sat buried in a ponderous textbook. Her sweatshirt featured a bleak clearcut with the slogan, "Pardon me, thou bleeding piece of earth."

"Perfect verse for a nurse," Belle said as she put down her coffee. "Do you have room for one more at the rally?"

The girl smoothed her shirt and gave an A-OK gesture. "We need all the help we can get. Maybe I should comb through the wards on the way and pick up the ambulatory patients."

"The premier's closing beds as fast as he can anyway," Belle said. A restructuring due to massive provincial cutbacks had left only one hospital out of three. "So what are you studying? Did you did pay by the pound?"

Mel hefted the book like a weightlifter. "You bet. More than for filet mignon. Medical texts are ridiculous. But this $150.00 model gives valuable pointers on geriatric care. I'm in my last year and hope to specialize in that field."

"You're in the right place. It's becoming the denture capital of the world."

Melanie piled her books neatly. "You look calm enough, so can I conclude that you didn't get to see Ian yet?"

With a shake of her head, Belle described her maniacal rendezvous. "You are well out of that relationship. Amusing though he might have been in a warped way."

"Well, I'm sorry that the leg ruled him out. He would have made a great villain, a regular sociopath. We'll just have to keep on looking." As she shrugged philosophically, a distant chime rang the half-hour, and they both watched students heading for the door, talking and waving.

"I guess it's nearly post time. How is Franz arranging the rally?" Belle asked.

"He told me to meet him in his office. I'll show you where it is." She hesitated, a slight frown crossing her face. "I guess you didn't get to the camp yet, Belle. You haven't mentioned it."

Belle gave her a friendly but firm smile. "I'm not a PI, Mel. My job and an old man called my father make demands on me. I had planned to go the other day, but then I got home in that storm to find my dog attacked."

"Belle, no! What happened? Is your dog all right?"

"Just a slight concussion. I think she stopped a break-in. Anyway, to keep it short, I got off the road in that blizzard, and Franz rescued us, drove us right to the vet. He saved the day."

"That was lucky!"

Belle sipped from her cup and rolled her eyes at the taste. "Yuck. I wish his mother made the coffee here. I went out to the island to thank him and was fortunate enough to meet her. Quite the lady. And what a house. How long have they lived here?"

"Came here in the fifties, he said once, like a lot of Europeans—'DPs,' my parents called them." She frowned in embarrassment. "Not too politically correct today. There was plenty of work in the mines in that boom time. I suppose the island came cheap. But it must be so inconvenient to live out there and commute."

"Did you ever meet his sister?"

Melanie turned her head in surprise. "His sister? How did you find out about her? That seems to be a forbidden topic for Franz, and of course, you have to respect people's privacy."

Belle felt a tiny twinge of guilt, but pressed gaucherie-override and pried further. "I saw a picture of her at the cabin. What is she like?"

"There's not much I can tell you about the mystery girl. We weren't friends. I might have seen her once or twice. Eva was studying history, and nursing is a fierce little world of its own; we stick together because of the heavy hours and clinicals. The school paper carried a story about her scholarship. Then she dropped out suddenly in her sophomore year, just disappeared."

"Grade problems?"

"Hardly. Eva was a top student. She had a couple of publications in a history journal. Could have been a breakdown. You've read that book about passages. Twenty, thirty, forty, as our psych prof says, the beginning of a decade can be stressful. And perfectionists crack. We've lost about 30 percent of our initial class." She shrugged philosophically, tapping her temple in the traditional gesture. "And sometimes I worry about myself."

A few minutes later, they headed toward a cubbyhole at the end of a corridor. Franz was on the phone, talking excitedly and waving his free hand. When Mel touched his arm, he looked up with a broad smile.

"See you outside. I'll just round up another supporter," she explained, disappearing with a wave.

Franz's handshake was firm and his smile welcoming. "Belle, glad you could make it. Pull up something and relax. The rally's not for another half hour. I've just been calling the marshalls. No parade permit from the city, probably afraid to step on toes, so we'll be marching down the sidewalks, stopping at lights. Kind of a hitch, but we'll improvise. Have you picked Freya up yet?"

"Later today, thanks to you."

"Any clues on the attack? Tracks, perhaps?"

"Not a chance in the snow. Just a fumbled burglary. We've had enough of them on the road. Or…" She drew out the last word like a long pull of toffee.

"Well?"

"Or maybe I've been asking too many bothersome questions about the drug traffic. I did go out to Brooks' place, the Beaverdam, and looked around in a half-baked fashion. I'm sure he noticed that I was snooping."

"After you mentioned drugs, I made some connections." He picked up a pile of student papers. "It's everywhere. Look here." He passed her a handwritten essay.

Belle squinted as she read and gave a derisory whistle. "My God, it's totally incoherent and all over the page, too. Did the writer get a bad mushroom? Surely you don't have to put up with this?"

"The university has to be very careful, Belle. I don't dare accuse the student of taking drugs. Unless he causes a row in class, he's not considered a problem." He paused at her expression. "Oh, don't get me wrong. Most of our students wouldn't touch the stuff. Then again, last Christmas two freshmen were arrested bringing back cocaine from the islands. Donkeys, are they called?" His eyebrows rose cautiously over the sense of his usage.

Belle laughed. "Don't talk the talk, my man. It's mules you mean."

He looked embarrassed, then coughed. "Yes, well, they seem like asses to me, if you'll pardon the pun. Poor fools were promised a free trip and a few thousand dollars to hide the bags inside a jar of cored pineapple. Pretty stupid, eh?"

Belle couldn't help grinning. "Would have made an unbelievable upside down cake. But to trade stories, what about the three guys who swallowed condoms of coke before boarding a plane from Acapulco to Toronto. Forgot their Boy Scout knot lessons, because they all collapsed at takeoff."

He flicked his hand over a bust of Shakespeare. "Classical poetic justice, wouldn't you agree?"

"You mean like 'hoist with your own petard'? My favourite kind of story. The biter bit and all that."

"Shakespeare is so popular in Germany that we would claim him as our own if we could."

A knock at the door introduced a huge native man with thick braids down his back. He wore a heavy hand-knit wool sweater under his parka and untied construction boots like many students. "Nearly ready, Franz?" he asked, glancing over at Belle with a shy smile.

"Come and meet Belle Palmer. She lives on Wapiti and knows the park area well." The man's large hand wrapped around Belle's like a warm heating pad. "William Redwing. He teaches Ojibwa in our new First Nations Studies Program. In the summer he takes groups low impact camping."

William's eyes crinkled. "My people have been doing it for thousands of years without leaving any footprints. How much more low impact can you go?"

"It just makes me sick to see what people leave around at campsites. Styrofoam plates and broken beer bottles," Belle said. "And how can archaeological sites be protected?"

"Exactly. That is our fear. We have verified that a burial ground dating from the mid-eighteenth century lies within the boundaries. Will somebody dig it up as an exhibit? Why not display Sir John A. Macdonald or René Lévesque? These artifacts record our history. Look at this beauty," he added as he lifted a dark gray rock from Franz's shelf.

"A tool?" asked Belle. The object was about eight inches long, sloped and chipped at one end.

"Hand axe is our guess," William explained. "Somewhere around 1500 A.D. Franz and I found it on the North River, just below the small falls. Under the pines the ground is as soft as a cushion."

"I know that spot well," Belle said, closing her eyes in reflection. "The flat outcrop comes down to the water for bathing, and the blueberries make great cobbler if you have bannock mix."

"A good campsite, a good tool, they don't change over the centuries," William added, turning the rock slowly. "Such a practical feel. See how it fits the thumb perfectly? Could have been used for skinning."

"I'm really worried about the pictographs at the narrows. They're fading with each year," Belle continued.

"It's sad, but little can protect that fragile art short of

erecting a dome to prevent weather damage like with the Peterborough petroglyphs. If you want to see an unspoiled site, Belle, go to Elliot Lake," William said. "Now that the mines have closed, there is water access to a very holy place, an overhang on Quirke Lake. The elders took the young warriors there on their way berry-hunting and left them on the ledge for their dream time. Several days later the elders returned with their fruit to hear the stories, see the pictures and welcome the new men into the tribe."

Belle admired a birchbark box on Franz's shelf, its intricate pattern woven with porcupine quills. "What meticulous quillwork. I've often been tempted to buy smaller pieces at the craft stores north of the Sault. Out of my price range, unfortunately."

"I can tell you that the labour is considerable, and what tiny portion goes to the artist is a moot point," William said. "As children, my sister and I were in charge of finding quills. 'Road kill!' she'd yell, and off we would run. Then my grandmother sipped tea under a kerosene lamp until dawn sorting the quills into sizes and colours. Some birch baskets can boil water." His confident expression challenged her.

"Now you're kidding. That's impossible," Belle said.

William explained the careful seaming, the folds and fastening to prevent leaks. "Suspend the pot over smouldering coals, and allow no contact with a flame. Be patient, and tea can be brewed."

Belle cocked her head at Franz, who agreed. "But it's scientific, Belle. The water cools the bark from inside. And remember that water boils at 100° C, about half the ignition temperature for paper."

At the noon chime, Franz picked up his papers and put his hand on the big man's shoulder. "Let me get a few people down the hall. William, you collect the troops. I'll be back in a few minutes. Last minute details. Make yourself at home, Belle."

She dropped her pile of reviews onto the desk and plopped into an old oak armchair, vintage university. Shelves of books lined the walls, mainly anthropological. *Indians of Early Ontario, North American Aboriginals, Man Corn: Cannibalism and Violence in the Prehistoric American Southwest.* Franz had chosen the right specialty at the right time. New government money was flowing to Native Studies programs: law, social work, history and mythology. A dusty 286 computer sat on a smaller desk, complete with a cheap dot matrix printer. Lucky man if he had free Internet access, she thought. Blondi's colour photo had a place of honour, her younger eyes clear and deep. Otherwise all was typical professorial clutter and piles of student efforts.

When Franz returned, she grabbed her papers. On the way to the rally, they detoured to Belle's van to deposit her things. Several hundred people were gathered in front of the university. Young and old, miners and doctors, waitresses and bookkeepers, and students and teachers joined hands to preserve the wilderness for different reasons: clean water, quiet, respect for wildlife or the priceless value of history. A few nervous campus police stood around, passing an occasional remark to each other and cultivating serious expressions. Signs read "Save the Big Trees", "New Park. Not!", "Keep Wapiti Free" and in front of a group quietly drumming, "Sacred Trust: the Pictographs". The smell of burning sweetgrass brought summer to the air. Melanie waved and hoisted her placard: "Trees Not Tourists".

"Take one, Belle. We have plenty."

The earnest spectacle reminded Belle of her University of Toronto days, when students had taken umbrage that an anti-

Vietnamese war speaker had not been allowed on campus. Back then, the students had spent twenty-four hours sitting in at the Administration Building, quietly studying and sharing tuna sandwiches. She recalled her ancient professor of economics growling as he tapped past on his Malacca cane, "Terrible. Very, very American. You should be ashamed." But there had been no tear gas, no murder like at Kent State.

"Should have made my own placard, I guess. Something about cutting down the last tree and putting it in a tree museum," Belle commented to Melanie, who looked confused. "Joni Mitchell. A bit too early for you," Belle added.

"Sure, I know Joni. My mother has her albums," the girl replied spritely. Suddenly Belle felt as ancient as the venerable trees they were protecting.

Franz lifted a bull horn and gestured for quiet. "If you don't know me, my name is Franz Schilling. I'm a professor at Shield, and I'd like to thank you on behalf of the Stop the Park committee for coming to support this watershed issue for the Sudbury area." A cheer went up. "As you know, the decision will be made this month on whether to open a new provincial park on the north side of Lake Wapiti, near fragile pictographs, sacred graveyards and the last refuge for wildlife like the lynx and the peregrine falcon. But the developers wait at the gates, imagining rich profits: lodges, motels, restaurants, condos. Will our heritage be turned into a theme park?" Boos erupted, which he stopped with his hand. "I admit that jobs will come with the tourists. But at what terrible price? Look at the dunes area at the Pinery Provincial Park near Sarnia. An entire ecosystem of beach areas with precious plant life is under constant threat from campers. And east of Superior at Pukasawa Park, rare arctic plant life, Northern Twayblade and Franklin's Ladyslipper, have nearly disappeared and the sacred rock pits, four hundred years old, have been levelled. Our precious Killarney, that emerald necklace of lakes, cannot support fish. You need a number to canoe the system, and the tourists and cottagers from Southern Ontario are pushing sanitary facilities to the limits. Now is our last opportunity to convince the Ministry of their terrible lack of foresight." People began clapping. The First Nations drummers started up like a faithful heartbeat.

Franz looked at Melanie as he put away his notes. "There's someone else we need to do this for, someone who can't be here today but stands with us in spirit." He lowered his voice before the stillness of the crowd. "Jim Burian was documenting risks to the trees north of the lake. He was a forestry student at Shield before his tragic accident a few weeks ago. So let's say a silent prayer and dedicate our march to him." He paused and people bowed their heads while even the drums stopped and left an eloquent silence over the scene. Belle felt a lump rise to her throat and pulled her parka tight around her neck.

Then Franz raised his hands and gestured to his left. "Del here has the petition, if you haven't signed it already." A tall woman in a bright pink snowmobile suit waved a sheaf of computer paper. "Follow us to the Ministry downtown where we'll present it, along with our final report, to Ann Dawes, who has kindly come up from Queen's Park. Remember to keep to the sidewalks and obey the traffic signals. We have promised that there will be no trouble. We're environmentalists, not rioters."

A voice rang out. "Not if the park opens, Dr. Schilling."

He shook his head. "A wise government must listen to reason. Let's go, people!"

With a single energy, the crowd flowed away from the

university and down onto Ramsey Lake Road. Cars gave cheery toots and drivers waved. Strikes were common in the union town, and the "them against us" philosophy hit a familiar chord. Right on Paris Street and on downtown they marched, singing, "This land is your land, this land is my land, from Bonavista to Vancouver Island." An hour later, as the crowd regathered in the handsome courtyard of the provincial buildings, Franz presented the petition. Melanie's eyes were bright and wet. "I wish Jim could have been here."

"So do I, Mel. But I think we did him proud today," Belle said, putting her arm around the girl.

After a rather wary Ms. Dawes had accepted the petition and backed quietly into the government building as if not daring to turn, people began to disperse. A few pickup trucks ferried groups of five or six to the university, with the police ignoring the obvious seat belt violations. Belle found Franz to congratulate him.

"I think it went well, too. Thank God there weren't any incidents. We don't need any bad publicity at this point," he said. "Of course it will be a few months before the final decision. The wait won't be easy. Thanks for marching with us, Belle."

Belle tapped Franz's arm. "I've been thinking about the park and about Jim's contribution. Really, I don't know where else to go with this. Is there any possibility, is there any reason that his reports might have earned him some enemies, people who stood to make money on the development he was trying to stop?"

Franz gave her a politely sceptical look. "Well, I'm not minimizing his documentation, or anybody else's. It was all integral, Jim's trees, William's sites, the whole ecosystem, not to mention the overriding threat to water quality. One is not

140

more important than the other, but together we hoped that these factors would make a powerful argument. I wish it were a thread to follow, Belle, but I think not." He waved over a small van for them.

Belle said goodbye to Melanie at the university parking lot. On the short drive to the Petville clinic, the radio warned people that the smaller lakes and rivers were thawing. Another snowmobile driver had gone down on a tributary of Lake Penage. On the happier side, the rally had inspired a phone-in poll that showed 65 percent of listeners disagreed with plans for the new park. Radio polls might not have much influence, but public support should help their cause.

At Shana's, Freya was pacing behind the counter, nails ticking on the linoleum, and she barked excitedly as Belle caught her eye. She galloped through the waiting room, galvanizing the clients and their tinier charges. Shana was panting as heavily as the dog. "Am I glad you're here. She's driving me nuts! Every sound HAS to be your car."

"Thanks, Shana. What do I owe you?"

Her friend sighed, but business was business, no professional courtesy between realtors and vets. "Oh, with the X-rays, that's the expensive part, let's say an even hundred."

Considering the days of boarding and the tests, it was a shameless undercharge. "You won't retire in New Mexico that way, Shana, but you have our thanks," Belle said and flipped her thinning VISA card onto the counter, first holding it up to the light. Was it becoming transparent?

Shana had another thought as she passed over the receipt. "Before I forget, her stools are a bit hard. Age gets to us all. I suggest a tablespoon of Metamucil each day with a tablespoon of canola oil."

Belle gave her an incredulous look, and they both burst out

laughing. The dog flounced out of the room after Belle and stood nose to the van door, taking no chances. This was the way home, and she was not going to be left behind; on camping trips, she often climbed into the canoe even on dry land. Freya planted a few nose prints on the glass before curling up on a rug in the back. Having forgotten to plan dinner, Belle bought a pizza (Chicago style, wow!), a jar of marinated artichoke hearts and a woody tomato from Israel, wondering if it were better to have peace and blizzards or meaty tomatoes and car bombs.

At home she stuffed herself while the Nostalgia Channel pumped out *Mata Hari*, a masterful propaganda vehicle featuring Garbo as the legendary World War One spy Gertrude Zelle. Lionel Barrymore strutted as the manly Shubin against the effete but more effective posings of Ramon Novarro. Hadn't Ramon been found dead in auto-erotic strangulation? Many critics accused Garbo of sleepwalking through a familiar role, yet her farewell to the blind Novarro before going in quiet dignity to her execution had the timbre of a Casals cello concerto.

THIRTEEN

J ust as well I didn't visit Jim's camp immediately, Belle thought as she looked out at the thermometer; I know what the Burians meant about not being able to face his belongings again. Now, with some mental distance, maybe I can handle it. The temperature was a fair -17°, about zero F and better yet, the wind was down. For once, Freya didn't pester her. The dog was so overjoyed to be home that she parked herself contentedly in her easy chair, oblivious for once to the snowmobile preparations. Trips to the vet seemed to traumatize shepherds, such territorial homebodies. "Who hurt you? If only you could talk, old girl," she said, rubbing the characteristic nose bump that made the breed look extra fierce when their lips curled in a snarl. A mumble, then a grumble came from the chair, and the dog tucked her nose under her tail, closing her eyes. Belle laughed. "Sure, talk a language I can understand. I could use a clue, you know."

Several groups of machines streamed by as she stepped onto the cedar deck, bearing a cup of seed for the bird feeder. The familiar four-part whistle piercing the woods signalled that the sparrows had returned, but the robber baron squirrels loved to lift the roof on the little cedar house and spoon into dinner. Belle scanned the ice. Fewer huts each week; the season would soon end with the thaw awaited by fish-belly-white Sudburians dusting off their BBQs and dieting to squeeze into their shorts. The beginning of April was about the limit for ice fishing, even on the large lake.

Ben's quarter section topo map pinpointed the cabin's location near Larder Lake, about ten miles from the Burian Lodge. As she passed the remains of the first village, Belle swore softly at the garbage, pink fibreglass insulation, wood scraps, metal pieces and the occasional broken window. Why couldn't the huts be licensed and monitored as on Lakes Nipissing and Simcoe? People made a bathroom and a dump out of her drinking water. The DesRosiers were back out in lawn chairs to catch the last weeks of fishing. "How's it going?" Belle asked, pulling up. As tanned as if she had spent a month on the sands of Montego Bay, Hélène passed her a hunk of herb bread mounded with cream cheese.

"Some good. I had three fine trout this morning," the woman answered with a sly grin, opening a cardboard box to show her prize. Ed kept quiet until his wife gave him an elbow. "Old man too lazy to jig the bait. He just leaves it in and loafs."

Belle licked the crumbs from her fingers and made a remark about male and female attitudes toward a more intimate activity before driving off in good humour. It might take a good hour to reach Larder Lake. How rich in land Canadians were, she thought as she covered the miles without seeing another person. Crown property held many small cabins like Jim's scattered over unlimited territory. For a small lease and minimal taxes, anybody could have a place to hang a toque if he didn't mind the inaccessibility and lack of hydro. She cleared Wapiti, slipped up the Dunes to the trails, eying Schilling's island on the way. Now it seemed so familiar. Smoke rose cheerfully from the stone fireplace as it likely had for nearly two hundred years. Was Marta popping another tempting strudel into the oven?

The route led past an old friend, Spirit Rock, a personal shrine for Belle. This huge chunk of glacial erratic had been her private place for meditation. Seemingly fallen from the sky, it dominated the landscape. She stepped off the snowmobile and strapped on the snowshoes lashed to the rear carrier. One day she was going to retire her clumsy wooden relics with their bindings so tempting to hungry little rodents. Trailhead Equipment in Toronto advertised high-tech beauties in its catalogue, space age metal alloys so light that she would be gliding over the snow like Fred and Ginger in *Top Hat*. Even at a pricey $300.00, if they lasted forever, or longer than she would, the bite might be worthwhile. It took several sweaty minutes to reach the rock due to the clumsy snowmobile boots, meant for warmth, not walking. Breaking trail without a crust was no picnic either; the snowshoes could sink up to a foot and turn into scoops. And people bought treadmills when they could do this?

Lifting fifty feet into a cadmium blue sky, Spirit Rock was solid and dependable, pure Cambrian granite. Rocks and water and trees, the triumvirate of Shield country. After living with their power, Belle doubted if she ever would want to abandon them. What honest land refused to show its bones? Eons ago the mighty boulder, dropped in retreat as the glacier smothered the land, would have glowed silvery shell pink as the rock down around Killarney, but a century of acid rain had weathered it gray and tanned its folds like the skin of an aged elephant. Still, where the rock chipped, crystalline rose shimmered. A tiny cedar tree, indefatigable as the stone itself, shot its four feathery inches out of a narrow cleft. What a miracle for this stubborn natural bonsai to find the right niche, the perfect mix of dirt and moss. Near the top of her monument, a triangular dent revealed where a chunk of several tons had fallen. Now the fragment was covered in snow, but in summer, Belle could lift the giant piece in her mind, rotate it to complete the three dimensional jigsaw. How long ago did the huge weight submit to gravity, groan and break free? One hundred, five hundred, a thousand years? Did some passing Ojibwa startle at its earth-shaking fall? Patient nature ground slowly but exceedingly fine, like the mill of God. Not like police departments.

Placing her hands on the cold, familiar face, she said quietly, "Jim loved this land. He tried to preserve its integrity so that your beauty could live forever undiminished by man. Help me to find his killer and understand his death." Lord knows, Mother, she murmured to herself, you can take the Anglican out of the church, but you can't take the church out of the Anglican. Bless that grand old Cranmer prayerbook.

After another half an hour on the route, Belle passed Larder Lake and turned to follow a deep groove in the snow that indicated an overblown trail. A few minutes later, she reached Jim's small cabin. Anyone who wondered where moose went in the winter could have found the answer here. At least ten piles of droppings littered the clearing, the striped maples well browsed by this "eater of branches".

Next to the cabin, no more than four walls and a door, someone had been quartering birch, stacking fresh pieces on the porch for convenience and protection. Sure enough, under the massive splitting log nestled the key, wrapped in a plastic bag. She opened the door with a sense of dread and regret, overwhelmed by the silence, then marvelled at the evidence of Jim's soul. A closer look showed the care that made the simple hermitage neat and practical. Chinked logs had been carefully whitewashed, and the tin sheet base of the oil barrel woodstove was swept clean of ash. She noted a small desk and a rustic bed, a sleeping bag on a padded wire frame, and a wooden chair with embroidered pillows. The picture of Melanie that Ben had mentioned smiled brightly from the desktop, bringing cotton to Belle's throat. Framed in art deco pewter, the pretty girl was clowning with Jim's brother Ted, mugging into the camera. Belle skimmed through the book titles: *Trees of Canada, Diseases of Conifers, Common Weeds, Peterson's Edible Plants, The Woods in Winter: Wild Animal Tracks and Traces*. And the usual Audubon guides to mushrooms, butterflies, insects and flowers.

Moving on, she rummaged through the small pantry. Rudimentary cold-safe provisions like Kraft Dinner and other pasta, dried beans and milk, coffee, flour and rice. An instant noodle package was crumpled in the garbage. Lunch perhaps on that last day. The pots were clean, nesting under the dry sink.

A pair of lovingly-varnished snowshoes hung on the wall, along with a tattered rabbit pelt, maybe a childhood trophy. Topo maps were pinned up marked with sites of interest: oak grove, white pine growth, moose pasture, springs and bear dens around the other Burian hunt camps. Of the several record books lining the shelves, one leather log listed hundreds of flowers Jim had noted, starting with spring's first, the bright yellow marsh marigold (the pickled buds resembled capers, he had told her) and the last to leave, the durable pearly everlasting. From a well-dusted shelf of specimens, Belle picked up a small piece of fungus, chicken of the woods, a savory treat when sautéed with eggs. On their hiking trips Jim had provided a never-ending banquet from the bush for an amazed Belle, who had thought that raspberries and blueberries were the limit. "What do you imagine the natives lived on before the white man traded his flour and sugar?" Jim had asked, with a gentle tease. And over the nights they had camped together on the edge of shimmering Lake Temagami, he had brewed pine tea, plucked pickerelweed from a swamp for a salad, fried up milkweed flowers and shaken off cattail pollen for pancakes.

Small memories of small rituals of the heart. Thank God she had seen him that one last day. These simple belongings impressed on Belle, as the funeral had not, that she would never see her young friend again. And she wept for the loss. Sitting on the hard floor of the cabin, Belle used her sleeves to brush away the hot tears.

The rows of diaries drew her from the pain. She skimmed the contents until she found a large looseleaf binder for the current year. The 30th, the day of his death, contained observations of tree size and number north of Wapiti. "Inspected medium growth birch grove by Marian Lake for evidence of frost cankers and borers." Other lists counted white or red pines over 24 inches in diameter. Belle pressed the bridge of her nose until it hurt. "Here's a trick to remember the difference between the two: white pines have five needles for five letters. It's easy," she heard him say. The lessons kept rolling back as if two friends were warming their hands together over a quick spruce fire. All of a sudden she narrowed her eyes, shifted the page to compensate for her myopia. "Think I saw Brooks near Damson Lake last night when the moon was so bright, a large duffel bag strapped on his sled. What would he be doing out here?" Then followed only a final few sentences, messier, scribbled in haste. "4:00 p.m. Heading back before storm gets any worse. Mom probably worried. Hope I don't have the flu." So Jim had been on his way home, not bushwhacking. How then would he have gotten off the trail when he could have navigated these woods in his sleep? And he had seen Brooks the night before, an important discovery.

Before leaving, Belle made a final sweep, ending at the medicine cabinet. Though the cabin had no bathroom, only an outhouse, a place for supplies was useful. Aspirin, bandages, nail scissors, iodine…then a cold pill blister pack, three missing. So Jim had taken medication. Was Monroe right? Could that explain the disorientation?

She left the camp as she had found it, resisting the urge to take even the small token of the chicken of the woods. The memory of their good times would be the best souvenir. Belle thought that she had better tell the Burians about her visit. Though they had said they wouldn't be out any more, she looped by the lodge anyway.

Lost in thought, she snapped to happy attention at the familiar white smoke trailing from their chimney. The "closed for the season" sign was still tacked on the door, but the Burians were back. She found them in the kitchen, Ben brewing coffee and Meg rolling a pie.

"I didn't know if I'd find you two here," Belle said. "I took a chance coming from Jim's cabin."

"Fresh sorrow and all, it's still the most beautiful place in the world to us," Ben said. "We couldn't stay in the damn city and rot the rest of the winter, eh, Mom?" He put an arm around her gently and pulled her close. "In a way, Jim will always be with us here. In every flower, every bush, every tree we see. This was his real home."

Meg's eyes held a tender hope which made Belle melt. "Did you find anything?"

"Data for his projects. Apparently he had lunch and then left around four, according to his diary. He wanted to get home for supper and save you the worry. And in the last line, he noted that he might have the flu." She paused as Meg's shoulders sagged. "Perhaps that explains why he took that wrong turn in the storm."

"The flu. Well, Ted had it the week before. Do you think that proves the police theory that it was an accident, Belle, that he was confused, feverish maybe?" Ben asked.

"I might agree except for one odd detail. His diary pinpoints Brooks as having been in the area the night before."

Ben gave the table a sudden pound. "Brooks! Jim worked for him when he was a boy. I never liked that man, but I find it hard to believe he'd turn to murder."

"If there are drugs involved, nothing is past imagining," Belle said.

As they sat and talked, Meg poured coffee, rubbing absentmindedly at her chapped hands, hardly listening to their conversation. Finally she cleared her throat and rummaged in her apron. "Belle, there is something. Haven't even shown it to Dad. Didn't turn up until the wash. Silly of me, but I had to set his things aright, even if I was going to give them to the Sally Ann. Couldn't throw away good clothes when folks is out of work. His pants, you see, I found this deep in the pocket as I was ironing them." She held out a tiny gold tear drop.

"A piece of jewelry?" Belle asked. "I'm no metallurgist, yet it looks like unworked gold. Pure. Natural." She turned it in her hand, sensing a warm magic.

"Something special he was having made for Melanie?" Meg wondered. "Her birthday was coming up. But he never said nothing to us."

Belle balanced the puzzling object, lifting it up and down in assessment. "Surely not even an ounce. Hardly enough for an earring. Let me keep it for now and think about it."

Belle followed a short cut of Ben's back onto the main trail, her skis slipping in and out of the wider tracks. Surely she deserved better suspension, more comfort and padding now that she was about to join the older set. She paused under a feathery pine, inhaling its sweet balsam perfume. A quirky play was writing itself, a repertory of Jim's death scene, his sculpted hand in the ice pointing the way to eternity. Painful or not, she knew she would have to force herself to visit the site of Jim's accident again. Afraid of missing the cutoff, she poked along, searching for the tell-tale pine loop. When saw it, she sighed, removed her helmet and reached for the snowshoes lashed to her carrier. Almost two feet of snow had fallen since Jim's death; the curious side trail had vanished.

Swinging her feet, brushing back heavy branches, she plunged into the deep forest. It was as remote as she remembered. Such a good place for a murder, she thought.

Just as her sweat was beginning to build, the lake appeared, pristine and innocent, oblivious that a life had disappeared into its depths. Nature, the great director, played no favourites, didn't care if its performers lived or died. It was completely amoral except for ruthless contempt for stupidity and carelessness. Then it would close the curtain and bid another act begin. How many minutes she stayed at the deserted lakeshore with the wind rising and teasing puffs from the unmarked snow she could not tell, except that at last her chapped face and ears warned her to return to her machine and put her helmet back on.

Jim hadn't been stupid, not with woodlore, naïve and innocent though he might have been with human relationships. Sitting sidesaddle on her sled, chin on her hands, Belle replayed the scene leading up to Jim's death. Frame by frame, she tried to recall each detail. On that trip, she'd been slipping in and out of the trail, following that tempting path Ed had discovered. Even with the light snow cover, the grooves had been inches wider than her own, and, she thought with sudden inspiration, larger than the tracks of Jim's Ovation. There had to have been another sled. But why had there been no sign of its having turned around or any sign of footprints? A murderer didn't vanish into the air in this country without a skyhook from a helicopter. Another answer, another question.

A pair of ravens, their blue-black feathers dishevelled like a chimney sweep's coattails, wheeled through the sky, croaking, likely on their way to the Burians where a few bread crusts might await. In the Ojibwa mythology, Raven was a famous trickster. Whoever had orchestrated Jim's death was a similar master of deceit.

Around four, Belle glided up in front of her house and parked the machine under the deck, covering it carefully, after refilling the fuel and oil. A trip to the bank in town was in order, to transfer funds from her father's Florida account where his social security was deposited.

When she saw the jammed parking lot, her blood pressure spiked. Inside, the only working machine had a line of ten, while at the wickets, motherly tellers tried to keep the crowd moving through the corded labyrinth.

The people were grumbly but not mutinous. Canadians subscribed to the "Peace, Order and Good Government" policy instead of the more militant American "Life, Liberty and the Pursuit of Happiness". The right to bear arms would never be inscribed in the Charter of Rights; the right to arm bears, maybe. During the wait, Belle's hand kept finding its way to the gold drop in her coat pocket. What might Melanie know about this tiny talisman?

A phone call to the Nursing Residence told her that Melanie had just left for dinner next door at the hospital cafeteria. Fifteen minutes later, Belle found the girl at a corner table, probing a grey chunk of shepherd's pie, heavy on the mashies and dotted with mushy peas. She looked up and smiled. "I'd invite you to join me, but I have too much respect for your good taste."

"I just got back from the camp." Belle shook her head. "I know…finally."

"Any luck?"

Belle told her what Jim had written in the log. "He seemed fine the last time I saw him, but that was days earlier. I guess the flu could explain some distraction, but to go so far off the track? And he mentioned seeing…" She glanced around the crowded room. Better not use names. Sudbury was small enough to be quite an intimate little family, especially where locals were concerned. She hummed to herself. "Our lodge friend up there in the bush." Melanie squinted up her eyes in a question, then caught on as Belle continued.

"What about your investigation at the university?"

"It's been slow. I start to bawl every time people tell me what a great guy he was. Gone through a box of tissue." She paused and wound a strand of hair around her finger. "Except…Father Drew, the chaplain who teaches one of the crisis counselling courses we have to take. He's a good man to talk to. He gave me to understand that Jim had consulted him once about a student who had a crush on him. More of a bother than anything else."

Belle perked up. A lady of mystery in Jim's past? Hard to believe. "Who was it? What did she look like?"

"Forget it. You know Jim. Never a word. I find it strange that he asked for help. Certainly he never said anything to me.

He gave me the impression that I was his, well…you know." She lowered her eyes and cleared her throat. "What's next, then, Belle? Do you have any more ideas?"

"At least the log convinces me that I'm on the right track. The next step is to find a definite connection between Brooks and the drug trade," Belle said. "And Mel, I have something to show you." She presented the drop. "Meg found this when she washed Jim's pants. Could it have been a gift for you?"

The girl accepted the gold like a holy relic, her face softening. "Jim's? I don't know. Where would he have got it? It looks like a tear from an angel. God, that sounds so trite. May I keep it?"

How could she say no? Belle told Melanie that she had to consult a few friends who worked with gold first, from raw material to finished product, to discover exactly what it was and where it came from.

Freya got some chow before Belle stirred up a quiche with shredded Emmenthaler and Black Forest ham for herself. Thirty-five minutes later, she hunkered in front of the oven, watching an edible television show. The savory cheese was bubbling, the chopped chervil and capers peppering the top. Finally she could wait no longer, tested it with a piece of spaghetti and doused on hot sauce. Then she watched Miriam's precious tape of *Wild Orchids* as a torrid Garbo pirouetted around the hapless Louis Stone. Not too convincing for the twenty-four-year-old to be in love with a man pushing seventy. Had MGM believed the public that gullible? Belle suspended her disbelief and sat back to enjoy the quintessence of the silents, the subtle techniques that made words superfluous. Silent films had been called "shadow plays", and these shades fluttered around the actors with stunning effect: while Garbo waits tentatively outside her lover Nils Asther's bedroom door, light suddenly washes over her as the door opens, and his shadow begins to move up her body; and as the image of his cupped hand falls over her breast —she disappears. Just like the solution to Jim's death is forever pulling away from me, Belle thought.

After the movie, she began her bedtime routine, marshalling an artillery of vitamins, a 400 mg E (not natural, but cheap!), halibut oil, a 1200 mg lecithin and a new B-75 bomber horsepill. She assembled them on the bathroom counter along with her favourite old-timey glass from Mother's Pizza in Barrie, bearing a wistful portrait of Mary Pickford, Canada's sweetheart. Slow down, Belle thought, and bite the big ones in two. Or learn how to apply the Heimlich manoeuver to yourself.

FOURTEEN

The local bar scene was a subject far from Belle's mind. Only in university, in cozy bierhalls or pizzerias, safe havens for women, had she "gone drinking" with friends. Everyone knew Sudbury's watering holes by sight and reputation, from the upscale Office to the restaurant-bars like Pat and Mario's to the outer limits like Eddy's down the alley from the Salvation Army. Later that night she would give Derek a call to find out the best dives to search for a link between Brooks and the local drug trade. He might have friends in "low places," as the song went. Of course, she would have to go alone. How else to meet people?

After a salty but satisfying breakfast of English muffins, wicked feta cheese and some tempting dried black olives, she drove downtown to check in with Miriam. Her lieutenant and her PC companion were humming in tandem. "Guess what?" the older woman called, sweeping her arm like a grand duchess. "We got the go to sell that apartment in the Flour Mill. Ten units. Low rent is the polite phrase, but well-maintained. I was over there this morning." She flashed Belle a few Polaroids. "200K if we're lucky. And the owner has other properties, too." She sprayed wildberry deodorizer around her desk. "Sorry. Mr. Balboni smokes a wicked cigar. Didn't want to be rude and lose the sale. The things you do." She coughed theatrically.

"Windfall, Miriam. We'll have to celebrate. Dinner on me at the restaurant of your choice when and if. Oh, the Garbo tape was a definite gem."

Miriam smiled like a Buddha and started dialing. Pushing aside the clutter on her desk, Belle clicked up her files on a lakefront distress sale. Nowadays lots had to be 150 feet minimum so that tiny places did not overtax the waterfront. This lot was 100 feet by the dubious "irregular". With the bedrooms a weak shot put from the road, it was like sleeping on the pavement itself. Since there was no land for a conventional septic, the owner had tunnelled creatively to put in an anaerobic bed across the road. Uncut, unruly, Tim Horton cups and other detritus nesting in the high grasses, it doubled as a wildlife sanctuary in clear violation of the code which demanded that a septic bed be green and reasonably clipped. A cement block sauna with a sinister hole by the chimney and a rusting trailer with broken windows crowded the last inches of the site. Even the house roof sagged, weighed down by ice dams and no doubt leaking inside. The elderly owners had become unequal to the upkeep. Bring on a dozer, Belle thought, but there was no accounting for taste. The wretched toenail of dirt might attract someone who just wanted boasting rights to lakefront property, thereby providing a retirement cushion for the old pair.

A few groggy hours later, the coffee pot exhausted, Belle trudged back from a lunch run down the block to fetch submarines, Italian salami for Miriam and for herself, a seafood special (fish masquerading as crab). Turbot maybe? In a recent diplomatic contretemps with Spain, a long-patient Canada had surprised the world by defending its fragile Grand Banks, impounding one boat and displaying the illegal nets at the United Nations building. Whatever its origins, the succulent flesh had Belle licking the last calories of mayo from her fingertips. A cold draft blew through the room as a young woman toting a gigantic leather book bag muscled through the door. Hefty but fit, with baggy jeans slit at the knees, a Metallica sweatshirt glimpsed beneath her parka, and several earrings, the intruder was Miriam's daughter, Rosanne.

"Bellesy," she said. "Haven't seen you since the school year started. I hope I haven't come at a bad time. Mom said you would let me on the computer."

Relieved that the clear speech seemed to discount possibilities of a pierced tongue, Belle got up. "Sure, Rosanne. I'm finished. Just don't access the hard drive or use the mouse as a foot pedal," she joked, peering at the pencil drafts the girl carried. "Early Christian Burial and the Catacombs?"

It was for a course on the history of education, Rosanne explained. "Our prof, such a cool guy, told us that since the subject was dead meat, all that Dewey and Maritain and Whitehead, that we could do our term paper on anything we wanted. I'm going to be a social studies teacher, but I have a gruesome side."

"Really?" Belle whispered as she watched the girl log on. Suddenly a neuron twanged across into a distant connection. "You took your degree at Shield, right?"

"Yep, graduated two years ago, but it took me that long to make teacher's college. The quotas are ruthless."

"Did you know Eva Schilling?"

"Well, sure. Not too many of us crazy history majors." She tapped away furiously.

"What happened to her? She dropped out, I heard."

Rosanne shrugged. "Who knows? You could say she was the new star of the department, scholarships coming out the …uh, ears. Some found her stuck-up, but, like, she just didn't seem to have a life beyond that dumb island and the library. We asked her to parties, but she always had to get a ride with her brother. Can you believe? Then in her second year she did a fade-out at midterms. No sign of the babe again."

"Pressure?"

"It's schizy to have straight As going. That's why I avoid it at all costs." She flashed an impish smile at Miriam. "Anyway, if she weren't in school, why would she want to stay on that island? Could be she's working out of town. In the States, maybe. Wish I could get one of those pretty green cards."

"Cheap cigarettes and liquor would be your ruin, Rosanne. But don't panic. Wal-Mart has arrived. Say, could she have married an American? There must be some Yanks at Shield."

"UN-likely. She was more like a nun or a saint, if you get my drift." A chime sounded from the courthouse. "Hey, two o'clock. I'd better get my buns in gear. Thanks, Belle. And I won't save or anything. Just work it up and print." Unwrapping an entire pack of sugar-free gum and wadding it into her mouth like loading a flexible cannon, she bent to her task. Belle whiffed cinnamon all the way to her van.

Tripping over a rubber taco toy as she entered her house inspired dinner: hamburger fried with chili powder, garlic and tomato juice, topped by Monterey Jack, all nested in crispy corn tortillas. When her charred taste buds had recovered sufficiently to permit clear speech, she called Derek Santanen.

"You gave me a hand when I needed it, Belle. That's why I'm being dead honest with you. I don't have nothing more to do with the trade, no old friends, nothing," he sighed elaborately. "I can't tell you what's coming down now, just the action before I was busted. Prob'ly all changed. They don't do nothing in the same place twice. Security." He spoke like a proud professional.

"Well, where was a good spot to deal then, pal-o-mine?"

"Hardy har-har. Like I told you last time, my buys use' to be at the Paramount." Chomping and slurping sounds followed this information. Belle wrenched the phone from her ear and inspected the receiver. "On Brewster Street?" she asked next. The rotten end of the downtown core. Winos, small fry drug dealers, and those with newspaper in their boots who with the price of a few beers fell into drunken brawls and an occasional murder—if the victim landed in a snowbank at thirty below and couldn't crawl to a warm place. Every big city and some small ones had their Brewster. The only time the place really stirred into life was the day the welfare cheques arrived.

"You want I should take you down there? Kind of a bodyguard like?" he offered generously.

"That might spoil the effect, Derek, but thanks anyway."

"Maybe, but lock your car doors. Hey, remember Brooks? He mentioned you last time I did some tune-up work at the Beaverdam. You didn't go looking after them machines I told you about, did you? Were you bugging him?"

"Why? What did he say?" Belle felt a frisson of warning.

"Nothing much. Just asked if I knew this nosy babe. Described you pretty well." He snorted a dubious compliment. Then his voice grew serious, nearly brotherly. "Stay away from him, Belle. Guy's a coward, and that's the worst. Gimme a crazy anytime. Least you're allus on your guard."

Belle thanked him for the crunchy concern and headed to her closet, sorting through a collage of clothes she hadn't worn since Rod Steiger had played a pawnbroker. What outfit would raise the fewest eyebrows at the Paramount? She chose a costume of circulation-cutting wheat jeans, a green silk peasant blouse, short leather jacket too small for her expanded winter body and fake armadillo cowboy boots optimistically purchased for the Calgary Stampede. "Sorry, guys," she apologized as she shoehorned them onto spreading feet spoiled by years of cushy runners. "You're not getting any younger." As an afterthought, she dug out the wig her mother had bought for her unsuccessful rounds of chemo. It was tasteful, neatly short-cut in dark brown curls for a soft, vulnerable look. As a final touch, she unearthed some makeup from vainer days and applied powdery blue eye shadow and a bronze lipstick, tucking them into a small handbag which usually held her coin collection. A final whiff of Chanel 22 followed her shivering body to the van. The boots were cold and stiff. Why did people dress this way in the North?

The van rolled along next to the railroad tracks which bisected the city, past a grim strip of soup kitchens and cheque-cashing places: a pawn shop's beckoning golden balls, a few greasy spoons with the cheapest breakfast outside Vegas and second-hand furniture stores with shabby rooms upstairs. Too cold for the roaches, though. She flinched as a freight chuffed by. When the transcontinental rail traffic pulled into Sudbury, this lowlife panorama greeted the passengers as they sipped daiquiris inside the insulated windows of the club car, or so a national magazine article had said. The town fathers had rumbled and frothed, countering that Sudbury had just made the top twenty best cities in Canada. But they couldn't very well drag the tourists from their seats and limo them around to the postcard spots.

Belle hesitated at leaving her precious van in this neighbourhood, relaxing only when she remembered the comprehensive coverage on her insurance policy. With steely determination she clumped to the door of the Paramount, passing three chubby Harleys parked out front. Bluestocking days still left one door reading "Gentlemen" and the other,

"Ladie's and Escorts". No grammarians need apply, but inside all was one. Beery fumes and raucous country wails greeted her along with smoky drifts of conversation and the occasional click of ivory rounds across a baize table. Large hairy males, tattoos undulating to the music, cigarette packs stuffed into their T-shirt arms, lifted bottles around a video game. Gang members? A few years ago a riot between rival clubs had made the national news.

She plowed through the layers of haze to order a Scotch and soda, although she knew her stomach might rebel. Only bar brands, but hoping a few of Derek's reliable Paws might quell indigestion, she munched from a large bag, rationing them carefully, treasuring the sensation of perfect crunch, salt and cheese. About twenty feet away, a horseshoe runway with a tape deck featured what the sign outside euphemistically called "Montreal Table Dancers". Most rare traces of Canadian exotica seemed to emanate from that colourful city. Watching the two women, one young and faintly pretty, the other a stretch-marked pro, called up an ironic comparison: "The best lack all conviction while the worst are full of passionate intensity." Pretty snide, Belle, she thought. These women were making a hard-won living shaking their worn gilt tassels instead of collecting welfare. Two pot-bellied men on furlough from their wives tucked bills into the bikini underpants gyrating in their steamy faces, hooting and elbowing each other, making crude gestures, giant rings of keys jingling from their belts like fashion statements. Belle swirled her drink and arranged her junk food snacks in a small design on her serviette. Suddenly a throat cleared.

A Willie Nelson clone smiled at her, his clean-shaven face pleasantly creased. You didn't come here as Miss Manners' foreign correspondent, she told herself. Take a deep breath, well, maybe not too deep, and pretend you're in a 1963 Grade C film. If he's not in his prime, he's in your superannuated ballpark, dear old ivied Wrigley Field.

"Buy you whatcher having, little lady?" he offered, and sidled up, nudging a silver-tipped boot onto the footrest. Belle raised an eyebrow like Roz Russell in *His Girl Friday* and offered him a Paw, in response to which he signalled the waitress for another Red Dog beer and a drink for Belle. Black stove pipe jeans and a red and white checked Western shirt with fringe made him a line dancing natural.

He studied the snack with a mischievous look, pretended to smoke it and raised his beer in a salute. "Some folks call it a six-pack. I call it a support group." He laughed pleasantly and so did Belle. It wasn't bad for a beer joke. "Ain't seen you around. Nick's my name." He extended his hand in a warm firm grip. "Nick Nomless."

"Are you kidding? You mean like in nameless?"

"You got her. Hey, it's better than no-name. Maybe my grandfather pulled a fast one on Immigration."

Unprepared with an alias, Belle rifled her MGM Rolodex. "I'm Susan Lenox. Sue."

"Related to that furnace guy?"

"Wish I, uh…" (not 'were') "…was. Nice to have free repairs in the family."

"New in town? Or just visiting?"

Improvisation isn't my forte, thought Belle. Definitely nothing fancy, just with enough money for an apartment, a car and a cheapish good time. "Yeah, moved up from Windsor a week ago. Secretarial work. Dull but reliable these days. Yourself?" With a little inner cringe, she congratulated herself on remembering the local dialect.

"Tolands Automotive. Diesel truck mechanic." He sighed.

"One helluva hot and dirty job. But gotta make the buck, ya know?" When the waitress brought another beer, he poured slowly to avoid a foamy head.

Time stopped as the beer rose, mesmerizing Belle for a moment. She chuckled and he looked up. "What's wrong?"

"Oh, you really spooked me with that glass. The strobe light made it look as if you had only three fingers."

"Well, I do, honey!" he roared, wiggling the survivors under his chin like Oliver Hardy. "Lost 'em in a transmission overhaul a couple years back. Don't slow me down none, though."

Belle brushed her hair back. Talk about tactful! Still, Nick seemed friendly and open. They danced for several numbers, including a Texas two-step which Belle survived by refurbishing her old fox trot from junior high, adding the Watusi, and mixing in a Peppermint Twist for polish. "They have some great line dancing at the Triple R over on Douglas. I go every Wednesday. Or, " he added, proud to offer a choice, "wanta have dinner at Don Cherry's some night, catch the Leafs on the big screen, and dance up a storm later?"

"I've passed the place. How's the food?"

"Chicago wings beat out Buffalo. Steak's good, too. Listen," he added, flashing an eager grin. "This dump is gettin' to me. Can't stand smoke since I quit a couple years ago. I got a place where we can be more comfortable," he said, clearly warming to a familiar line, and at the same time wiping at his eyes convincingly.

Belle touched his arm with a discreet pressure, not too much, but sincere as hell. "Nick, sounds great, but it's a work night for me. I just wanted to break out of my apartment for an hour or two. First time since I got here. And," she moved closer and lowered her voice, "I wanted to check out the action. You understand?" She mimed a toke.

He laughed, still in a good humor despite her rebuff. "Tough luck for the old guy, I guess, but maybe later. So, little lady, what's your preference? Grass? Coke? Pills? It's not the big city here, but the selection's good."

"Coke, I guess. Special occasions only."

"Sure, I can tell by lookin' atcha. Gotta watch that poison. Anyways, I find a bit for friends now and then." He paused and cocked a grizzled eyebrow. "You ever snowmobile?"

"In Windsor? It's practically the deep south. I've always wanted to try it. Is it dangerous?" she asked, playing wide-eyed Sally Field in *Gidget*. Not that Sally ever did drugs.

"Nah." He waved his hand in dismissal. "Reason I ask's 'cause I make my buys at a lodge my friend owns. Get my drift?" He chucked her under the chin. "It's not far. We can go on my machine some time. I got a major serious mother of a 750."

Nick gave her a few lessons about snowmobiles, switched to boilermakers, and Belle excused herself to go to the washroom as a prelude to leaving. The older dancer was peering into a tarnished mirror, freshening her makeup. She wore a pink leather sequined bikini sliced wickedly up the thighs with matching pasties covering her nipples, her medical history written in ragged stretch marks, an appendix scar and probable breast enhancement. The pneumatic pair charged out like twin B-58 nose cones. Belle applied a small pat of powder on her nose. She smiled over at the woman in sympathetic sisterhood. "Tough night?"

The other woman mashed on a candy apple red map of lipstick. "You said it. I hate the hours, but it keeps me in shape."

Belle laughed. "I'll bet. With my desk job I could use some exercise. But dancing all night would leave me in traction for a week."

The woman fluffed her hair, a vibrant blond with ruby

touches. "You can't smoke, and I try to eat sensible. Watch the cholesterol and all that new stuff. Stamina's important. Sort of like an athlete in training. It's not so bad. We work four days on, three off. And decent breaks every twenty minutes. Better dough farther north, though. Once in the Kap I pulled down a thousand a week. 'Course that was when the paper mills were steamin'. But I can't follow the business like I used to. Got a little one. Mindy's ten last week." For a moment Belle wondered if she were going to haul out pictures from some nether region.

"Yeah, it's tough to work and raise a kid." Belle lit up a cigarette and inhaled deeply, meeting the dancer's reddened eyes, sore and tired, brightened momentarily by thoughts of her child. "Say, any chance of a score? I just moved here and don't know anyone."

The woman appraised her carefully, then shrugged. "Hell, you look OK. Too old for a lady cop. They just started takin' 'em on the force." Belle blinked into the mirror, smoothing a third line under her eye which had joined the usual two. "Hey, no offence. Anyhow, that guy you're with, Nick, you can trust his stuff," the woman advised as she left.

A final drink later, Nick escorted Belle to her van, weaving too much for her liking, his arm around her shoulders as he sang about swimming the Pontchartrain. The Global Village. At least Timmins' Shania Twain was making it big in Nashville.

"Hey, how's about a good night kiss?" he asked, his breath a flammable combination of beer and cheap rye. Belle pulled away and flopped into the seat while he tugged at the door. "Hey, Sue. What's the matter? I bought you a couple drinks."

"And I gave you some Paws. Caveat emptor, Nick," she said as she locked the door and turned the ignition.

"Coffee at what, baby?" He pressed his face against the glass, a confused expression shaping his mouth into an "o" like a cartoon pup booted out of the house.

A white and blue patrol vehicle trolled along Brewster Street. The window rolled down, and even in the faceless dark, a commanding tone assessed the scene. "Some trouble here?"

Nick jumped back, losing his balance. "Uh-uh, had to see my friend got out safe." He had started to slur his words.

Steve eased out of the cruiser, taller and wider than Bigfoot, his hand near the snap on his holster. "Back off. The lady doesn't seem interested to me."

"Hey, sorry, officer, no big deal." And Nick disappeared back into the Paramount.

Steve glowered at Belle, his voice as furious as his mood. "Do you have a secret life I should know about? What are you doing with these scumbags?" He shot her an appraising look. "Who are you supposed to be? Madonna, Dolly or Joan Baez?"

She yanked off the wig and tossed it onto the passenger seat. "Ouch, that hurts, your comments, I mean. You might not be over the hill, but you're closing in on the top." Why not take the offensive? "I wanted information. What's the harm? He hinted at some lodge owner as his source. How many could there be, and what have you been doing about it?"

"I told you we were onto Brooks," Steve said evenly. "Other informers have been naming him."

"Like Nick. The guy you just ran off," Belle tapped her fingers on the steering wheel. "He's hardly going to trust me now, Lancelot."

"Is that gratitude! Next time do your own wrestling. Anyway, this is my last warning. Brooks is in our sights. Problem is to catch him in the act or find his goods before he flushes it. He's careful. It's a matter of time and timing." He shielded his eyes as the wind chased a whirl of snow down the street and the siren of an ambulance split the air. "How about a hamburger? I missed dinner by chasing a drunk half-way to Cartier, and I'm due for a break."

"Maybe a soda water. I'm so overdosed on salt that I'm going to go all prickly like a blowfish."

As they ate at a nearby truck stop, Steve told her about his new daughter. Belle wondered if the old saw would work, that he and Janet might conceive their own now that the stress was removed. "Anyway, we brought Heather home from Thunder Bay last week."

"What's she like? Do you have any pictures?"

"Give me time. She's a real doll. Three years old. Half Cree and half Italian. Almost as weird a combination as yours truly." He examined his double cheeseburger, adding ketchup. "There is a problem. She may have suffered some fetal alcohol damage." His worried eyes revealed more than his voice. "Nothing you can put your finger on now. She's too young for the tests, but the doctor says she could be…what do they call it? Not retarded." He shovelled his fingers through his thick black hair.

"Developmentally delayed?"

"Bunch of crap. All I know is that it's been pretty rough." He explained that Janet had taken a leave to spend time with Heather. By the time Steve got home from work, he was an intruder. The child wouldn't let him dress her, feed her, bathe her, even touch her.

"If I go near, she bawls up a storm. What's wrong, Belle? I've always gotten along with kids." In his work with Big Brothers, Steve took groups to Toronto for Jays games and coached a baseball team. Many of his lads had completed college or university; two had even joined the force.

Belle listened to his quiet, frustrated voice, which

demanded reasons to rationalize feelings. "Hear what I'm saying, Steve. You're a big man, a monster to her. Your voice is strange and deep. What might have scared her before she came to you, you don't want to know. Right now Janet is bonding to her, and it's leaving you out. But it sounds normal so far."

"So what can I do? Stay home all day and inhale helium?" He smiled weakly.

Belle touched his large hand, so helpless against a tiny one. "Of course not. But be patient. This is only the beginning, and it must be scary for her. My advice is to leave her alone, but show affection to Janet. Heather will see that another woman trusts you. It's just like this pup a friend of mine had…" While parents told kid stories, Belle turned to dogs. "Nothing is more tyrannical than a dog or a child," she said. "They're always testing limits, so establish the hierarchy immediately and stick to it. Then when they see you as benevolent head of the pack, they'll do anything for you."

"Isn't it too late for that? I told you she's terrified."

"This time you have to do an end run, if you'll pardon my mixed metaphors. Janet's top dog. Show her affection. Once Heather sees that she trusts and accepts you, you're in."

"Sure, Belle, but you forgot one thing," Steve added. "Dogs can't talk. And if they don't work out, you can take them to the pound."

She finished her club soda, stifled a burp and reached over to shine his badge with her serviette. "Never lost one yet."

FIFTEEN

The strengthening sun pierced the horizon like a jewel, dazzling Belle's sleepy eyes with its renewing warmth. She spun the handle to open her window and inhaled the pure, liquid ether of the morning. Fearful groans, a basso profundo tympanic plumb from measureless fathoms, echoed across the lake's impenetrable depths. The ice had risen. Freshets draining the back country were undermining its integrity, wrenching the earth free from the winter's icy grip. Travel on the lake would still be safe for a wary week or so, but after that, the rotting ice mass would blacken into honeycombs and marry with the water, signalling time to watch for the blessed signs of spring.

As she was outside grabbing at some birch logs under the tarp, Belle heard the phone ring five times and then defer to the answering machine. How civilized to be freed from its imperative jingle, to enjoy a hot meal in leisure instead of being interrupted by a ten-minute long "two-minute" consumer questionnaire. The tape played a familiar voice speaking slowly and precisely, unintimidated by the technology. "Hello, Belle, it's Franz. At a lake near my camp I found something interesting. It's a clear indication that you were right about the drug drops. We can go out there this morning if you are free. I'll be at my office for the next two hours. It's now…eight o'clock."

Belle called back immediately. "Have you had breakfast?" he asked. "Why don't we meet at Connie's?" It was a thriving truck stop on the Kingsway, a main artery through town.

Franz's Jimmy pulled into Connie's crowded lot at the same time as Belle's van. As he held the restaurant door for her, the pleasant scent of a subtle European cologne, perhaps 4711, drifted past. With the smooth pink look of a shave on his cheeks, he placed a shearling coat on an extra chair and sat immaculate in pressed chinos and Pendleton wool shirt. Belle stroked the coat with envious sounds. "Yes, I bought it on a trip to the States last year," he explained as they ordered the mucker's special. Three eggs, five sausages, a pancake, homefries, toast and coffee.

A pair of ladies in fox and raccoon coats, dressed for a shopping spree, looked over in amusement. "Haven't they ever seen a woman eat?" Belle sliced into the tender sausages and took a bite with a grateful, dreamy look. "Going to heaven to meet my mother and worth the price." She crossed herself and thumped at her heart, placing a hand behind her ear. "Is that the sound of sludge forming? Well, what's the news?"

Franz poured coffee from the urn left on the table in American pancake house style. "First, madame, hear the wonderful results of the rally. I have over 5,000 signatures on the petition, an excellent response from the area. But strong lobbyists on the other side will generate publicity, too; merchants, hotel, motel and restaurant operators who want the tourists."

"I saw a full page ad placed by local businessmen in the *Sudbury Star* last night. What shameless propaganda. And of course Brooks is a star member. What did they call themselves? Parks for Progress?" She scowled and attacked her pancakes. "They'll turn Wapiti into the Canadian National

Exhibition fifty-two weeks a year. Condos are coming, did I tell you? A sleazy developer I know is oozing around after the zoning right now."

Franz clenched a fist and abandoned his continental reserve for a quick pound on the table. "But that's why this evidence is so important. If we can discredit just one of them, turn the direction of public opinion, we might keep our lake for a few more years."

"Well, don't leave me in suspenders, as Uncle Harold used to say. What on earth did you find?"

Franz said that he had been hearing more small planes at his camp near Cott Lake, where he had been preparing lectures and marking papers. The next morning, he searched the area and found the debris. "I left it in place so that you could understand the logistics. Cott's too shallow for ice fishing and miles from the main trail. Very isolated. And my cabin is nearly invisible from the air with all the spruce and cedars. That could explain why they were so careless. From the tracks, I'd guess a machine met the plane."

"The strikes against Brooks are adding up," Belle said, ticking off points on her fingers. "First, expensive renovations on the lodge, not just a cheap facelift. Second, a stable of new machines, hardly rental jobs. Where did he get them if he's been broke? Another possibility is that he's operating a chop shop or feeding one. And third, I met one of his contacts at the Paramount the other night." She had Franz laughing over the script.

"You met him there? Oh, Mata Hari, wasn't that unwise? Do you list the martial arts among your many talents or did you carry a pistol?"

"Bah, I wasn't going to go home with the man to watch David Letterman. Even gave a false name. He got a bit rough, but an officer I know came along in his patrol car."

"Another knight entering the lists?"

Belle tapped his knuckles playfully. "Not where Jim's death is concerned. Steve sure let me down there. But look, even if Jim had witnessed something, perhaps a transfer like you describe, how did someone arrange such a picture-perfect accident without leaving one bruise? It just sounds so coincidental. How could anyone even know who he was?" She frowned pensively as she mopped up the last of the eggs, then unwrapped the gold drop and presented it on top of a napkin. "Breakfast at Tiffany's. One new clue. See what you think of this. I've been carrying it around like a talisman."

The unflappable Franz raised his eyebrows for a nanosecond, his pupils widening. "And where did you get this small treasure?"

"Jim's mother searched his pockets a few days ago when she did the wash, poor lady. What in God's name is it?"

He moved it delicately between his fingers, shifting it to catch more light, as his expressive mouth formed a *moue*, more French than German. "Gold, by the appearance and silken feel. For a piece of jewelry, perhaps, though it is so small. A gift for Miss Melanie or maybe just a curio."

"That's what we thought. But it never hurts to double check. For a starting place, I have a friend in the jewelry business." She retrieved the drop and let Franz whisk the cheque from her hand.

"I am too fast for you today. Your treat next time." He checked his watch. "We had better be off. The ice has risen, but conditions will worsen as the day warms, especially with bright sun." To save the long drive home for her gear and the Bravo, he suggested she park at the marina and ride with him over the ice road to his island. "I have an extra snowmobile," he said, "an old Elan of my father's. Low on suspension, but ticks like a sewing machine. He used to assure me that a Singer was under the hood. When I was a small boy, I believed him."

By the time they reached the marina, lake traffic was headed the other way, people helping each other haul their huts off. "This is not my favourite time of year," Franz complained as the Jimmy bumped along and he waved at a few drivers. "When the ice is breaking up, I have to stay in town for a week to ten days." Belle wondered if he were hinting for an invitation. What an interesting guest he might be, though. There would be no end to the conversation. And he liked dogs. "Then at ice-out, I pick up my boat at the marina and so it goes until December." Belle dreaded ice-out, too, prayed against a northeast wind which could skirt the rockwall and blow dangerous floes onto her dock, grinding the satellite dish and everything in its path like a juggernaut. Insurance companies did not cover these acts of God.

As they climbed the wooden stairs to the house, Marta greeted them, her creamy white hair thickly braided and wrinkles of concern lining her cameo profile in the harsh light of day. "Be careful," she warned. "Franz told me where you are going. The ice is thinning everywhere. My son knows the safe places." Inside, she gave Belle an extra suit, a pair of boots, and a thermos of coffee.

The old warhorse of the elder Schilling roared into life, shaking temperamentally and spewing out oily gray smoke. "Not very ecological, I suppose," Franz said as he gallantly presented the keys to his own machine. Belle removed the custom cover like opening a birthday present and crooned, "Where have you been all my life? This was featured in the *Ontario Snowmobiler* magazine. A Grand Touring SE. What do they call it, Franz, the Mercedes-Benz of sleds? What a yuppie you are!" She brushed appreciative fingers over the thick seat padding and adjusted the oversized backrests. "How fast are we talking? What kind of track? And what other cute little bells and whistles? A CD, perhaps?"

Franz seemed embarrassed about her reference to his conspicuous consumerism. "It's not really a racing machine; it's designed for touring."

"Oh, right, just for plain Jane cruising. A retirement model, no doubt. With 670cc? You could smoke my baby Bravo into cardiac arrest," Belle moaned, testing the controls.

He sighed elaborately, but a nuance of a smile crept over his lips. "If you insist. She has extra wide and long track, much more suspension than the standard models. I need that for my bush trips," he offered as a rationale in the face of her disbelieving sniff. "My back's not what it used to be, so gas shocks, too. I think that's all. Oh, thumb and handwarmers."

"Not to mention reverse gear, you greedy man," Belle snarled, toying with the complicated cockpit of controls.

"Of course, so enjoy it." He thumped the hard, duct-taped seat of his father's old machine. "Your pleasure is my introduction to a set of kidney pads." A call brought Blondi from around the cabin, her tail wagging eagerly for an outing.

"Franz," Belle objected, "she can't run that far."

"No fear. Just watch." He attached a lightweight toboggan as the proud animal picked her way gingerly down the steps, carrying her famous sunglasses in her mouth. She climbed into the sled happily and settled down with a doggy sigh.

Franz attached the glasses. "She can run the last few miles for exercise. I always take her to the cabin as company, so the extra horsepower is helpful to pull the gear, you see," he said with an "I told you so" look. When the Elan stalled, he began tugging his starter cord repeatedly, muttering what sounded like arcane Teutonic curses while Belle merely pushed a button and smiled smugly as her engine purred like a cat curled before a fire.

The last vestiges of the winter runs were disappearing. Marshalls from the Drift Busters were removing the red poles across Wapiti that marked the major trail. The year before, the trail had been marked by using discarded Christmas trees complete with shreds of tinsel, a curiously surreal diorama which elicited howls from the environmentalists. Approaching the Dunes, Belle lost all mature restraint and thumbed the gas full-throttle, a move which snapped her head back in shock and rearranged her spinal cord. What a race horse!

At the top of the Dunes, Franz caught up with her like a faithful Sancho Panza. The sight of him bouncing barely inches off the ice, his back probably screaming, drew her sympathy and amusement at the same time. He waggled his finger like a teacher, yelling over the motors. "I thought you would fall under her spell. Why don't you get a new model? You would like it, you know."

"No wonder so many riders exit the gene pool every year. Horsepower corrupts; absolute horsepower corrupts absolutely. But stop tempting me. Why buy a VSOP cognac when Ontario brandy will do?" She stood up like a jockey in a steeplechase and revved the engine. "I might be spoiled now, so thank God the season is nearly over."

As he pointed out on the topo, Franz had chosen the safer land trail instead of the faster route across five lakes. Crossing the bridge over Thimble Creek, Belle stared into the rushing water shimmering with ice diamonds. This was still frozen on her last trip, she thought, but she's coming up like gangbusters. Wapiti's going to rise quickly. The Ministry of Natural Resources, keeper of the hydro dam keys, let the lake fall all winter and didn't close the sluice gates until the ice had vanished, minimizing dock and boathouse destruction and allowing cottagers their rockwall repairs with a backhoe in the narrow window of opportunity.

After half an hour, Franz pointed to a small side trail and signalled Blondi to jump out. "My cabin is that way," he said, "but here's the trail I cut to Cott." The sun was brilliant, and the winds seemed tropical. It had been seven months since Belle had enjoyed such warmth. Several minutes later, they drove into Cott, skirting the shore carefully. It was a swamp lake, soft and treacherous in spring. A plane landing would be impossible now with the thaw. Franz guided her to a thick spruce growth. "Look at what I found," he said, rummaging under a bush and pulling out some plastic bags. "Broken open. And they just left it. Why not? One quick gust and gone…"

"With the wind."

He tasted the residue with a wet finger. "Cocaine, if the usual mythology is true."

Belle took the bag and dipped in, wincing at the bitterness. "Who says television doesn't have educational merit? Hey, should we rinse our mouths with snow?" she asked. "Anything else?"

"Just these two bags. Oh, and cigarettes." He passed her a half-full pack of Luckies, sodden with moisture. "American. I've never seen them for sale here. Too expensive." They scuffed their way to the middle of the lake, noting the landing marks of the skis. Blurry steps packed the ice where a conversation might have occurred, and a snowmobile trail, covered by fresh snow, pointed to the end of the lake.

Belle punched his shoulder lightly in her excitement. "This could make the connection. At the very least, it proves that Jim's theory was on the money. Steve should see this, with your permission," Belle said, and packed the evidence into her pocket after Franz nodded. "A raid on Brooks could come soon, by the way."

Some coffee warmed them while Franz tossed pine cones for Blondi to chase. "Come up next winter, and I promise to be a better host and show you around my camp. I have a few fine spearheads from a quartzite dig at Sheguiandah on Manitoulin. 7000-8000 B.C. Much sharper work than the hand axe you admired."

"I'll look forward to it, Franz. Why don't you come for dinner tonight and tell me how you found them?"

He sighed reluctantly. "This is unfortunate timing. After my four o'clock class, Mother and I are off to Toronto to see *Phantom of the Opera* this weekend for her birthday." Belle suggested an excellent Portuguese place on Bloor West, recommending the octopus. The dog resumed her place in the toboggan, and Franz followed Belle back to the island, lurchingly slow and steady on the old chestnut.

When Belle collected the van at the marina, it was barely three o'clock, so she stopped at the police building. Originally built as an armoury after World War One, it squatted downtown on its treeless square like an ancient toad. According to Steve, the staff hated the place; not only was it cold, uncomfortable and overcrowded, but security was a joke. Last year several prisoners had escaped, to be caught hours later playing PacMan at the bus depot. A classic tale of felonious stupidity, Steve had told her, like the guy who robbed a convenience store, then left his footprints in the snow right to his house.

At the main desk, a sergeant doing crossword puzzles pointed her to a sub-basement after asking a five-letter word for "criminal". Water pipes covered in shredding asbestos led her down a dungeon hall, her steps echoing ahead in the gloom of a single, dangling fifteen-watt bulb. Steve stuck his face out of a door with a look of suspicion. "What brings you to my palace? A social call, I hope."

"Where do you chain the man in the iron mask? And I thought asbestos had to be removed," Belle responded, flopping into a comfortable brown leather chair cracked with age. She adjusted the stuffing to cover a spring and brushed white flakes from her shoulders.

"We've been lobbying for a new building for years. Just don't do too good a job of it. Need a crime wave to raise our profile. A nice mass murderer or an arsonist. This year the money went to the Seniors' Complex. So?" He looked at her quizzically.

"Presents. Franz Schilling and I found some drug traces in the bush today." She placed the bags and cigarette pack on the desk, shifting a plastic plate with a crust of pizza.

Steve didn't even examine it. Her news pressed his irritation button one time too often. "Are you still prowling around?" he yelled. "And disturbing evidence again?"

"Let me get to my point if you're in that kind of a mood. We found this up at Cott Lake. It's a miracle the stuff was still there. A brisk wind would have buried it. Come on, look at it. Don't make me feel like a fool."

"Wow, a cigarette pack! For me? I suppose you want us to check for DNA."

"And the bags?"

After the usual rituals, he settled into serious mode, sighing and tapping a pencil onto a date on his calendar. "Congratulations. Every now and then a blind squirrel finds an acorn. We can't cover thousands of kilometres of bush in the hopes of catching someone in the act. We have Brooks set up for

Saturday night. Saturday, Belle, is that close enough for you?" He drew a stick man on his paper and confined him in a box. "If you want to watch the fun, and I know you will, be at the Beaverdam around eleven for the raid. But stay clear."

"Yes, sir!" She offered a snappy salute and backed out of the office. Saturday Night Fever at last.

Belle arrived home about six o'clock to find the house inhospitably cold and unwelcoming. A rising wind had blown up and sucked the wood to ashes with the draft. Wood was a benevolent dictator to its grateful servant, usually good for ten hours or more before a temperature drop would trigger the propane furnace. She would have to restoke it for the night.

Belle refilled the stove with soft fat pine for quick coals, then took Freya for a short walk. At last the bitter temperatures were gone, even if most of the snow remained, as it likely would until May. Her boots crunched down the road, as she listened through the silence for sounds which carried miles in the clear air and insulating snow, the long, piercing whistle of a train headed south with lumber, or north with shiny automobiles for those who had cut that wood. She heard the familiar tinkle of Morris's windchimes, a summer memory. Mo must have come out early to open up. Taking note of the cottages, she pictured their snowbird owners making a last forage to the cheap American supermarkets, or buying a breadmaker or air conditioner to offset costly supplemental health insurance premiums. Yet what were their electric bills when they had to leave the juice on all winter to protect the foundations against frost damage?

Back inside, Belle heaped maple and yellow birch over the new coals and heated tasty and filling Habitant pea soup as a accompaniment to a toasted cheese sandwich. As a treat for Freya, she opened a can of expensive dog stew, giant hunks of beef swimming in gravy. Then as Shana had suggested, she sprinkled on the Metamucil, dropped in a tablespoon of canola oil, and stirred the mess queasily. Freya materialized out of nowhere at the grind of the can opener, a thread of drool dropping from the corner of her smiling mouth. "Dig in, babe. It's better than some people get."

Tidying up her computer area after dinner, Belle rummaged through documents and notes from the office. But as she sorted them, strange papers caught her eye. Shield University memos addressed to Franz. One concerned a blood drive, and the other warned of a rise in parking rates. How embarrassing. She must have scooped them up that day in his office. No need to return them since the relevant dates had passed. The next sheet made her sit down in shock. It was a receipt for nearly six thousand dollars from the Forest Glen Wellness Center in Harrisville, New York. A private nursing home? Or were they all private in the States? She pulled out her atlas. Just over the border from Cornwall, maybe ten hours' drive. Probably an old place in the Adirondacks.

Was it Eva? Was she in treatment for the nervous breakdown Rosanne had suggested? Was this any of Belle's business? "Oh, here, Franz," she could say. "Sorry I picked this up by mistake. Who's the lucky patient?" Still, she was pricked by her usual rude curiosity. Perhaps there was an Internet contact in New York, someone who could do a bit of handy digging. The likely source for snooping came quickly to mind, the Dorothy L. Sayers mystery discussion group, three thousand strong. Though each person had a special *nom de plume*, she hadn't chosen one (Miss Marple had been taken and she couldn't remember Mary Astor's role in *The Maltese Falcon*). "dorothyl@listserv.kent.edu" she typed. Her message was brief, even enigmatic, but DLrs loved that touch: "I am marooned in Ultima Thule and need an ally to sleuth around near Harrisville, New York. Is the game afoot?" In case the frosty lines might garble the connections as often happened in winter, she added her phone and FAX numbers.

Belle hopped into bed and tuned her radio to the last innings of the Jays against Oakland. Mr. Five Million had pitched flawlessly, retired twelve in a row, then pulled a groin muscle. Mr. Four Million had fanned four times and tossed his bat into the stands. So much for their top guns. Management would have to curry the Syracuse farm team with a fine tooth comb. The radio crackled in and out as usual, reception fading as far-off stations smeared the signal at critical "three and two" calls.

Then an infernal shriek drilled into her ears like the squeal of chalk on a blackboard. The mandatory smoke detector, only this time as often before, smoke was not the problem. Gnats, little spiders, dust, anything could give the fussy monster a tantrum. Belle climbed onto a chair and wiggled the box in quasi-scientific fashion, muttering and coaxing to some success. Then only minutes later, as the Jays scored twice, the screech sounded again. "You son of a…you're not keeping me up all night," Belle said as she located a screwdriver and disconnected the detector. In the morning she would give the rascal a thorough shaking or better yet, buy another.

SIXTEEN

A message from a Geoff Garson, aka the Saint, flashed on the screen when Belle selected "new mail" the next day. A retired librarian from Notre Dame in Indiana, he was delighted, even flattered to accept the "Mission: Impossible." Choose a librarian, she thought, for patient, meticulous work; they thrived on rooting up uncommon facts, the more obscure and useless the better. His information later that week showed that he was indeed an ace researcher, but it also brought some troublesome questions. Belle's fax machine slowly churned out a picture and fact sheet. "Forest Glen Wellness Center, formerly Forest Glen Sanatorium. Founded in 1878 as a TB facility. During the 1950s converted by Dr. Brian Whitewell to a premier psychiatric hospital. Fees $75,000 U.S. yearly, excluding special treatment plans. Patients approximately 30. Single suites only. Two hundred wooded acres in the Adirondacks. A small stable of horses, tennis courts, jogging track, exercise rooms, indoor and outdoor pools. Specializes in schizophrenia, false memory, personality disorders, emotional trauma recovery. World reputation brings clientele from Europe, South America and the Far East." Belle inspected the building with a magnifying glass. Stately Georgian brick, tastefully modernized through several eras. Two wings flanked an impressive portico over a stretch limo. She polished the lens and looked again. Manicured cedar hedges, classical topiary (a brontosaurus?), layered flower beds and lawns to kingdom come, probably rolled to within an inch of their lives by a gardener imported from King's College, Cambridge.

In an impulsive mood, buoyed by her sudden success, Belle got the phone number from the operator, surprised that it was listed. "Forest Glen," answered a plummy voice bearing the cachet of the Received Standard English pronunciation as only Miss Moneypenny could deliver. "How may I help you?"

Belle gulped and modulated her tone to quiet confidence. "I'd like to speak to Miss Schilling."

The voice turned chilly and tense. "You don't sound familiar, Madam. I'm afraid Miss Schilling has a specific list of callers."

"Sorry," said Belle and hung up. A foolish trick. Would the woman inform the family? So Eva was there. But how could Franz afford the fees on his university salary? And as an over-taxed, under-serviced Ontarian, she knew damn well OHIP wouldn't foot the bill. A private medical plan? Doubtful. Few Canadians had that animal. More to the point, why was she there and what was the prognosis? She typed another message to Geoff: "Excellent work, Saint. Loved the picture, too. Any prayer of more personal data on a patient, Eva Schilling? Do you have contacts who work there or know someone who does?"

Belle spent the afternoon taking a very demanding primary school teacher (was there any other kind?) on a tour of Valley East bungalows under $120,000. Ms. Bly, a cod-faced woman of fifty, who might have been Don Knotts in drag, had precise objections to all six places. One was too near the fire station, too noisy. Another had the old siding, sashless windows, too drafty. One used oil heat, too smelly. Another had a barking husky next door. One had poplar trees, "common and filthy pests". And the last, an older custom-built home with quality touches which Belle hoped her client would appreciate, got the loudest sniff.

"What fool wants hardwood floors? My mother used to spend all Saturday on her hands and knees rubbing that sticky beeswax around. Polishing, always polishing. She was a regular slave to it," the woman said, writing in a small notebook. "I don't fancy ceramic tile either. Much too cold on the feet."

Belle hummed an evil internal melody and nodded with a slight sincerity since she agreed about the floors. Northern Ontario wasn't Santa Fe, and it wasn't Back Bay. Having a dog had put the last nail in the notion of oak parquet when she had built her house. Claws on floors reminded her of the odd cringe she felt whenever she ate raisins.

After arranging another tour the following week by planting in the woman's head the concept of living a wee bit farther north in Capreol ("So many wonderful bargains since the sad closing of the Canadian National Railroad facility"), Belle stopped for gas at the last station before home. As she waited for her charge slip, she glanced at a four-by-four Chev pickup with supercab and eight-foot box across from her. What a boat. Probably mortgaging his soul to feed those twin tanks, Belle thought, smirking at the $90.00 on his meter. Then again, if you can afford a giant in the first place, you don't worry about the cost of his keep. The license plate read 1BIGMF. How did he slip that past the Ontario censors? Suddenly she did a double-take. With Brooks at the wheel, Nick rode in the passenger seat, flashing her a toothy smile and showing no hard feelings. The lodge owner glared her way, whispered to Nick, and arced his cigarette onto the asphalt as they drove off. Belle braced for an explosion, but it snuffed out in the slush. Nothing like upping the ante. Now Brooks would know that she was pursuing the drug connection. Steve would have her head if anything sabotaged the raid.

After another fill-up at the liquor store, she reached home in time to throw the ball for Freya and use the leftover taco mix for a tomato soup and macaroni casserole. A can of precious hominy bought in Buffalo added a southern touch. To her surprise and delight, Melanie called to report that she was dropping her roommate off at the airport around noon the next day and wondered if she could visit.

"It'd be great to see you. Bring a *Toronto Star*. We don't get delivery out here" was Belle's answer.

What was on the Nostalgia channel, she wondered, spooning into the food? W. C. Fields in *The Dentist*. A Slim Jim in this early talkie, with his bulbous nose in training, he grabbed the giant block of ice from the delivery boy and set it absentmindedly on…the stove! When he returned, it was an ice cube, which he shrugged off as perfectly natural, scissoring it up with the tongs, and depositing the tiny piece back in the ice box. Of course, the film was a minefield of ethical blunders. He treated his daughter like a slave, locked her in her room, threw tantrums on the golf course, thrashed caddies and gyrated ham-handedly over helpless women in his dental chair while he pumped the pedals with abandon.

Still chuckling, Belle cranked open her bedroom window, amused to find another ladybug. Warm weather in September had sent hundreds clustering around her patio doors in an unusual infestation less bothersome than mosquitos or biting flies. She inspected the creature to see whether it had two spots, nine or none, then dropped the bright little memory of summer onto the thick branches of an aloe plant on the sill. "Flying home is out of the question, ladybug. You'll have to stick it out until spring. Now find an aphid and behave." The oblique reference to fire led her downstairs to check on the woodstove. It never hurt to be too careful. She assured herself that the damper was up, stood in front of the stove, gripping the wood-tipped handles, and said, "Check, double check, triple check" chanting as far as "octupal" in an effort to make sure that the round spinning "keys" were adjusted properly. Obsessive-compulsive, or just plain cautious? Just the other day a family in Chelmsford had gone to town while the stove roared, worked itself into a chimney fire and turned the house into ashes. She recalled her father balancing back and forth in front of the gas range when she was a child, looking, leaving, looking, leaving, never trusting his eyes. But then again, his aunt had died in a gas leak.

Finally she climbed into bed, prepared for a shudderfest over the latest Cornwell novel. The sleuth was a pathologist whose diehard fans ate gruesome realism by the pailful. A few graphic chapters taught Belle to slice a Y incision, pull out assorted organs, weigh them and set aside the stomach contents for analysis. She began to grow queasy and took a large slug of Scotch to disguise the reek of formaldehyde. No more Cornwell before bed. Something refined, Ngaio Marsh maybe. She rattled through assorted prayers for people she hadn't seen in forty years, then surrendered to a deep sleep, imagining the faithful loons calling in their mating dance. But they wouldn't be back yet, skating on the ice. Once she and Jim had seen a nest with a loon's egg clinging perilously on a tiny atoll hardly bigger than their boat. Perhaps the human proximity, quiet as they had tried to be, had disturbed the parents, because a few hours later, the prize had vanished! To a safer place, or the stomach of an otter?

She woke in shallow awareness as her clock read two a.m., smelling a light, comforting smoke drifting in the window. A few snuffles and snorts sent her back to sleep, only to wake more fitfully with a pounding headache. A change in weather? Sinus problems? In her stupor she debated chugging aspirins, but decided to wait it out.

Such pleasant time passed while she and Jim hunted for the egg, yet what kept dragging her from the dark and quiet river passages which led past the cherished pictographs? Jim was cozying the canoe against the cliffs, bracing with his paddle so that she could take pictures of the red ochre figures which seemed to be distorting despite her efforts to focus the camera. Slowly she became aware that Freya was coughing and whining and licking at her. And the dog had never, ever, asked to go out during the night. Belle rubbed her eyes, burning with something more pungent than sleep, and forced herself up to hit the light switch. The room seemed to be blurry, foggy.

Suddenly all too awake, she felt the marrow freeze in her bones, despite the blood temperature of the water bed. Smoke was seeping through the ventilation panel cut to the living room. A fire, with her trapped on the second floor, the worst nightmare! She clawed free from piles of bedding, dropped to the rug and crawled to the patio door to rip into the plastic sheeting taped inside to conserve heat loss and shove the door open. The frigid air cleared her head momentarily. Fearing that the lights might go out at any moment, she retrieved a flashlight from the dresser. The bedside water glass doused a T-shirt, which she wrapped around her face. Freya stayed behind her, sneezing and hacking.

Yet the door to the downstairs was cool. Fire or no fire? Belle cracked it slowly against the thick smoke which followed the draft, backing down the stairs on her knees, blessing the thick broadloom that had cost her a trip to Curaçao. Why didn't she have a contingency plan, a rope ladder from her balcony? Ed had always teased her about it. Like a scorched worm, taking a gulp through the soggy shirt, she flashed a teary look at the living room stove. Smoke was billowing out of the keys. Something must have blocked the chimney from above. Holding her breath until her lungs ached, Belle tightened the keys and turned the damper to shut down the blaze.

As her lungs finally rebelled against her brain and opened wide, she pushed outside with a gasp into the softly dropping snow, oblivious for a moment that she stood only in T-shirt and underpants, standard bedtime attire. Spasms of coughing punished her shoulders and back as she braced against the deck post. "Wow!" Belle yelled, lifting her feet one after the other like a phony fakir on burning coals. Holding her breath again, she reached inside to the hall closet to grab her snowmobile suit, boots and mitts. Could a squirrel have fallen down the pipe? There was no protective mesh at the top, couldn't be because of creosote build-up. But no roast beast smell filled the air. Shivering more from fear than cold, Freya stopped hyperventilating as Belle hugged her and stroked her fur. "Breathe on your own, girl. I just couldn't do CPR on that hairy mouth." Safe now, the air clearing inside with the door open, she debated whether to put out the fire with water, or climb to the roof and stuff down the chimney brush. The smoke damage would be horrendous.

Breakfast and some creature-comforting noises in mind, Belle walked down to Ed's, blowing her lungs clear as the sun's red eye backlit the trees. Sailor take warning? As she trudged, she missed the amenities of socks and long underwear, but blessed the fleece-lined moosehide mitts that did the job at any temperature. Northerners knew what was important.

She hated to wake her friends, bang into their morning

stillness, but what were pals for? "All right, you slackers, everyone out for volleyball," she called, pummelling loudly at the back door and causing fearful yelps from Rusty, asleep in the mud room.

Thumps and bumps came closer as lights flashed on in sequence through the house. "What the hell?" Ed said. "Are you crazy? Say, what's all over your face? " He sniffed at her as he pulled her inside. "Were you smoking in bed again?" He fastened his robe as Hélène shambled in from the bedroom, her eyes puffy with sleep.

"It's safe enough on a waterbed. I got smoked out. My chimney is plugged at the top. There's no fire. I shut the stove down, but can't do much more until daylight. Can I get warm here?"

"Thank God you're OK, Belle," said Hélène, giving her a firm hug and passing her a tissue for her face.

"Thank Freya. She warned me, saved my life. I was too groggy to know what was going on," Belle added. She availed herself of their bathroom in an unsuccessful attempt to scrub off the smoke.

"What about your alarm?" Ed asked as they sipped coffee and stuffed themselves with hot blueberry pancakes. Squirts of whipped cream added to the impromptu picnic. Heavy food was appreciated when cold work lay ahead.

"It kept going off for no reason, well, not exactly no reason. Bugs, I guess, so I jerked it. And naturally I forgot to reconnect it."

The DesRosiers drove her back in the truck. While they aired out the house, Belle shovelled hot ashes from the stove into a bucket and used asbestos gloves to carry out the smoking logs. Then she collected the fibreglass cleaning rods and brush and climbed an aluminum ladder next to the house.

Ed scolded her as he followed. "Why do you leave this up? Thieves could get to your bedroom balcony."

"I clean the chimney every three weeks, and I'm not excited about digging out the ladder after every blizzard. Besides, Ed, I have glass patio doors. So do you. We live out here because we want to see the lake, not hole up in a fort with arrow slits. Someone wants in, they get in."

Checking for tracks on the roof under several inches of new snow proved fruitless. Ed said, "What a mess around the chimney, all trampled. You won't get clear prints here." His probe with the brush revealed a soft mass several feet below the top which he pushed down the chimney. "Have to take the pipes apart in the living room. She's caught up on the damper."

"If the chimney had caught fire, the house might have gone up in flames. Still, it's deadly enough. Most people in fires die of smoke inhalation," Belle said, shivering in the brisk wind on the roof as she surveyed the grounds. "What's that by the big yellow birch? Looks like it was tossed off the roof like a javelin." It turned out to be six-foot wooden stake for delphiniums, probably from a pile under the deck, except that the end was sticky with black creosote.

Dismantling the pipe, fanning themselves against the smoking rags and despairing of the falling cinders, they cleared the mess and reassembled the pipes. Belle had goosed the propane furnace, but with the doors still open, it was barely above freezing in the living room. Luckily the computer room and TV room had been closed. The fish would have to hang tough until she got the stove going again.

"So where did those rags come from, Belle?" Ed asked as he pitchforked the pile onto the snow.

"Looks like old towels I hung over the propane tank. Used them to wash the van last fall."

Hélène looked on the verge of tears. "Please stay with us for awhile, Belle," she pleaded. "Or Ed can—"

"You've been great. But I'll be OK. And yes, I will report this."

Finally alone with her thoughts, Belle left a detailed message for Steve. If he had been mad in the past, this would send him into overdrive. He'd blame her for going to the Paramount, for snooping at the lodge. Derek had warned her about Brooks' interest, and now she'd seen Nick with him. "But what exactly does he think I know?" she wondered aloud as she watched her fish slowly tour their kingdom, blissfully unaware of their near-death experience.

Steve skidded down the driveway after lunch. "They told me you'd been hit again. Look at all the tracks! Grand Central or what! Did you have to trample everything? I got here as fast as I could. Since morning I've been north of Parry Sound where a gas transport accident blocked 69 for hours." In his irritation, he ignored Freya's barking. Usually he loved to play with the dog.

Belle felt a defensive surge. This was her territory, her violated home. Why did he have to make the situation worse? "It's been snowing heavily, so any tracks are gone. What do you want to know? Someone stuffed the chimney. From what we found when we pushed down into the stove, it was towels left by my propane tank. I've been through a rough night, and I had the funny idea that you were my friend." She bit her lip and turned away, knowing she was in for a grilling.

He reached into the squad car for his notebook and wasted no time pinpointing the obvious question. "And your smoke detector?"

She sighed deeply. "No contest. I did something stupid. It's reconnected now in case you feel like jailing me for building code violations."

Taking a look around, Steve seemed ready to continue the third degree as he scribbled her remarks and his observations, but with a glance at her sitting slumped on the deck stairs, he took a deep breath. "The burglary attempt or whatever that you didn't even bother to report is one thing. That's common enough in cottage country in the winter. This looks serious, but I can't see why they didn't cut the hydro. Must have had a kind heart or been real amateurs." He put a hand on her shoulder. "Everything should be fine if you mind your own business until Saturday, our big night. Make it look like the scare worked. Lock the doors; look over your shoulder. Maybe have a friend stay with you?" He paused to consider her snort. "No, eh? Well, fine. Freya's track record is good enough."

"And I do have a shotgun."

"Load it with rock salt. You won't do any real damage." That got her smiling. "Come on, now. We'll put Brooks and his sleazy friends away until the Leafs win the Stanley Cup."

Belle met his eyes and cleared the phlegm from her throat. "I'll lie doggo. Not a bark."

After Steve had to make three tries up the slippery drive, somewhat to Belle's satisfaction, she called a painting firm listed in the *Northern Life*. With business slow, they promised to come the next day with the colours she wanted. The job could be done quickly if she didn't mind the smell. Then a small Golf drove down the driveway. Melanie got out, and Freya capered around her, friendly as ever with females, even strangers. Size? Conformation? Pheromones? Voice? Who knew what lurked in the genetic memory of a canine?

The young woman presented the newspaper and widened her eyes at the sight of the lake. "What a paradise, Belle, but it's colder here than in town. Natural refrigeration. Your sign's sure easy to find. Neat owls." Her chirpy tone changed as she noticed the smudges on Belle's face. "My God, what happened?"

"Just a smokeout. Somebody stuffed my chimney. And I didn't even have a ham in the rafters."

"Are you OK? How did you get out?" They walked inside as Belle made coffee and told her story once more. Each time it became more exciting and elaborate, and each time she realized her dumb luck.

"Hope you don't mind smoky coffee. Maybe it'll be exotic. I've had the place airing, but as you can see," she said as she pointed to the dirty stone-white paint in the living room, "there is damage. And I'll have to wash the pine on the ceilings, too, or negotiate for a cheap steakhouse franchise." They sat on the leather sofas which Belle had swabbed hastily with soap and water. She looked down tiredly and scuffed the rug with her foot. "Good old commercial stuff. Totally resistant against dog hair and wood debris, but I should call a steam cleaner." She rubbed her bloodshot eyes.

"Aren't you afraid, Belle? It looks like someone is out to get you." Melanie's warm expression reflected a genuine concern.

"Yes and no. It has to be Brooks. But we're getting closer. Franz showed me a spot near his bush camp where a cocaine exchange was made. It won't be long until Brooks is sitting in jail, his friends, too. Maybe one of them will talk about Jim's death and make the connections we've been after. Meanwhile, I've got Canada's best security system." She snapped her fingers at Freya, who trotted out Mr. Chile and obligingly laid him at a bemused Melanie's feet. "Guess I'll cruise on propane for a while to be safe. I know it's stupid, but that woodstove has me nervous. It'll probably cost the earth to keep the place at 20°, much less my usual 25°." She pressed at her temples and gave a small moan.

"What's wrong? Did you fall last night?"

"It's just a stupid headache. Carbon monoxide, maybe, or my sinuses overreacting. It'll go away with time and a few pounds of aspirins."

"Let me try something." Melanie moved next to her and cradled her head with a touch that was curiously cool and warm at once. "I've been taking a healing course, reiki, it's called. One of the techniques might help."

Belle made no protests, and after a blissful ten minutes, she sat up with a stunned grin. "You're a miracle! What did you do, and can I hire you?"

Mel seemed pleased at the praise. "I'm not discounting conventional medicine, it's my job, but I'm sure therapeutic touch can help any patient, especially where stress is involved. It's more than just massage."

"I'm impressed. Anything else to it?"

"I'm glad to talk to someone who takes me seriously. At the hospital I have to walk a narrow line so that I don't sound like a crackpot. But I've been experimenting with sending healing messages from afar, in one case to a nephew who had been in a coma from an auto accident. I surrounded him in white light, tried to rejuvenate him with an aura." She blushed. "Do I sound like Shirley MacLaine?"

"Hey, I'm not laughing. Flo Nightingale lived before her time, too. And your nephew?"

"He's in rehab in Toronto. Should make a complete recovery. Prayer, natural energy, modern medicine, luck, who knows? I like to visualize a bright white fluffy cloud around me wherever I go."

The girl's too good to be true, Belle thought. Protected by a cloud. Why not? They used to call them vibes; now it was auras. Melanie spoke also of cleansing the mind of grudges, bitter failures resupped from an old menu. For this she recommended buying a candle for each harmful person or experience. Forgive the trespass, and watch the burdens of the past burn away harmlessly. Ageless witchery mixed with common sense psychology. Every day in every way, getting better and better. Murders, however, needed resolution, and sometimes, though "Mordre will out," according to Chaucer, it needed a helping hand.

SEVENTEEN

A few days later, Belle pulled up in front of Shirmaz Jewellers and Gifts, a tiny shop in the older Donovan area, long bypassed by commercial concerns defecting to the malls. Small, square, compact homes, living relics of Sudbury's frugal past, showed the blue collar priorities of keeping warm while avoiding a crushing mortgage. A wiser time, perhaps, she thought, waving at a sturdy grandmother shovelling snow, woollen babushka on her head. Omer Shirmaz ran his eccentric store more for hobby than profit. He and his wife Thema lived upstairs in the frame building, a shaky, enclosed staircase running up the side.

A bell jangled as she entered. "Omer, hello," Belle said to Sharif's double. What elixir did these men sip, growing handsomer by the years, refining their manners and elegance? Any woman transformed into a queen under their shadowy gaze; the smart ones they complimented for their beauty, the beautiful ones for their brains. Immaculately combed, his dark pewter hair bearing a touch of pomade, a hint of frankincense or myrrh in the air, Omer wore a warm vest with a gold watch chain peeking from the pocket. The fine timepiece along with a stamp collection had been his only baggage arriving from Leningrad at the end of World War Two. An envelope of rare Czarist stamps had bought him his shop, he had told her. "My Russian grandfather was the village postmaster, a very important position. I had the complete 1866 issue, one to twenty kopeks. Not a blemish," he had said as his voice turned to velvet. "My dearest black and lilac, I miss like an old lover."

He bowed to give her hand a zephyr's brush of a kiss. "A delight to see you, my young friend." Belle could swear that he winked. "You are looking so well. Don't tell me you are going to offer me your mother's Doulton ladies at last? Or have you come to check my price list?" Discontinued figures appreciated substantially in value and might make a newspaper ad in Toronto worthwhile.

"This is another matter. Your expert opinion is required."

The deepening lines around his kohl-dark eyes crinkled in curiosity. "Come into the back room and let us be more comfortable. I will hear the bell if she rings."

At a heavy oak table in a cubbyhole heaped with boxes and newspapers, they sat close together, an ancient brass chandelier casting its flambeaux of crystal in an effect eerie and intimate. Omer found a dusty bottle of Slivovitz and poured them both a small glass.

"I always think of you when I eat plums," Belle said, raising a toast.

"Every morning an inch, and you will never have a cold. I guarantee it. Fabled Turco-Cossack remedy."

"An inch! Best not tell the breathalyzer." She licked her lips as delicately as she could, then placed the gold drop in Omer's palm. "Here's a mystery for you."

He examined it with his loupe with no change of expression. "Pure, very pure. I can test it if you like, but see how soft? Never for jewelry. Where did you get it?"

"From a dead man's pocket. Where did he get it?"

Not a blink. "Alchemy was a romantic but false science. There are only two directions. Fine gold from rings, plate and even teeth, can be melted down in a crucible. That is my domain. Or from the richest vein, dripped straight from the ore by intense heat. I have heard that it is possible. You would have to ask a geologist."

Belle tossed the drop lightly in her hand, embroidering the moment with a wry smile and a final sip of brandy warming her throat. "It's part of a very maddening puzzle. I just can't make the pieces fit. What would it be worth, just hypothetically?"

He fished in his vest and put a dime into her other hand. "A bit heavier than your drop. 2.4 grams, not quite a tenth of an ounce at the current $280.00 U.S. quote. Negligible."

"For larger amounts of this raw gold, Omer, a constant supply...out of the proper channels, would there be a buyer?"

"There is always a buyer for everything, and a price for anything. The war taught me that. Northern Ontario has more prospectors than doctors, but this is a small town. Many noisy tongues. In Toronto? Montreal? Without question, though at a considerable discount."

He looked at her with such intensity through those intelligent, trained eyes which had shut out the horror and valour in his past that she felt that she had been holding her breath. Suddenly his steady voice brought her back and rekindled her imagination. Light splintered onto the table. "You said that it came from a dead man's pocket. Are you sure there is not blood on it?" Although they both knew that he spoke figuratively, Belle found herself staring into the tiny drop as if to plumb its heart. From the time man had first glimpsed this hypnotic metal, blood and gold had been quick and greedy partners.

By Saturday, Belle had stayed quiet enough to receive the Mutt of the Year award. Her enforced retirement had led to washing all the downstairs windows, cleaning the stove and fridge, scrubbing the floor (twice), sucking out the fish tanks, and writing four overdue letters to family friends over eighty, none of whom had an estate of substance. All that remained was to cut Freya's claws, a mutually squeamish chore; Belle commanded the dog to lie motionless on the kitchen floor while she maneuvered the clippers to avoid hitting a vein. Every snip received a moan of torment, a quiver of fear. "OK, go, girl," Belle sighed finally in her own relief, and the dog yawned from nervousness and raced away as if given a deathhouse reprieve.

In search of a newspaper to pass the time, Belle drove to the airport smoke shop for the *Toronto Star*, passing a familiar green Jimmy in the long-term parking. A peek inside revealed a Shield University parking pass and the blanket she recalled from Freya's rescue. Another play in Toronto, she wondered? More usual to drive unless time were a critical factor. From the smokeshop, she saw one of her neighbour's daughters and strolled over, raising her arms like the roaring polar bear image in their logo. "Hi, Patty. How's life at Polar Bear Air?"

"A wild ride. With this awful weather, everyone's hustling to get a final holiday any place south. Recession nothing! You should see the bookings for the Caribbean and Mexico now that the peak time's over. Wish I could go, too."

Belle folded her paper in studied disinterest. "Lucky folks. Say, I saw a friend's car in the lot. Professor Franz Schilling. Was he heading for the sunny beaches or just off to Toronto?"

The young girl drummed into her computer without a second thought. "Let's see. He was routed through to Kingston. Maybe on business. Back on our 10 p.m. Sunday flight."

Stranger and stranger, but just over the border to New York. A visit to the troubled sister. Why lie about it, Franz?

The stigma of mental illness? He seemed enlightened enough, but one never knew. The paper engaged her for the rest of the afternoon, especially with the dollar in the sub-basement thanks to Canada's monumental debt load and a resource-based economy.

An hour later, Belle was still wandering around the house, toe-tapping, checking her watch to distraction. Would it ever be time to leave for the Beave, to coin a poem? And why ever go alone? Entertainment should be shared. She picked up the phone. "Now, I know you're in bed by dark, Hélène," she joked after she described the fun, "but make an exception. Going around nine thirty should give us a couple of hours before the witching hour for the raid."

"I can jump start the old man," Hélène said. "Cut off his decaf at supper and watch him hop it on caffeine. We're having Referendum Soup, so he should be hot enough about that."

"Referendum Soup? Are you serious? Sounds too controversial for *Canadian Living* magazine."

"Made it in Thunder Bay visiting my son the night the votes on the last one were counted. See if you recognize anyone: take a big hambone, add plenty of beans and prepare to eat it for the rest of your life. Trouble is, it's delicious." A tinkling laugh came over the phone.

Belle had her own culinary memories. She defrosted a cube of pesto from her summer basil and spinach crop, chuckling as she recalled the day she had made the sauce. The spatula parked on top of the whirring blender had fallen in and in three seconds plastered the oily green sauce over the counter, cupboards, floor, ceiling and her naked self on an unusually torrid afternoon. In consideration of these efforts, she had had no scruples scraping the costly mess into ice cube trays. A thin spaghetti dressed with the ill-fated pesto and a salad of endive grown in some abandoned local mine by a creative entrepreneur went onto the table, showered with freshly-grated Romano.

A reliable Pinewood Studio film from the late fifties was on Nostalgia, so she settled in. Around nine o'clock, she stepped out onto the deck before deciding how many layers to wear. Luckily it was warmer and surprisingly windless as the darkness deepened, yet a feathery ring wreathed the moon. She hoped it would not be a bad one rising.

Down at the DesRosiers' shoreline, Belle winced as her machine bounced over a snow-covered log that had drifted in before freeze-up. "We're just about ready. Have a coffee," Hélène said as Belle leafed through the *Sudbury Star* to find Ann Landers. A hockey game blared on the giant TV. Belle could hardly believe her benighted eyes. Near the eastern windows sat, seedlings? An optical illusion? Would spring ever arrive,or would this be the first nuclear winter?

"What have you got, you fox?" she asked. "Aren't you jumping the gun?"

Hélène beamed and pinched off a tiny leaf which she waved under Belle's nose, releasing a precious scent of peppery oregano. "Can't keep us Frenchmen down. Ed promised me a small greenhouse as soon as the ground thaws. So I'll be able to keep these tomatoes, herbs, broccoli, cukes right nice under glass until the last frost."

Belle warmed up with the coffee, nosing the smallest dollop of rye. "Last frost. Right about mid-July before the first frost the day after."

"Oh, *fais dodo*, as my Great Aunt Jacinthe used to say. Get to bed with you. Shut it." Hélène watered her babies with perfect confidence. "We'll have a dinner of this, and I'll remind you about your lack of faith."

Judging from the communal roar of machines from all directions, Saturday night at the lodge had started. Twenty people passed the trio as if they were moonwalking. Some thought travel was safer at night because of the lights, but so many speeders overran their beams that it made little difference. The lake assumed a surreal perspective by starlight, a silvery rink dotted with shore twinklings. Across at the Reserve, the lights which greeted Belle every morning before dawn were still flickering. Nearing Brooks' island, they could hear booming bass thumps, gradually developing into a passable imitation of Alabama. A large birch fire snapped in front of the lodge, a cheery spot for hardier souls who wanted less music and more privacy. For a moment Belle imagined that she smelled a smoke too sweet for wood as she glanced at a young couple toasting marshmallows and snuggling in the fire's glimmer.

Pushing through the main door, they carried their helmets into a wave of music and laughter, standing stupefied for a moment in the sudden heat, until Ed commandeered a wooden booth in a side room. Belle's watch said ten o'clock. Their pitcher of draft arrived with a bowl of popcorn, packed with palm oil, Belle bet, knowing that virtuous canola could not have hit the sticks this fast. Shoving their jackets under the table with their helmets and kicking off their boots, they relaxed in their overalls like the rest of the crowd. As a cheap alternative to live music, the karaoke setup gave volunteers their standard five minutes of local fame. A balding porker in red underwear beneath Farmer John's began warbling "Tie a Yellow Ribbon," lurching offstage to polite applause, followed by two young lovers who rivalled Kenny and Dolly in "Islands in the Stream".

"In the steam," Belle said as she excused herself for the

bathroom, ducking a second later as she saw Nick. Luckily he was occupied with what looked like the stripper from the Paramount. At least he wasn't a cradle robber. Belle chose the door with a winking doe instead of the rampant buck. So this was the fabled septic system. Well, let's give it a go, she muttered under her breath, and checked out a stall, glad to find a lock which worked. A hand-printed sign in block letters admonished users NOT to flush paper. Miriam's brother had left his tank unpumped for seventeen years and, thanks to two fastidious teenagers and a wife, ended up with an 800 gallon tank of papier mâché and a clogged field bed redug at the cost of the St. Lawrence Seaway. Belle merrily waved goodbye to an ox-choking wad of tissue to serve Brooks right.

When she returned to the table, the pitcher was gone and so were the DesRosiers. It appeared that they were dancing to the unforgettable "Hello, Darlin'", Belle's favourite. "Just for old time's sake," Ed sang with a rise to each word, dipping Hélène dangerously as he might have done to the sounds of Don Messer and the Islanders back when he and his only sweetheart had been dancing at their Senior Prom.

Belle's concept of raids came from scenes where a bumbling array of Keystone cops stampeded into a speakeasy and rousted everyone into a paddy wagon, careering off into the distance as "The End" hit the screen. On an island, logistics might be easier. True, someone could vanish into the night, but not if the cordon were tight, if Steve had brought enough officers. It wasn't the common variety toker with a bit of hash in his pocket wanted here, though the odd minnow might stick in the net meant for a grandfather walleye. Belle finished off the popcorn while the DesRosiers fanned themselves from the exertion, Ed making a hula hoop motion with his bad hip. "Feels good tonight. Must be a high coming in," he noted.

Belle snickered and waved some of the fragrant air toward them. "The high has arrived."

Hélène grinned in mischief as her nostrils flickered. "Well now, Dad. So this that happy grass they been talking about since those Beatniks. Maybe I should try it before I hit seventy. Never too late, they say."

Ed slapped his hand down in mock anger. "Better not, lady. You want that high, a good Alberta rye'll do you just fine."

The signature song that had put the town on the country music map, Stompin' Tom Connors' "Sudbury Saturday Night," sent an explosion of cheers across the room, inspiring one man to snare a Canadian flag from the wall and parade around, joined by a bearded giant brandishing the Fleur de Lys. Here was one place in Canada that French and English were having a royally good time; separatists, take note. The crowd started clapping, and Belle found herself singing along, sorry that her low profile kept her from serenading the crowd with something by Reba.

Just after "The girls are out to bingo, and the men are getting stinko, we think no more of Inco," the noise suddenly stopped as if the electrical plug had been yanked. All eyes moved to the door as several officers walked forward, spreading out in an unsmiling phalanx. From the kitchen came a yell and a tinkle of glass, chairs started scraping and a young girl cried out. Steve stood before his men and spoke calmly into a bullhorn. "Please relax, folks. You won't be delayed long. We have reason to believe that some illegal substances are changing hands here." A male voice bellowed the most frequently occurring word in *Pulp Fiction*, but Steve ignored it and motioned toward the wall. "Just line up, please. Men over here. A female officer will search the women in the side room. Once you're cleared, you can leave. Your tax dollars at work." When boos erupted from the back, he smiled and made a "That's the breaks" gesture.

Though Belle passed through the cordon quickly, she became separated from Ed and Hélène. The lodge cleared rapidly to the sound of snowmobile motors roaring into the black silence. At the ramp to the lodge sat a police van which had travelled the ice road, and three men, handcuffed behind their backs, were being guided into seats, their heads ducked for them as they entered. One might have been Brooks, but shadows could be misleading. Belle rubbed her hands by the embers of the campfire until Steve strutted up, unable to conceal his satisfaction.

"Got the bugger," he said proudly, smacking his fist into his glove. "Two of his dealers will plea bargain their snow pants off when we get them to the station. Five more were carrying small amounts, scared enough to tell us anything. And here's the cream! In the housing for the electric guts of that fancy septic system, we found his main supply wrapped snug in layers of plastic. Guess he didn't think anyone would be poking around in there. Five kilos of coke. A small bale of pot. And some of these babies." He held out what looked like a perfume sample vial, tiny and jewel-like.

"So what's that, swami?" Belle asked.

"Meet the newest nephew of Sudbury's drug family. Big city crack cocaine. One teeny rock to a person, please."

Belle shuddered. "Anyone on that stuff wouldn't have the sense to come in out of the cold. Any stolen snowmobiles turn up?"

He gave her a comical look as if wondering where she had learned about that. "Just one, but it's enough. Rumour says he managed to get rid of everything but a Mach Z, saving it for someone who could afford the price and use the machine out where registration wouldn't be checked. Anyway, we're tracing it to a theft in Sturgeon Falls. I'll bet that if we cut him some slack, he'll admit to the two incidents at your house, Belle. This may be his first charge, but the judges have developed pretty tough skins for dealers lately. He could draw a mandatory fifteen-year sentence without parole." He left her to return to the final details of the evidence collection. No use going to all this trouble and blowing the fine points.

Belle found the DesRosiers having coffee with one of the cooks in the kitchen. "Damn cold out there, girl. Where the hell have you been? Didn't want to leave you."

Not long after, all were home suffering only a popcorn and beer bloat. In a hedonistic papaya bubble bath, Belle warmed up, contemplating her toes, probing the big one into the faucet. When it stuck for a moment, she imagined another humiliating finale worse than choking on vitamins: "Woman starves to death in bathtub. Found by neighbour returning from Florida with Miami Dolphins T-shirt gift. Had been gnawed on by desperate shepherd." Would Freya do that? Why not? The "doggy dog" way of the world. Dreamily content, relaxing to the sweet perfume, she thought of the gold again, appearing and disappearing in the elusive bubbles. As the surface of the water turned to milky film, a whiter line of surface tension delineating her legs, one half-submerged, the other bent and invisible six inches below the knee, Belle had a vision of her body frozen in the ice.

EIGHTEEN

The gray mailboxes at the junction of her road stood an inconvenient six miles from the house. Half the time Belle thought in kilometres, half the time in miles. Another decade and the logic of metric would be second nature. She took two pieces of mail from the box, cheques for her father, the Canada Pension, which everyone paid into, and the Old Age freebie—$400.00 a month just for wrinkles and myopia!

When she got to Rainbow Country with the shrimp, her father was spruced up in the blue plaid shirt she had bought him for Christmas. Her careful eye noted the clean undershirt, braces and freshly ironed pants. "Good news, Father," she announced. "Your pension cheques arrived. And, at last count, you're on the yellow brick road to becoming a millionaire. The stock market is soaring."

"Take all the money out of the bank and bring it here, right now, right now." At his stern face, she nearly stepped back. Then his eyes sparkled, a royal blue which belied his years and waning health. No wonder her mother had fallen in love with the man in the picture on the dresser, serious, wearing a tweed suit and metal-rimmed glasses, holding a meershaum pipe. "Just kidding. Gimme ten bucks, though. I owe the haircut lady."

While she was setting up his meal, she encouraged him to talk about old Toronto. "Hogtown, she used to be called.

208

Rough and ready. Small houses, family stores, horses still pulling wagons down Avenue Road. Big night out to go downtown for a Chinese feed at the St. Charles and see a show at the Odeon. Or maybe Sunnyside Park in the summer. Did you know your old man was a great dancer? Some bad times, though. Those riots at the Christie Pits in 1938, damn Nazis beating up the Jews. My brother Fred and I got Abie Schneider out fast on the trolley. Took him right home with us. And Ma gave us all tomato soup and crackers. I remember Abie was crying."

"And your years in the film business, all those people you met. Didn't you tell me that you shook Gene Autry's hand?"

He held up his knobby fist proudly and offered it to her. "Shake the hand that shook the hand. All the biggest stars came through the office."

"Right. And all those glossies of Elvis, was that really his signature: 'To my girlfriend, Belle'?"

That got him laughing, an unusual sight which cheered her in this quiet room. There would never be another home, another room for him. "Norman, my name was Norman then," he corrected her. At the nursing home in Florida, they had mistakenly called him by his unused first name. Then his girlfriend (his consort, he had called her) and he had decided that George was more British, more noble. How many people changed their name after 80?

"Like my haircut?" he asked, and she gave it an appreciative rub.

"A regular crew cut. You don't look a minute over fifty." And he didn't, thanks to his baby-smooth skin.

"No shave, though," he added with a definite pout.

"Ontario is broke. You'll probably get one later today." Belle arranged the lunch she had brought and filled his glass of water from the immaculate bathroom. It always seemed as if Joyce had just cleaned. Lysol was redolent and the porcelain sparkling.

As her father enjoyed his shrimp, Belle picked at her roast pork sandwich, hardly tasting it, although the bread was homemade, the mustard piquant and the meat tender and lean. With a sigh, she wrapped it for Freya.

"What's the matter? Not hungry? That's not like a Palmer," her father said, clearly "with it" enough today to notice her lack of appetite while tucking into his favourite meal.

"I'm OK. Just too many things on my mind." She folded up the soiled napkins and set out more for the gooey pie and ice cream, sighing in resignation. You couldn't keep things from him. She hadn't wanted to tell her father about Jim, thinking that the report of a death might upset him. "A friend of mine was killed going through the ice on a snow machine. No witnesses. Out in the middle of nowhere. Everyone says it's an accident, but it stinks. He was the last person who would make a dangerous mistake in the bush." She paused to mush up the pie, chopping away the tough crust so that his last few teeth could handle the assignment. "But on the other hand, there's no motive. He was a serious and private man, a university student and about as nice a guy as you could find. Why would anyone kill him?"

Her father shovelled in some coleslaw with a shaky hand, chewed for a pensive moment with his eyes closed, then beamed as if he had just scratched a lottery winner. "Easy. *Greed.* Don't you remember that movie? Longest silent ever made! Got me interested in the fillum business. I was only a kid but knew right away the job was for me."

"What do you mean? What greed?" She drew her chair closer and turned down the disco trash from the exercise show on television.

"Think, girl! What was the motive? Gold. That big tooth, Zasu Pitts lying on a bed of shiny coins." His eyes glittered as if the curtain had lifted on a favourite picture long faded to shadows. "Aren't we in Northern Ontario, where gold sits under every tree? Old Sir Harry Oakes died for it. It's gold all right, always was, always is. You'll see. Just keep your peepers peeled." He munched his last French fry and reached for the container of pie.

When the local news started, Belle cleaned away the lunch debris and unsnapped the prison of his lap table. "How about a walk down the hall?" she asked. It was crucial to get him back on his feet to juice the circulation. The nurses had reported that he was not cooperative during his exercise periods. Perhaps extra motivation would help. "You've got to get practising again if you want to go back to the restaurant when the weather gets better."

A smile broke out on his face as he looked up like a trusting child. "Really? OK, let's give it a try. Where are my shoes?" He shook one red plush bedroom slipper, all his swollen feet could wear. Belle searched the closet, peered under the bed, even plowed through his underwear drawer. How could a large item vanish from a private room whose sole occupant barely tottered down to meals each day? Yet some of the more mobile female patients roamed the halls "cleaning house" in their cobwebbed minds, collecting loose articles and driving the nurses crazy when they had to sort out the belongings.

"Never mind. We can slog along with one. Come on." She hoisted him up, gripping his wasted arm. Even five years ago, his biceps and calves had bulged, huge bunches of muscles due to genes more than exercise. They used to strike poses together, their arms and legs and faces identical DNA maps. A purposeful grunt helped him to stand, leaning perilously, then shuffling forward, all 170 stomachy pounds. They inched into the hall, past dim rooms with heads lolled back, toothless mouths agape, or worse, quiet bundles of blanketed shapes forever dreaming of a precious time far and away.

"Take the hand rail," she told him, as they rocked along. Only thirty feet to the nurses' station. Suddenly he stopped and looked down. Her gaze followed. His other slipper! "It dropped out of your pant leg?" Their laughter echoed down the silent hall. "A miracle! Didn't you feel it? What else is up there? No, I don't want to know!" Belle put the shoe on him, and they rounded back to the room in time for the weather report.

As she left by the front desk, Belle had a word for Cherie, the nurse on call. "He looks good. Thanks for the extra effort in dressing and grooming him."

"Sorry we didn't get to his shave. All hell broke loose in the kitchen. Dishwasher overflowed. Oh, by the way," she coughed delicately, and swivelled her head to see if they were being overheard, "that doctor we were discussing the other day?" Belle nodded. "Rumour says that he was involved in abortions a few years before the hospital started providing them without hassles. No charges were ever laid, though. He's a slick one." Her eyebrows arched knowingly. In big cities like Toronto, abortions were available if a woman had the nerve to brave the gauntlet of pro-life pickets. In smaller towns and solidly Catholic areas, the procedure could be difficult to arrange.

Belle left the building, still trying to sort out the tangle of clues, hunches and tips revolving in her brain. Something was trying to take shape, to drop out of a pantleg. Although she had latched onto it as a tempting possibility, less and less did the drug angle look viable. Brooks' gang was rounded up, squealing like shoats (or was it stoats?) for legal aid, but nothing about Jim had been forthcoming. Steve would have told her. Maybe she should speak to Brooks directly; surely he was out on bail by now. And the gold? Perhaps not the romantic dream of an old man at all. Jim's drop haunted her, the last tangible reminder of her friend. As Omer had said, the area was full of treasure hunters searching new places yet undreamed and old places long played out. The generous meteorite which had blasted the Sudbury basin had planted many precious metals, gold and palladium among them.

One of Belle's favourite summer haunts, Bonanza Lake north of Wapiti, had been mined briefly around the turn of the century. Since it was accessible by old logging roads, Belle and Freya beat through undergrowth to climb the steep trail to its hills once or twice each summer. Not only were the blueberries spectacular, but the pellucid green lake attracted wise loons, who knew well ahead of the scientists that the PH of the troubled waters had been slowly improving. True, the only mine shaft she had actually seen had been filled in with rubble and ringed by rusted scraps of a fence, but she had traced along the walls of the water-filled excavations the petering-out of the quartzite. Aside from picking up a few specimens and taking a swim in the lake, Belle never ventured further into the dense bush, rife with bloody-minded flies and festooned with poison ivy.

Tom Beardley would know. A retired chemist, he played prospector on the weekends, ferreting out tiny mining claims more for fun, boasting that he was an explorer, not a gold baron. A lucky find near Timmins had netted him twenty thousand dollars once, which he had blown quickly on a new Bronco, but that had been his only major discovery. Now and then Tom taught a night course in metallurgy at Nickel City College; Belle had met him there in the cafeteria on a break from a real estate seminar.

Tom's wife Dorothy answered Belle's call. "Tom? Sure, he's back from Wawa today. Never misses the Jays on television. No sooner unpacked than he's rushed down to the Diamond Pipe to meet some of his gangster friends. Tell him for me he'd better not be home later than fifteen minutes after the game. And I'm listening." The radio warbled in the background. Belle knew that Dorothy's jocular threats held little sting. Tom had nursed her through several breast cancer operations and made sure that they escaped every February to the Portuguese Algarve, a favourite Canadian destination because of its bargain villas.

The Diamond Pipe on Bathurst Street was jumping as Belle strolled in shortly after seven, so as not to interrupt the game. Her friend sat with Paolo Santanen, demolishing a platter of Buffalo wings. Tom, a huge man with a matching gut but strong as a Terex truck, looked as if he had not only pounded in the last spike of the Trans-Canada railway single-handedly, but all the others as well. He clapped his massive paws on the table and set his unshaven jaw in Paolo's milk-mild Finnish face. "They'll never make the grade without another couple of pitchers, my son. And sure as hell they trade any of their duds, those bozos'll win the Cy Young award for their new team. Maybe it's the coaches' fault, who knows?"

Nearing eighty, the small and wiry Paolo was developing a bow to his back, and he moved with slow deliberation. Derek had come along when he had been well into his fifties. Last time he and Belle had met, he had wiped tears from his eyes as he thanked her for helping his son get the Snopac job. "I want to die the day before I go into a nursing home, and the day before Derek ever gets in trouble again," he had confessed privately as his wife Gerda boiled up some potatoes. Yet tonight Paolo seemed full of fire. "Jays got power to spare. Let 'em get five runs in the opposition, these boys'll bring 'em up. You ain't got no trust at all. Don't you know baseball's a game of faith?" Belle moved forward to catch Tom's eye.

"Belle? I haven't seen you in months. Too busy grubbin' real estate to talk with old pals?" With a friendly wink, he nabbed an extra chair from the next table and patted it. "Now how's my Freya?" He and his short-haired pointer Duke loved to go birding. Three fat partridges that he had dropped off last fall, ivory breasts more succulent than chicken, had made a memorable stew.

Paolo took her hand and squeezed it wordlessly as he met her eyes. She signalled the waitress for a beer by hoisting Tom's bottle. "Good, for all of her ten years, but getting on like her mom." She nibbled at a wing he offered. "Yow, hot stuff. Listen, I need some information from you, some mining expertise."

He roared into high gear, flexing his masculinity and nudging his friend. "The Midnight Prospector strikes again. And you said I was over the hill."

"Stop showing off, you old coot. I need to know about gold north of Wapiti, the Bonanza area maybe. Is anything still there?"

"Up where the new park's goin' in? Nah, she's all played out. Bonanza. Some joke, that name. Never did find nothing much, though they thought at first they had another boom like Cobalt. 'Course, that was long before my time. Closed up about a hunnert years ago. Nothing left now but a couple of filled-in shafts and rubble."

"That's it? You mean the quartzite piles at the top of the hill? I've taken some pieces for my rock garden. White and brown."

"It's pretty stuff. The brown's siderite, a crystalline carbonate. That one heap's all most people ever see. Couple other shafts a few hundred feet farther into the bush. Pretty dense and overgrown. Could be flooded, too. Dad said they were almost ninety feet down. Tanned me once as a kid when he thought I'd been fooling around there. Say, listen to me rattling on. What do you want to know about that played-out claim for? You don't want to poke around those rotting timbers. The gasses are toxic. Methane, for one." He gave her a serious look which spelled worry.

"Could there be any gold left?"

"Well, the companies gave up and never went back. That tells you something. Odds are against it. They mined out any veins as far as they could."

Belle narrowed her eyes and tapped his wrist gently. "But if someone found a streak, even a smallish one. Don't ask me how; I never took geology. Why would they keep it quiet? Why not cash in?"

"Are you kidding? Someone still owns rights to that land. And it would be 'thank you very much, buddy. Now get lost.' Except it probably wouldn't be worth the company's money to pursue a peanut find even with high tech. Cost them five million to get in, they'd need to make fifteen. This isn't the Klondike of 1898, girl."

"So how could anything be retrieved profitably?"

"Well, hell, you could blowtorch it out," he boomed and gulped his beer with an approving belch. "A rich little vein, pocket gold mine. Drip her into what we call 'buttons'. Ounce or two. Easy to carry. 'Course, you'd have to sell on the black market at less than half the price. Be worth it, though, damn government taxes. Lots of fun, too."

Paolo had been listening with interest, nodding at the excitement as he tried to get their attention. "You know, that could be. A chum of mine, after he retired, used to spend weekends loading tailings from an old site in Kirkland Lake into his pickup, take it back to his garage to crush. Called it the Lost Deutchman Mine. And you know, he made hisself enough to live on a good ten year. And good for him, I say. Pensions weren't worth nothing back then."

Belle placed Jim's drop in front of Tom's bottle. His eyes widened, reflecting the yellow flame of the table's light as he touched it lovingly, rubbed at the sheen. "That's the ticket. The real thing, as they used to say before that there cola."

"Could this come from that method you describe? Dripped off? It sounds so primitive."

"Nothin' more simple and more valuable than gold. Whoever made this has a pretty little girl for sure. Lucky devil."

Belle pocketed the drop as a baby Jay belted a lead-off double to galvanize the crowd. What had Omer said about the drop having blood on it?

NINETEEN

The sunrise had a definite MGM lock on the pastel lavender of Liz Taylor's eyes as Belle refilled her bird feeder on the frosty deck. She was getting jumpy and frustrated at the confusing trails surrounding Jim's death, the widening circle of ripples. Someone waited at the centre, sure of safety or anxious of discovery, deadly in any case if the smokeout were an indication. The sudden ring of the phone made her spill her self-righteous decaf all over the table. "It's Geoff Garson. Pardon the violation of netiquette. I had to hear your non-electronic voice, Belle. E-mail is so cold and mechanical."

"And I got your information. The picture came through showing every brick. Top notch sleuthing. But don't tell me that you uncovered more?"

"My housekeeper's son's friend, I will spare you the nepotistic connections, is an orderly at Forest Glen. From his report, and I know you will handle these facts with discretion since I wouldn't want to get the lad in trouble, your Eva came there about a year ago. She had been through some trauma, possibly sexual because her psychiatrist specializes in rape, incest, abortion, sad dysfunctions from A to Z, or your Canadian zed. Rather a Dr. Ruth of the Dark Shadows."

"That would have been a show to remember. Any visitors?"

"A brother comes every month or so, only recently with the

mother. A breakthrough maybe." He emphasized words with delicious drama, Clifton Webb as Waldo in *Laura*. Of course, he could be a quarter-ton Marlon Brando, for all Belle knew.

Her notepad filled as Geoff continued. "My source is only an orderly, but those seen-and-not-heard types know the inside gossip. Like the servants in a Victorian household."

"Right, *Upstairs, Downstairs*. A fortunate choice."

Geoff pressed forward, not at all shy at inventing a scenario. "Playing amateur psychiatrist, Belle, is this a case of molestation or an unreported rape? What do you know of her family?"

Belle doodled idly as she recounted the visit to the island, the curious saint in her shrine. "Hard to figure, Geoff. The father's dead years ago. The girl was a lonely figure. No friends, no interests outside her studies. Her brother is beyond reproach, in my opinion. The mother seems loving and warm. It doesn't make sense."

"What was that saint you mentioned? Dymphna, was it? Never heard of that exotic lady; so many have been delisted for lack of documentation. Still, give me a moment. That was my territory at Notre Dame."

It turned out that Geoff was not only a retired professor, but also a Jesuit priest. She could hear him leafing pages. "Ah, the patron saint of the insane. Gheel, the Netherlands. This is getting very murky, Belle."

"A saint for the insane? This is exotic for a lapsed Anglican like me."

"Hmmm. Let's see. There are hordes, one for every human woe. St. Peregrine for cancer, St. Apollonia for toothaches, St. Fiacre for haemorrhoids…"

"Stop the rogue's gallery! I'm quite suggestible." Belle protested. She promised Geoff the latest L. R. Wright mystery, a Canadian favourite set on the Sunshine Coast in B.C.

Although Belle had a gift for fishing for red herrings and clutching at hypothetical straws, and although she still found Brooks a truly odious man, dog lover or not, she could no longer consider him a serious suspect. He was home on heavy bond, minding his manners, a candidate for several years in prison after his trial. At least his daughter Brenda might get a second chance, maybe even bring those Puddingstone kids to life. Although he wouldn't admit to the break-in, he had agreed to talk to Belle in hopes of gaining judicial brownie points. And the meeting might fill in some gaps in the picture.

She reached the Beaverdam shortly after nine. Brooks sat slumped in front of his father's fieldstone fireplace, oblivious to her entrance. His head sagged, giving him a bizarre chinless look. A beer sat beside him, and ashes flicked onto the handsome slate floor.

Belle smiled at his red checked shirt; trust a man to prize an old friend too much to toss it out even if it told dangerous tales. "I've been looking for a spot to fit this little piece of evidence," she said, matching the swatch to his sleeve, watching him recoil as if she'd been a snapping turtle.

"Big deal. I'm already goin' down far enough. Sorry about the dog, though. That was an accident. I wanted to tell you that." He stroked an old raggedy collie who gazed up at him with warm, liquid eyes. "Just went over to teach you a lesson, smelling around in the business. Make it look like the place had been robbed."

Her savage glare backed him off with a whine. "Hey, now, missus, nothing bad. Just throw a few papers around for show. When I opened the door, and you know, you should lock your doors..." He cowered as Belle slammed her fist on the table and stood up to leave. "Your dog ran out and laid into me something fierce. And he's big. Was going right for my throat when I saw the shovel. Just hit him once. Not hard. Then I heard a car and got out fast."

"Self-defence, no doubt. And the dog's a she."

"Why, sure. That's exactly what it was."

Jim's accident had surprised him as much as anybody, and though he admitted to using small lakes north of Wapiti for transfers, the warmer weather had ended that. One plane had come close to getting stuck. "How about Cott Lake?" she asked.

"Cott? Up by Bonanza? No need to go all that way." He paused and poked at the fire reflectively, his voice almost avuncular. "Jim was a nice kid. Never had a boy of my own. He used to do some scut work here when he was in high school, baiting and gassing up for the tourists. One thing I can tell you, his death didn't have nothin' to do with drugs. I'm no killer."

She gave him a sideways stare, like a wary gunslinger. "No? Then why did you come back and plug up my chimney?"

"Huh. I heard about that. Not my style. The whole week I was over in Thunder Bay selling two machines." He drew on his cigarette and coughed. "Hey, your dog is OK, right?"

Belle drove home, frustrated at not learning more, but admitting to herself that Brooks was telling the truth. Pacing from room to room, unable to concentrate, she remembered the appointment with Ms. Bly. She called Miriam, who agreed to take the woman to Capreol, glad to get out of the office on a slow Friday. Even the coffee tasted bitter and metallic, and when she thought about lunch, she felt no hunger, just the slight nausea which came from too much caffeine.

Maybe she was suffering from cabin fever, SAD or Seasonal Affective Disorder. A change of place might recharge the brain cells, a trip to Toronto, a cruise of the mall outlets. Sure, run away and shop yourself into oblivion, Belle. That wasn't the problem anyway. She had failed Jim, failed Ben, Meg and Melanie. Buffaloed, outfoxed, decoyed with this conundrum, riddle, enigma shrouded in a...in a wallow of clichés. With a self-accusing sigh, she picked up her mother's copy of *The Diviners*, thumbing through it absently, when a line from Catharine Parr Traill caught her attention, something irksomely didactic about getting up and doing when all seemed lost. An Englishwoman's view of the wilds of Peterborough, well, wild enough in the nineteenth century.

The temperature stood at -10°, but spring days warmed up fast. In her father's old-fashioned terminology, a "constitutional", forerunner of power walking, might help charge the batteries. The last time she had gone into the bush on foot had been New Year's Day. The dog seemed to read her mind, hyperventilating and nipping her elbow in an annoying dominance move. Belle wapped her toque at the dog's ample rump. "Yes, I get the point, Freya. Just give me a minute. I wasn't born with a fur coat." As an afterthought, she tucked a plastic bag with Hélène's jerky into her zippered forearm pocket. A snack would taste welcome in the cold. As she walked out onto the deck, the tall cedars, faithful monitors of wind, stood quiet. Good, then. She would march down the road for half an hour, and perhaps spot the gigantic red-headed Woody, insistent in his poundings, or hear the gentle thrummings of hairy and downy relatives.

Once on the road, Belle felt the wind chew at her back, an ominous sign. Maybe at the corner it would subside. Wind was worse than cold. Her eyelashes were icing, plastered to her face; her glasses had fogged, though she was careful to blow straight out. But Freya enjoyed collecting her P-mail, delivered since the plow's last trip, and making her own deposits. "Not there, Freya! Of all places!" Belle yelled as the dog picked the one open driveway in half a mile; Richard Earhart must have spent a heavy two hours snowblowing with an underpowered city style machine. Back and forth eternally with that narrow twenty-four inch swath. He didn't need this extra ignominy. Belle searched for a broken branch in order to perform her dip and flip manoeuvre, resolving to buy a cheap hockey stick next trip to Canadian Tire. Then ticking off the cottages in her mind as she passed, she was glad to see the unmarked, protective expanses of deep snow. It was unlikely anyone would haul off anything substantial, but absentee owners feared vandalism far more than the loss of an odd television or VCR. Insurance companies insisted someone check a vacant house regularly. A number of restaurant gift certificates had come Belle's way in recompense. Caroline's place looked safe and tight, only a fox track down the driveway. Her generous retired neighbour had pressed upon Belle the remains of her liquor supply, her satellite decoder and a stylish but impractical fox fur hat. The blessed woman was probably driving over that golden bridge across Tampa Bay in quest of a plate of crispy grouper!

A sudden rush, and Carlo sailed by in a roar with yet another Mustang, a '65 original, grey primer paint, no bumpers, its rear windows tinted; he was leaning towards her and blowing kisses. Belle had to laugh at his cheek. At the top of the second hill, she spied snowshoe tracks rambling invitingly into the bush. Anni Jacobs' web of paths. All four seasons the old widow led her dogs on daily forages, a boneheaded golden lab and a hyperactive beagle, who made Belle smug about the superiority of shepherds. Some paths had originated from logging roads fifty years earlier, an illegal horse-drawn operation of Ed's Uncle Louis. Lazy, hazy days when an entrepreneur could rob the bush unhindered by laws.

After a hundred feet, another trail appeared, perhaps looping back onto the major route or leading to the top of the bluff. Freya was already energized by her neighbours' traces. Belle tested the surface with her cumbersome boots and found the middle of the doublewide snowshoe path firm enough. The trail pointed up, twisting under thick spruce and between birches. Breaking twigs was not Anni's ecological style. Breathing heavily, but warming as she went, Belle ducked under larger branches and bent stubborn alders, which snapped back in her face. Her heavy mitts were becoming oppressive, so she stuffed them into her pockets, welcoming the cooling evaporation on her hands.

The farther she climbed, the more her admiration for the old woman grew. Surely she must be pushing 70. How many hours and days and years had she devoted to these highways? They were so fresh and numerous that the old woman must come out every day, one foot rounding the other in the hip-swinging snowshoe dance. Belle's heart was racing as she paused, and Freya dug her nose into a bush, sneezing at the powdery snow. Here the dogs had angled off to smell up a squirrel, to scare a few feathers off a fleet partridge, or to lay masculine claim to a familiar gummy pine.

An hour later, twining around the mountain, she emerged at the top, a balding outlook which presented the lake like a sparkling Christmas platter. Many miles out, a few toy figures on sleds scooted across, and a truck had heavy going pulling a large hut over the softening ice. The day had warmed at last. Taking large gulps of air into her lungs, which no longer pricked her nostrils or choked her, she gave a loud hallooo. Freya barked, and down at the lakeside, hidden by trees,

Anni's dogs answered, the deep lab duelling with the bugling beagle. Remembering the jerky, Belle fingered out a piece and presented it to Freya, tasting a chunk herself. Peppery and tender, it bore little relation to the prohibitively expensive store-bought cardboard. Then with an eye to this new kingdom, she noticed striations of moose antler marks on the smaller maples where the tormented creatures often rubbed the velvet to soothe their pain. In the summer, red froth pinked the papery white birches six feet up. Touching her stinging temple where an alder had switched her face, she wiped her own fresh blood and joined it to the birch. Name it, name it Moose Mountain, something told her.

Why not make some trails of her own? Belle knew every mushroom, lichen and birch gall on the paths nearest her house, the trails that Ed and his son-in-law tamped with their snow machines in winter and their quads in summer. With the clear vista through the woods and the security of a snowshoe track, she could link the trails by a key blaze or landmark, then follow before spring rains wakened the bugs and unfurled the concealing leaves. For the first time since the Great Freeze, she felt connected to the world, clicking on all cylinders. Best of all, she had forgotten for a moment that Jim Burian lay frozen in a quiet crypt waiting for a grave under blossoms he would never touch.

Fresh paths for the brain, she thought, breathing evenly and slowly. Explore the magic trinity of criminology unchanged since the death of Abel: motive, opportunity, means. Backward, work backward, oh time in thy flight. Means in the bush equalled a snowmobile, and if she guessed right, a second machine with reverse. It must have been very difficult and time-consuming to back up that far without a slip. Opportunity? Brooks, of course, originally the number one suspect, but no more. Cott Lake must have been a set-up. Why would Brooks lie about a particular lake after admitting the transfers? And speaking of opportunity, there was the nagging question of where Jim had eaten that fish and vegetables Monroe had found stuck in his teeth. If that had been his last meal at his cabin, there was no trace of it there, only the noodle packet. On his way home, he hadn't eaten dinner in the middle of nowhere.

Finally, motive. There the problem stuck as it had from the beginning, fast-closed into the ice. Jim Burian had done no apparent wrong, had made no apparent enemies, but "apparent" was a word with deceptive nuances. As for that, pursue another tautology: greed, love and revenge. Greed for gold, the luminous drop, the scam that Tom had described. Another Lost Deutchman Mine? Old Bonanza?

Then love, the lingering romantic, a love so quiet it was never admitted. Eva had been at Shield at the same time as Jim. Was she the girl he'd discussed with the chaplain? What had happened between them to cause her breakdown? Jim was incapable of harming anyone.

Behind love, the invisible grumbler in the dark. Revenge. But how could revenge enter into this scenario? The puzzle had assumed the convolutions of a pile of pick-up sticks. There was one last place where she might find enlightenment.

Belle steamed home, challenging the dog to keep up, and gathered her snowmobile gear. It had been an unusual violation of bush courtesy for Franz not to have invited her to his camp that day at Cott, when they were practically on the doorstep. Yet he was always so polite and proper. What was it he hadn't wanted her to see? Her microwave clock read eleven, and he had mentioned long lab periods on Wednesdays.

In spite of a minefield of wet spots and water channeling at the shore, Wapiti was safe enough. The ice was still a foot thick. The smaller lakes would be another story, especially as the sun warmed, so she would opt for the slower trail route to Cott instead of the fast trip through five lakes. Belle hauled two-by-eights from her scrap pile to bridge the crack at the shore and eased the Bravo onto the ice. A larger machine would have powered across without supports.

The ride across Wapiti took longer this time, since Belle detoured around several acres of slush fields at the half-way point. One machine, buried up to the seat, had given its owner a long walk home. At the top of the Dunes, she stopped and glanced over at the island. No Jimmy, just as she had hoped. As she drove, she planned every step. A quick turnaround after a search of the cabin and maybe a stop with the Burians at Mamaguchi. Her spirits sank as she passed the turn to see no smoke from the lodge and no fresh tracks. Just in case something went wrong, a friend at that relay point would have been a bonus.

On the slow and winding hills of the overland route, Belle saw very little outside her mind's theatre, as she concentrated on the task ahead. Finally, she located the last turn to the camp. From the condition of the trail, it had been perhaps a week since Franz had visited. Belle made a tour around the outbuildings. Between a toolshed and a small sauna rose an oddly shaped mound of snow. Strange woodpile. She swept off the tarp and lifted a corner to reveal a pile of mottled rocks. After being washed off in the snow, the piece she chose was heavy with gold streaks.

Wasting no time, with a screwdriver from her tool kit, Belle forced the hasps which fixed the padlock to the cabin door, stopping in amazement. Franz's camp was the polar opposite of Jim's simple retreat. In the main room sat an expensive

Swedish red enamel stove, more beautiful than practical with its stack of baby logs and pine splits. The decorative Nordic heater couldn't handle larger pieces and would have to be stoked often. A pillowy calico couch and wicker chairs added comfort, Coleman lanterns hung from the ceiling and chests of drawers lined one wall. A curtained pantry and kitchen nook were stocked with the usual imperishable foodstuffs as well as a double-burnered propane cookstove. On the wall beside the curtain hung a magnificent hunting rifle with a precision Zeiss scope that could drill Bambi's eyes at three hundred yards. The single bedroom contained a mate's bed with down comforter, another lamp, shelves of books, and in a prominent spot, like an icon, a print of Degas' ballerinas, double-matted with v-grooves and an ornate Victorian frame. From what Belle knew of local costs, it was pricey. An oddly feminine touch. Then she noticed that the dancer could well be Eva's double, protected forever from the tumults of maturity.

In a workshop dusty with crushed ore and tools, Belle lifted another quartzite sample and traced the thick vein with her fingertips. A propane torch lay on a wooden workbench beside picks and chippers. Following a gleam on the floor, Belle knelt to gather a bit of molten metal that had worked into a knothole, small sister to Jim's drop. A birchbark basket on a high shelf contained a chamois bag of the fabled buttons. Even at two or three ounces each, a slim reward for such painstaking work. Franz had been a busy and patient man to finance his sister's hospital stay with this laborious process. How far was Bonanza from the cabin? The topo read two to three miles, yet where else would this heavy ore have come from in a place where snowmobiles or small quads were the only transportation? And how many well-timed and cautious trips had been made to run his cottage industry? She filled her hands with the buttons, warm, sensual, atavistic delights. Gadz, she was turning into Zasu Pitts, she laughed nervously. Soon she would be rolling in them on the bed. In her absorption, she didn't hear the door open, or the footsteps enter.

TWENTY

In the frosty silence of the room, a gravelled throat cleared. "Belle. I didn't want it to be you." She wheeled and stumbled, letting the buttons roll on the wooden floor, the elation from her discovery giving way to a palpable fear. "No classes today, a bad cold and laryngitis. Mother had gone to town, and I couldn't focus on my research, just sat looking out the window. You drove by my island so fast, so unlike you, this haste. A clear purpose in mind. Perhaps that drop told you its golden story. I trailed you, hoping that you might be heading to the Burians' lodge or to Jim's camp. I walked the last hundred yards. The cedars hold secrets well." His red and rheumy eyes fell softly on the buttons. "Lovely, aren't they?"

Belle would have felt more confident if she hadn't seen the large pistol in his right hand. "Luger," he said, a catch to his voice. "My father's. Canada is not a land of handguns. A classic example of German design, form and function. And it never failed him in the war. I have always kept it oiled and clean out of the same reverence for workmanship." He brushed its muzzle with his lips, then motioned her to a wicker chair in the main room.

"Why did you kill Jim?" Belle asked, dropping onto the hard cushion.

"Not even a guess? You have enough of the pieces concerning my sister. That receipt which disappeared from my office."

"That was an accident. I picked it up with my books."

He coughed as he waved off her confession. "Of no concern now. You traced the hospital, of course."

"What happened to Eva?"

"Why do I have a feeling that you already know? Still, if you insist on playing the innocent. It's an old story. She became pregnant and in the fourth month had a miscarriage. There is some question in my mind that it was not an accident, that she used my mother's herbs. Tansy, for example, is a historical abortifacient. Even the common yew. Whatever the cause, it was traumatic. Eva is a gentle spirit, wished from childhood so much to please, but guilt overcame her small soul. After the pain was over…" He sat down heavily in the other chair. "It flows through in my nightmares in a red tide, all her precious blood. She became catatonic, you see. That beautiful, intelligent girl couldn't even communicate her basic needs. All she did was sing one of Mother's old lullabies and rock herself. When she wasn't sleeping for most of the day." His voice broke.

"Why didn't you get her treated here? Or in Toronto? Why all the trouble and expense of going to the States?"

"Do you know the number of psychiatrists in the North? When she fell ill, Sudbury was down to three practices. She would have been lucky to be a faceless number in a weekly group therapy session with a dozen other needy souls. Do not be naïve about a two-tier medical system. It's here already for those who can afford it. And I can. I bought the best doctors and the latest techniques. With our prayers she'll be home soon."

"Home to what, Franz? To find her brother a murderer? And are you implying that Jim was the father? That's absurd!"

He forced an ironic laugh. "Perhaps an improvement on

231

his more bitter fate. Let me explain. Eva was a delicate child, asthmatic, sheltered. She attended a convent school in Ville Marie for most of her education. Even when she came home for the summer, isolated as we are on the island, social activities were few, not that she cared to make friends. Mother became concerned and sought to break into that solitude by enrolling her at Shield."

"And Jim?" It occurred to her that Franz was moving all too circuitously, using his consummate logic to avoid the truth. Belle was piecing the story together herself, much too fast and much too late.

"Jim was the first friend she found, and she became instantly infatuated. He was scarcely her equal, for all his country knowledge. And that scarred face." Belle narrowed her eyes and felt a dull rage rise in her heart as he continued without apparently noticing. "From spending most of her life immersed in novels, knowing nothing of the realities of life, Eva took matters of the heart seriously. She was an inveterate romantic like our sensitive young Werther. A first terrible love, an equally terrible rejection. Yes, she tried every sad ploy her old-fashioned books advised, poetry, flowers, invitations. I saw them and wept inside, tried to tell her the lessons we all learn, that there will always be another love. When he didn't respond, even avoided her, she went into a serious depression. Why didn't he see how fragile she was?"

"I'm not following you, Franz."

He was shaking, crying without tears. "She was a sister, a child, all things to me. I tried to comfort her, one night when Mother was away…"

"And then?" Belle saw the danger of pressing him too far.

He shuddered, his face pale and clammy, drained by pain. "A scandal would have killed my mother. Eva was her little saint. You saw that shrine. My mother believes the father was Jim, and I have left it that way for all our sakes. It is a shame which will not happen again."

"And the gold?"

He nodded and slumped his shoulders, letting the gun fall into his lap. "For twenty years, my father had been searching the Bonanza third shaft, hidden in the woods, protected so handily by poison ivy. After he retired, he became obsessed with locating the vein. He told me where he thought the gold might be, but before he found it, he died of a stroke. I continued his work in a desultory fashion, more as a pastime, always careful to brace the timbers and wear a mask in case of fumes from the rotting wood. And about three years ago, after that small earthquake in Quebec, a rock shift here revealed the vein like a timely miracle. I spend the winter refining what I have found in summer. No tracks that way. The vein is almost mined out, but the gold has saved my sister."

Belle remembered the earthquake. Centred near Chicoutimi, it had struck with evil happenstance the day after her foundation had been laid. "Now I see why you fought the park. Less chance of being observed."

He bristled as if insulted. "Not at all! Why would I have wanted this land despoiled by such a commercial operation? All of my efforts have been based on a sincere and rational opposition. When Eva comes home soon, I will leave the rest of the metal to heaven where it belongs."

"Perhaps you should have left the whole situation to heaven. You've told me your twisted reasons for killing Jim. But why wait so long? Eva's been away for over a year."

"Quite so. After his insensitivity had plunged her into a depression, I let him pursue his common life, allowed him the courtesy of a second chance. Yet he kept intruding like a self-

233

appointed nemesis, bringing me his data on the park, eager as a puppy. And when I got back that day from fishing, there he was, propped here by the stove with a book. Hadn't wanted to take a chance with the storm and the cold or flu, whatever it was. He'd been bored and looked in my workroom for something to read. Once or twice he'd stopped by and knew I kept some technical works there."

"Did he recognize the value of the ore?"

"I told him that it was only pyrite samples. Jim was a forester; rocks held no great interest for him. He pretended to believe me, but I couldn't take the chance that he didn't. He was honest, if he was anything. Still, it was his fault that I needed it for Eva. Why would I let him destroy our family again?"

"And the drop?"

"Squirrelled it away. I say that proves his intentions. Why else take it?"

"How did you get him to that lake?"

He massaged the bridge between his eyes as if easing a headache. "Not very cleverly, even for me. He stayed for dinner while the storm lifted. And even with a fever, his appetite was sharp enough for my lake trout and a salad." He paused and turned his eyes to the wall.

"A salad? Out here?" Belle asked in confusion.

"My mother's herbal studies have many uses. In winter, however, our choices are limited. What would I have on hand at the camp? To shredded carrots and cabbage, I added some sprouts, potato sprouts, chopped up, innocuous in appearance. The deadly nightshade family, and the beauty of it all, with no apparent taste. It's so common you wonder why children don't poison themselves."

A wave of nausea forced bile to her throat, and Belle

struggled to control her voice. "My God. And then?"

Franz related the details with the clinical detachment she had come to expect. "After about half an hour, Jim developed a headache, then vomiting, abdominal pain, finally stupor. I don't think the nightshade would have killed him, a man in such good health, but the question quickly became academic. Around midnight I convinced him to try to reach his parents' lodge and use their radio phone to call the air ambulance. Except for a bit of wind, the storm was over, and the lodge was only half an hour away."

"But you didn't go there."

"Of course not. I rode behind him on his Ovation, holding him close, barely able to tow my larger sled. I had to stop several times to cool the engine." Sweat trickled down his forehead as he wiped at his face and coughed thick mucus into a handkerchief. "Jim was barely conscious, unable to notice the route, so it was easy to take a turn to that little swamp lake. I know the territory well; ice is always thin there with a spring running all winter. I stopped at the shore and disconnected my machine. When I got on again, I gunned the throttle and we went out a good distance before breaking through. My flotation suit let me swim back to shore, and minutes later I was at my cabin. I didn't need to watch him go down. The final act, clumsy though it was, was over at last."

"And you reversed to cloud the tracks, counting on the blowing snow for cover, in case anyone might have noticed the discrepancy of the wide set over the narrow."

He nodded. "You were the only one who suspected. And what was there to find? Without that damn drop, you never would have put the whole story together." The corner of his mouth rose enigmatically. "Dead men do tell tales after all."

"Melanie never believed in the accident."

"True, but she didn't connect me to it either." He closed his eyes. "She's so rare. She has Eva's sensitivity, but an incredible strength. I don't know how that callow puppy deserved them both." Then he stood up suddenly, shook himself as if to slough off fatigue, and pulled a length of rope from a hook on the wall. "I tried so many times to distract you, Belle, but you persisted, just like Jim."

"So the cocaine was planted."

"Purchased on one of my trips to New York. Then a flight from one of the tourist outfits. I paid extra to set down on Cott."

"And my chimney?"

"Whoever engineered the initial break-in, Brooks if you were right, made a helpful suspect. How could I know you would turn off your smoke alarm? I thought merely to divert you until you tired of your investigation." He bent over. "Put your arms behind your back, please, and don't make this painful for yourself. I would rather not act violently." Breathing heavily through his mouth and giving an occasional sniff, he pressed the gun to her temple with one hand while the other looped the rope around her wrists and then her ankles. "The arrangements are simple. You are going to have a serious accident in the deep shaft I no longer use. You go down, and your machine follows. There is plenty of rubble for camouflage. I doubt if you will ever be found unless by an anthropologist of the 22nd century. A predicted wet snow will cover the new trail, long before anyone will start searching."

As the realities of his plans unfolded themselves, Belle suppressed an urge to scream. "Jesus, you're going to throw me down a mineshaft! And you call yourself non-violent?"

He looked offended. "I am no friend to pain or the indignities of force. Carbon monoxide from my engine can be hosed into the sauna. A quiet and relatively quick door from the world that some people actually choose. Out of caution, I don't want to inflict obvious damage."

"Another murder, Franz? Where will it take you?"

"Let me give you a familiar and telling philosophy: 'I am in blood stepp'd in so far that, should I wade no more, returning were as tedious as go o'er.' To put it in the simplest terms, my obligation to my family outweighs my feelings for you."

Out of some Saturday night sitcom formula, Belle tried to keep him talking, as if the DesRosiers, Steve and the entire Musical Ride of Mounties might soon crash through the door with a flourish of trumpets to rescue her. "Congratulations on your Shakespeare. Is this where you tell me that it's nothing personal?"

"But it isn't, you know. My compliments to your successful investigation, despite its cost to us both. I wish I could have been a better *Ritter*." He tugged on the bonds to secure them and brushed her face with a gentle hand. Then he opened the door and called. "Blondi. *Hier.*" Some scrabbling from the porch and the dog padded inside, responding to his signals by resting at Belle's feet. He took off the sunglasses. "Don't worry about Freya. I shall call at your business and express loud concern about a broken lunch engagement. Your machine and riding clothes will be gone from your home; any of fifty stretches of open water could have claimed you. The way the melt is coming, searchers will have to wait until your body surfaces, which it won't. It is ironic that you will be perceived as a victim of your most sensible gene pool theory." He lifted a pair of snowshoes from the wall and swung the door open. A minute later, a motor faded into the distance.

TWENTY-ONE

B elle's temples began to pound like pumped-up bass speakers on a cheap stereo. Her breath puffed out little clouds, but despite the chill, rivulets of sweat poured down her back; Blondi sat alertly, trusting to her master's commands, docile so far, but if alarmed? Belle raked, combed and curried her German vocabulary, doubting that the dog was bilingual. Franz and his mother kept their language alive at home. Then she felt like giving her head a smart rap, had her hands been free. So what if the dog were friendly. Would Blondi untie her bonds?

Belle shifted uncomfortably with her aching hands lashed behind her and her feet rapidly becoming numb blocks. She eyed the painted sides of the venerable old chair. As cottagers well knew, wicker grew brittle over the years, especially in unheated storage. She manipulated and pulled methodically until a twig loosened and her wrist mobility improved. Yet though she tested the hold and ground her teeth until they screamed, no way could she free her hands from the rope or the rope from the wicker. Even if she fell over, could she inchworm out the door and home twenty miles? But concentrate on the improbable, use some of Franz's famous ingenuity. What does it have in its pockets? Paperclip? Nailfile? Lighter? Five-pound Swiss army knife? She'd dropped the screwdriver at the door. Not one tool, nothing but the jerky, still zipped into her arm pocket.

Blondi bared her teeth during Belle's grunts and twists, but with luck this expression signalled nervousness rather than ferocity, the dopey canine smile she had seen on Rusty. Dogs had an amazing ability for precise nibbling with those small front teeth, as legions of fleas had learned too late. Freya had even worried a bumblebee, peeling back her lips with instinctive precaution. Blondi might be induced to nibble at the bonds if the jerky made them tasty, and she got encouragement.

After some painful gyrations, Belle unzipped the pocket enough to finger out a piece of the dried meat, turned greasy by body heat. She smeared it clumsily on her bonds, snaking it into the cracks of the old rope. The dog watched intelligently, ears pricked for her master's familiar motor. Then one paw quivered, and her nose wiggled.

"Here, Blondi." The dog rose cautiously. Good choice, the same in both languages, Belle recalled. Now to coax her to eat. Thank Teutonic gods that Dr. Scheib had drummed the distinction between "*essen*" and "*fressen*" into her callow freshman brain, one for humans and the other for animals. She gave a firm command: *"Friss doch!"* No response. Then Belle tried a lesson in pet psychology. Would the proper Marta speak rudely to her pet? "Sorry, girl. You're a person, aren't you? Let's see, now." She searched for a more casual, suppertime syntax for a moment, then commanded: *"Guten Appetit, Blondi."* Magic! The dog came to rapt attention in front of her, apparently puzzled at the absence of a dinner bowl.

Belle moved her head and eyes in her only sign language, hoping that Blondi retained enough vision to interpret the vague signals. Working dogs were trained to react to the slightest movements, border collies ushering their mindless

239

flocks through complicated sets of gates at a wave of their master's hand. Finally Blondi got the idea, circled the chair and smelled the ropes. *"Guter Hund!"* Belle encouraged her.

Doggy interest was confirmed when copious drool lathered Belle's hands. Finally the animal made a tentative nibble, as if to test reaction. Belle crooned her approval and minutes snailed by. A strand snapped, another, and finally the rope dropped to the floor. Not a tooth had touched skin. While the dog licked her lips and cocked her head, Belle untied her feet, rubbing her ankles and wrists before standing stiffly. For an electric second she thought she heard a motor and froze. But it was only an airplane, likely the four o'clock flight to Toronto.

"Thanks, girl. You never wanted this." She scratched Blondi's ears and rewarded her with the rest of the jerky as a tail switched energetically, knocking pillows from the sofa. She was more of a protector than an aggressor, trained to defend the island, not attack a friend of the family. Belle prowled the room in a controlled panic, grabbing first at the rifle, Franz's weapon of choice. *"Hostie!"* Just like a law-abiding Canadian to have locked the ammunition firmly into the cabinet. Her mind stuttered through a low blood sugar fog spiked by adrenalin jolts. A hatchet near the woodpile gave her the notion of smashing the rifle, but Franz still had his pistol and perhaps another long-range weapon on the property. The logistics of her Bravo vs. his Grand Touring racer, the unequivocal equation of speed plus miles, guaranteed that he would catch her well before Wapiti. Suddenly a sharp "awk awk" sounded from the roof. "Raven!" Belle said. "Trickster. Help me. What would you do?" A fluttery shadow passed the window. Not an animal itself, but the idea of an animal. The idea of a gun. A gun in appearance only. She fumbled for a splinter of wood to tamp in unseen. Nothing but kindling, and no time to whittle. Then she remembered the gold buttons in the workroom. Soft, malleable. A match to the propane torch; then she rolled a soft cylinder and jammed it up the barrel with a pencil. From jerky to jamming, finished in under ten minutes, her watch read.

Belle left the cabin on the run, flexing her wrists, the angry red welts tingling in the cold. The Bravo sat untouched, key in the ignition. Luckily the route to Bonanza headed right, not back to Wapiti, or she would be driving toward him. Since Franz had said that he didn't normally visit the mine in winter, it made sense that he would be tamping down a path with the snowshoes to facilitate the trip with her body on the toboggan. I'm not a body, not yet, she mumbled through clenched teeth. Suddenly an image she had wanted to forget pushed into her mind, the still, gray form borne away in silence, Meg's scarf for a winding sheet.

Bonanza couldn't be more than fifteen minutes by machine. That might give her a conservative hour, including the time already spent in getting free. Her only prayer was to drive hellbent towards civilization and hope to meet a fishing party. Which trail to take at the major fork, the five lakes or the safe way she had come? She opted for the lakes, risky but faster: Merrill, Damson, Warren, Basil and Marion. That Franz would take the wrong trail would be a foolish assumption. He had too much bush sense not to identify the most recent path.

Belle wondered grimly what lay ahead; in the several hours that had passed, the new slush might well be impassable. Nor could she power across open water with her small engine. But Franz could probably cruise Lake Erie in June, and on ice he could clip a good 120 km/h to her feeble 80. Luckily the five lakes were her familiar friends, winter and summer. A few were connected by narrows; on the others the trail followed short portages through the woods. No time now to admire the sun glinting off the quartzite cliffs at Merrill, the giant icicles dripping like transparent stalactites, slant-frozen with the winds. Now she had to anticipate every curve, every rock, every gleam to spot slush or open water. And she had to fly, fly on her underpowered little baby. She would be camping with Jim in the eternal wilderness if Franz caught her in his sights on the stretches.

Belle pushed the Bravo at top speed until her thumb screamed for mercy, her eyes tearing behind the visor as she scanned the first lake. Merrill was about two miles long, narrow and ringed with massive red pines, one cliffside sliced like an eroded layer cake. A few sticks drooped at angles in the ice, makeshift tip-ups, showing that winter folk knew it was heavy with fish. Merrill led directly into Damson, a charming spot with a nineteenth-century trapper's cabin burned at the point. Canoeists favoured the clearing, which allowed space for tents and the strong point breeze which blew off the bugs.

Belle exited Damson in minutes and sloped up the portage to Warren. Heedless of the damage to her kidneys, she took the bumps too fast and was thrown off on a wickedly-banked curve with a bad rut. The dead man's throttle stopped the engine as Belle landed up to her waist in melting snow, floundering like a child in a ball pit. For a moment she couldn't move in the cumbersome suit and boots. She did an Australian crawl back to the machine, grabbed a dead maple branch, and started digging, hoisting, digging, turning, digging, until she hauled the machine back to the trail after losing precious moments. Last time that had happened, she had wrenched her back muscles so badly that she had had to hibernate in bed for three days. Today her right wrist seemed to have taken the punishment, draining her pain reservoir when she turned the steering or hit a bump on the trail. She hadn't felt her feet since leaving the camp.

A cruise down a hill of soft brushing white pines brought her in sight of Warren, the halfway point. Stopping to clear a rotten birch deadfall from the trail, she detected a faint purr from an indistinguishable direction, a deadly kitten prowling behind her? Another flight to Toronto? Not so soon. She caber-tossed the log back across the path. It might slow him, or with luck, might disable the machine. As she streaked down Warren, the sound droned again. She risked a glance back and glimpsed Franz on that beautiful animal, parting the standing water on the ice like Charlton Heston commanding the Red Sea. Luckily she was just entering the landlink into Basil. She ducked a spruce branch and navigated the trail crazily, skirting trees and bumping the occasional rock emerging in the thaw. After Basil, only Marion to go. Five minutes? Ten? Then safety in numbers. Ahead on Wapiti, the lazier folk, bless them, might still be hauling off their huts, while others fished in the open like Ed and Hélène. Her heart did a little dance of hope. Basil was only a mile long, the smallest lake, connecting into Marion by a waist of open water at a perpetual spring, and she was across it in what seemed like seconds.

The Bravo nicked one of the warning signs which routed riders over land at the spring danger spot to Marion, and Belle heard the fibreglass hood crack smartly. She whispered in quiet desperation over the thrum of the motor: "If you get me back, sweetheart, you'll get the best tune-up, the most expensive oil change, platinum plugs if they have them, those sliders which I never put on, and OK, OK, even a new track. Trust me!" The trail snaked twenty feet off the lake over a small hill worn to bare grass under the hot sun. Belle braked for control on a sharp turn as the machine chewed turf.

Back onto Marion, the last lake. Three miles until the final portage to Wapiti. Her vision blurring from tears, the white and green and black of the scenery jerked along like a silent film. Half-way across she stopped to clear her faceshield and glanced around, confused by a profound silence. Franz was fewer than one hundred yards back, braced against his machine, taking careful aim with the rifle. Even if he missed her, he had the rest of the lake to catch up. And with his speed, he would close in, until even the pistol would suffice. Belle aimed for a wet spot, throwing spray up on both sides, her only protection from the powerful sight of the rifle. Then she heard a shot. But was it a shot? So muffled, thundering in all directions. And with the curious geographical acoustics, it echoed again and again as the hills replayed the ugly sound. Belle kept ducking in reflex, amazed to feel no pain, to see no fabric and blood and bone tear away. Then she charged up the trail, spurred by the line from *Now, Voyager*: "Don't let's ask for the moon. We have the stars."

The blessed sight of the Dunes set Belle cheering until she fogged the facemask and tossed it onto the ice. In one long heartbeat she sailed onto Wapiti, waving off the flying sand, huddling behind the windscreen to prevent frostbite on her exposed face. When she had ridden the remaining few miles to the familiar escarpment near her camp, she peered back cautiously. No one followed.

Blasting through the door, she ran through the house to bury her face in Freya's smelly ruff. "So you are still sulking and didn't even give me a welcome. This time I don't care." With the dog following her around sniffing both Blondi and jerky, Belle grabbed her single-barrelled shotgun from the hall closet and loaded it for bear, or something more dangerous. Only then did she call for help.

Her binoculars, trained on the lake while she waited, revealed no riders. Steve drove into the yard with Al Morantz, and soon after, an O.P.P. helicopter landed in the yard and took them to Marion Lake in minutes. With its wap-wap-wapping drowning her words, she struggled to describe what had happened. Far below a tiny figure stretched like a broken marionette, the ice sprinkled with pink. With an eye to safety, the nervous pilot set down on a level, sun-drenched blueberry field, the scraggy shrubs poking through the snow.

They plowed behind Al through the slush at the edge of the lake to reach the body. Steve spoke quietly. "I never met the guy, but murder didn't seem his style. I mean, a professor? And where were the connections? The accident was textbook, and the drugs angle had us running in other directions."

Morantz moved closer and stooped down; for a moment Belle wondered if he were going to turn Franz over. She hoped not. "That barrel you plugged really did a number on him. I'd say a piece of metal cut the main artery. Wonder that he has any blood left. Fast way to go. Couple of minutes, max," he said, scribbling a few notes.

"Stop. Please don't go on." Belle turned from the scene to study the puffy cumulus clouds moving across the sun, sending shadows onto the lake. Mel was right. Everyone could use a protective aura now and then. "What's happened to our medical system when someone commits murder to assure his sister of treatment?"

Steve looked at her in disbelief. "What kind of a crazy spin are you putting on this? It was more than that. He hated Jim, killed him for the feeblest of reasons. And let's not start analyzing his relationship with his sister."

Belle flexed her wrist, shivering as she sipped a cup of

coffee from his thermos. "You're right. And I hate him for taking my friend. It was just so clear that he loved Eva with a passion that nobody could understand."

Steve shot her a sceptical look. "So much the better for that. Say, you don't think the old woman helped, do you?"

Who would tell Marta about her son, knock on the door of that fairy tale world on the magic island, illusion though it might have been? For such a short time, Belle had enjoyed it too. "One glance will tell you about her bad heart. Franz wouldn't have risked using her...or telling her. He didn't need to. Time and chance put him together with Jim the night of the storm."

Like Marley's ghost dressed by Alec Tilley, Dr. Monroe arrived in the next helicopter with two stretcher bearers trotting at his heels. He seemed perturbed that he hadn't brought boots and was soaking his Mephistos. "Of all people, Miss Palmer," he announced as he set down his bag and touched a well-manicured finger to his lips. "How curious to find you involved in another death on the ice."

"I'm thinking of writing a book," she said pleasantly. Then she touched Steve's arm. "We have to get Blondi."

TWENTY-TWO

To the relief of all shovellers and scrapers and frostbitten faces, May trailed forth its leafy lacework at last. Marta had sold the island to a rich Torontonian who owned a chain of video stores and wanted a rustic and private retreat; her plans were to live in an apartment in Kingston to be nearer to Eva until the girl could leave the hospital. News of Franz's death had slowed her recovery. They might join an uncle with a small farm in the Annapolis Valley. Belle would always remember the grace and dignity in those lost, sweet moments over strudel and coffee.

Relating these details, Steve lolled on the deck in a dusty lawn chair dragged from the boathouse-cum-garage. He had refused a beer and was nursing a coffee. "Call me a bad Canadian, but I can't drink beer until July. Anyway, steam keeps the bugs away." With a benign smile, he urged a blackfly out of his mug. "They pollinate the blueberries." Belle scratched suspiciously at her arm while he continued. "The department flew me to New York to confirm Franz's story. I've never seen a girl like Eva. Innocence headed for tragedy. Time has stood still for her. She seemed to understand what had happened, even asked questions about whether her brother had suffered, and of course, about Blondi."

"I don't know how she can reconcile with her mother. They're saint and sinner in each other's eyes. Yet who else do they have? Franz was so gifted, so courtly. A prince in another time and place," Belle mused sadly. "If Eva had been stronger, if the blizzard hadn't delivered Jim to that cabin while Franz was away…"

"A prince of darkness perhaps. Would you stop defending the man? Don't act like he was forced to kill. Who knows what Jim made of the gold drop anyway? Probably nothing. That was all self-serving speculation. The good professor intended to dump you down a mine shaft!"

"Yes, and I saw his beast, Steve, all our beasts. The banality of evil. More tired and desperate than cunning. Driven by doing what he thought best for his sister. And when that was threatened—"

"Spoken by a woman saved by a hunk of dried meat."

She had to laugh. "If you taste it sometime, you'll know why it worked. But give Blondi credit." He nodded in approval, and she added, "Something told Blondi that Franz was wrong to order her against me. A good dog resists evil. And maybe she can help her owners find a new life."

They watched in companionable silence as two merganser ducks flapped across the waterfront in a mating ritual. "They nest somewhere along my shore, maybe in those heavy firs. I think it's the same pair every year, but who knows? Anyway, speaking of nests, how's your chick? Any improvement on the fathering scene?"

With undisguised delight, Steve rummaged in his Sudbury Wolves jacket for a fat pack of pictures. "Got a few hours?" The snaps covered all the parental bases: daughter waving a piece of toast, bouncing a ball, even splashing in a bubble bath. "Know what? That stupid jerk at the photo store gave me a funny look about that last one. Kiddie porn. It's getting ridiculous." In a final picture he actually held Heather, her face a curious mixture of strangeness and resignation.

"This the shot just before she burst out in tears?" Belle asked.

"Not quite. But I did what you said with Janet, that PDA."

"Pardon me?"

"What kind of a permissive high school did you go to? Public display of affection. Hand-holding, arm around her shoulders, little kiss now and then. Kid watched me like a baby hawk, but for sure she seems to trust me more. Pictures don't lie."

"Hey, I had a thought. Would Heather like to meet my dog? Could be an icebreaker. They use pets at the nursing home to coax residents out of their shells. I'll bring her over some night and babysit so you can see a show or go to dinner." He beamed, clearly elated at the prospect of a private evening with his wife. Belle went inside to fetch a couple of carrot muffins spread with butter and Meg's gooseberry jam. "I know this is going to be good, and I've waited too long."

Later that afternoon, Belle found Freya snoozing on the floor of the computer room. "Too chubby to squeeze into your chair, old girl?" she snorted. "Aren't we all. 'Menopause Manor' my sign out front should read. Except that I didn't give you a chance to have one. Maybe the vet can make arrangements for me. Let's do some chores. Get the old blood boiling before the buggies drain it off."

A week of spectacular Florida weather (23° C!) had melted the snow in all but the deepest woods. Belle had ferried Hannibal and Big Mac in a giant canning pot to their new home at Science North where a two-hundred gallon tank and plenty of admirers awaited them.

Meanwhile, Sudburians were dancing in the streets, or the equivalent, packing up kids and gear for Victoria Day at the cottage. The sodden ground, festooned with smut and dead leaves, looked as exhausted as everyone else. Time to scratch its back with a rake, her least favourite activity. From far above came familiar squawks. Belle shielded her eyes to scan the sky, watching a tiny vee move closer, keeping time with its vocal metronome. The geese were back, maybe fifty birds aiming due north across Wapiti to their breeding grounds on Hudson Bay.

Freya dashed hopefully but without success after a squirrel, which had the gall to dart up a cedar and scold mercilessly. The triangular flower garden, many weeks' labour in cutting railroad ties with a chain saw and driving in spikes with a fifteen-pound mallet, waited for her approval of a small shoot in the fresh earth. A bleeding heart? She gave it a gentle tweak. Something was alive! The expensive fringy parrot tulip and double daffodil bulbs she had planted in October? Or was this the narcissus? A garden diary might be just the ticket for the amnesia of a seven-month winter. Maybe even a wildflower diary like Jim's. Tomorrow Belle would take the dog to the swollen stream down the road to see if she could spot a marsh marigold.

Belle relaxed on the deck, trying to remember where she had left her bug dope. She opened the *Sudbury Star* to check the local news. The fickle gods had approved the damn park after all. It was slated to open next summer, once access roads had been bulldozed and the shelters, washrooms and dumps constructed. Next stop, Disney World North? Was it Victor Hugo who said that not all the armies on earth could stop an idea whose time had come?

Three o'clock. Belle had almost forgotten. She drove to Rainbow Country, greeting the sun-worshippers as she took the stairs two at a time. Someone was missing. Dapper Billy Kidd, a feature sitting in a lawn chair from May to October between his daily walks. "Where's Mr. Kidd?" she asked

Cherie. Her eyes moistening, the nurse pointed at the name board where a black space remained beside room 210. "I guess you hadn't heard. He fell last week. Broke his hip. At that age, they don't last long with a serious injury."

Do all you can do, thought Belle, as she wheeled her father to the van, presenting him with a small Canadian flag like the one she carried. In another year he could reclaim his citizenship. "I have a surprise, Father. Somebody famous is coming through the old burg today, and no, it's not the Queen." She parked on a hill overlooking the hastily refurbished arena, trundling the old man out of the car to a vantage spot behind a chain link fence. He crinkled up his face in mild irritation. "Who the hell are you talking about? I have to go to the bathroom!"

"There he is!" she said as a trim figure walked over a decorative drawbridge leading to a commemorative plate glinting in the sun. His retinue mumbled into their radios and surveyed the underbrush for terrorists poking out of the poplars. "The Prime Minister!" Belle announced. And they waved their little flags and cheered. It was a glorious day.

HÉLÈNE'S HERKY JERKY

1. Combine:
     2/3 cup Worcestershire sauce
     2/3 cup soy sauce
     1 teaspoon black pepper
     1 teaspoon garlic powder
     1 teaspoon onion powder
     2 tablespoons green jalapeno sauce
     1 teaspoon red pepper flakes (optional)

2. Slice 3 lbs. beef (top round) or moose meat into 1/4 inch-thick strips. The thinner, the better. Frozen meat cuts more easily.

3. Marinate meat overnight in fridge.

4. Place drained meat strips on oven rack. For extra heat, sprinkle with one teaspoon of hot red pepper flakes. If you don't have an auto-clean function, put down plenty of aluminum foil. Cook 6 to 8 hours at 150°F, removing smaller pieces first. They get crisper the longer they bake.

5. Store finished jerky in air-tight plastic bags or similar container.

LOU ALLIN was born in Toronto but raised in Ohio. Her father followed the film business to Cleveland in 1948, and his profession explains her passion for celluloid classics, which shows up frequently in her writing.

After obtaining a Ph.D. in English Renaissance literature, Lou headed north to Cambrian College in Sudbury, Ontario, where she has taught literature, writing and public speaking for the past twenty-three years. Like Belle, her sleuth, she lives beside the breathtaking vistas of a sixty-four-square-mile meteor crater lake where she canoes and snowmobiles, hikes and snowshoes.

Northern Winters Are Murder is her first Belle Palmer mystery and her first work with RendezVous Press.

Also available from

RendezVous
Crime

Do or Die

Barbara Fradkin

Inspector Michael Green must solve the perfect crime, committed in the unlikely setting of a quiet university library, while trying to hold his career and marriage together.

ISBN 0-929141-78-4, $11.95 CDN, $9.95 U.S.

Speak Ill of the Dead

Mary Jane Maffini

Nominated for an Arthur Ellis Award!

When crusty young lawyer Camilla MacPhee's best friend is accused of the murder of a vicious fashion columnist, the real killer may be the one on the run from her tenacious sleuthing.

ISBN 0-929141-65-2, $11.95 CDN, $9.95 U.S.

Down in the Dumps

H. Mel Malton

Nominated for an Arthur Ellis Award!

The book in which we meet Polly Deacon, a most unusual heroine, whose peaceful life is violently interrupted when she finds her friend's abusive husband lying dead in the town dump.

ISBN 0-929141-62-8, $10.95 CDN, $8.95 U.S.

Cue the Dead Guy

H. Mel Malton

In the sequel to *Down in the Dumps,* cabin-dwelling sleuth Polly joins a dysfunctional theatre troupe, only to uncover more murder and sordid histories in her country district.

ISBN 0-929141-66-0, $10.95 CDN, $8.95 U.S.

VISIT RENDEZVOUS PRESS ONLINE:
WWW.RENDEZVOUSPRESS.COM